SIX ANGRY GIRLS

SIX ANGRY GIRLS

ADRIENNE KISNER

FEIWEL AND FRIENDS
NEW YORK

A Feiwel and Friends Book
An imprint of Macmillan Publishing Group, LLC
120 Broadway, New York, NY 10271

Our books may be purchased in bulk for promotional, educational, or business use. Please
contact your local bookseller or the Macmillan Corporate and Premium Sales Department at
(800) 221-7945 ext. 5442 or by email at MacmillanSpecialMarkets@macmillan.com.

Library of Congress Cataloging-in-Publication Data is available.
ISBN 978-1-250-25342-2 (hardcover) / ISBN 978-1-250-25343-9 (ebook)

Book design by Mallory Grigg and Trisha Previte
Feiwel and Friends logo designed by Filomena Tuosto
First edition, 2020

10 9 8 7 6 5 4 3 2 1

fiercereads.com

TO SENATOR ELIZABETH WARREN

RAINA PETREE,	:	IN THE COURT OF
	:	COMMON DECENCY OF
Plaintiff,	:	CAMBRIA COUNTY
	:	
v.	:	CIVIL ACTION-LAW
	:	
BRANDON ROTH,	:	Docket No. 2020CIVIL0908
	:	
	:	JURY TRIAL
Defendant	:	DEMANDED

JANUARY 4: COMPLAINT

EVERYTHING WAS FINE.

Until it wasn't.

Everything was great, actually, until Brandon had to go and ruin my life.

School was back in session from winter break, and I was ready to live it up in my final semester at Steelton High. I'd killed it as Katherine Minola in the Stackhouse Players' winter production of *Taming of the Shrew*. (Everyone said so, including the reviewers in *This Town: Steeltown* and the *Tribune Republican*. And nothing usually impresses those people. *Nothing*.) The admissions department at Carnegie Mellon had caught wind of my performance and *everyone* said they'd be fighting NYU and even Juilliard for me, even if I hadn't applied to Juilliard. My evenings were filled with talks with my best friend, Megan, about theater craft and Brandon and college and Brandon and method and Brandon. (Brandon and theater were kind of tied together for me, since he'd been the one to encourage me to audition for my first play in elementary school, way before we were even going out.) At the end of last year, I'd just been elected Drama Club president to replace Cate Berry, who got cast in a movie and moved to LA. I'd narrowly edged out the awful Claire Fowler by two votes. She'd been my chief rival since she won the lead at fifth-grade summer camp (and every blasted summer after that), but I'd finally triumphed over her. Life had hit perfection by New Year's Eve, and it was only going to get better.

Or it would have, had it not all come crashing down because of dick Brandon.

I came back to school on day one of the new term ready to persuade Mr. Cooper that we should ditch *Almost, Maine* (which we had done for the spring production two years in a row) and perform *Radium Girls* instead. I had notes and a USB-saved PowerPoint. We had a full hour for clubs and sport meetings right after lunch, thank you, Football Boosters, so I planned to corner Mr. Cooper before he got an earful from Claire about *Arsenic and Old Lace* or, God help me, fucking *Our Town*.

I practiced my pitch on Megan between bites of my sandwich.

"*Almost, Maine* sucks!" said Megan. "Isn't *Arsenic and Old Lace* done everywhere? We need something different."

"Well, *Radium Girls* is super popular, too, but we've never done it here," I said. "And I want it for my portfolio."

"Yes. Heaven forbid we not have something in our portfolio," said Megan.

(She might have been hearing about said portfolio since Claire first bested me at aforementioned camp.)

"You need to show diversity—"

Megan held up her hands. "Yes, yes. For Carnegie Mellon's competitive drama department. I know, I know. You've convinced me. Down with John Cariani. Ring in the reign of D.W. Gregory to Steelton High's spring production."

"Yes," I said, but I was pleased she had been listening to my presentation. The PowerPoint had crashed her laptop.

"Go get 'em, tiger," said Megan as the bell rang.

I strode out of the cafeteria and down the hall with a purpose. This was *my* year. We were going to do the play I wanted, and everyone would thank me for it. Even Claire. I rounded the corner by the guidance office to hit up my locker before my date with Mr. Cooper. I practically exploded with joy to see Brandon standing there.

"Hey!" I said, rushing over to him. Before he could say anything, I threw my arms around him and pressed my mouth to his. That was not allowed in our sacred hallways of learning, but if you were fast the teachers didn't say anything.

The asshole even kissed me back.

"I thought you were doing some fancy extra chem lab today?" I said.

"Oh yeah. Mr. Bower is out sick, and the sub didn't want any active flames. Something bad happened in his past involving eyebrows. I don't know. I'm going to stop in to Mock Trial. New session is upon us. We have so many members this year, we might have a whole crew dedicated to researching for the competition team."

"Awesome," I said.

I meant it. Brandon had wanted to be a lawyer ever since we started going out in eighth grade. He was the only kid I knew who read Supreme Court decisions for fun. His passion for law stuff kept me going in theater, even when I wanted to try something else like debate or Mock Trial myself. But Brandon said it was better to stick with one thing. He always said it'd distract him if I branched into his activities. I respected that. I could be incredibly distracting. Though I always thought I'd kill it up there in front of a real judge.

"I'm going to convince Mr. Cooper that we can't have yet another year of *Almost, Maine*—"

"Listen, Raina?" he said, putting up his hands. "Can I just stop you right there? I actually need to talk to you." He looked at the floor. He dug the toe of his loafer into a gray hole in the dirty hallway linoleum.

"Uh. Sure. You okay?" I said. Oh God, did his grandma die? She'd been sick since shortly after her ninetieth birthday party. Brandon's mom was stressed about it every time I ate dinner over at his house. "Is it your grandma?"

"No, no. Nan is fine. It's just . . . well, you know how I went to Model UN camp this last week?"

"Yes," I said. He hadn't been home for New Year's Eve, but I'd made the best of it with Megan.

"Well, some stuff happened there I didn't tell you about. Because I didn't think it mattered and because of your Stackhouse show and everything. But now . . ." He trailed off.

Dig went his shoe. Dig, dig.

"Stuff? What stuff?"

"Ruby Carol and I hooked up."

His dialogue came out all wrong. Rushed. Forced. No emotional connection at all. I didn't believe it.

"Ruby Carol. From Model UN," I said.

"Yes."

"You hooked up," I said.

"Yes," he said.

"But you were happy to see me. You were *really* happy to see me just this Sunday," I said. I hadn't been ready to sleep with him until this year. But once we got started, woooo boy. Brandon's parents both worked late on Sundays, so we had his house to ourselves and believe me—I always got a great start to the week over there.

"We were safe. I would never . . ."

"You were *safe*?" I said. My voice bounced off the silver lockers and the diversity mural and the skylight outside the auditorium. "You *had sex* with her?"

"That's what I said." He glanced around. "Maybe you should lower your voice . . ."

"No, you . . . there are a lot of meanings to 'hooked up.' And you can shove my loud voice up your *ass*." I stepped toward him, forcing him to back up against my locker. "Why are you telling me this shit in the hallway? Between classes? *Before drama period?*" I said.

"Apparently there are pictures of me and Ruby. My buddy Kyle— well, you know he's an idiot—he posted them someplace. And I'm tired of it being a secret. She wants to go to Duquesne, too, so we wouldn't have to break up in May, even. We're together."

His blocking was all off. The movements were slow. Labored. Rehearsed.

"But we've been together for five years. CMU and Duquesne are in the same city. *What about last Sunday?*" I gasped.

The bell rang. I could feel the staring eyes of the people who were trying to pretend they weren't milling around in the hallway to watch the fight.

"Five years is a long time. We're just not in the same place anymore," he said. "We were both bored, Raina. Admit it."

I would not. I could not honestly say that, ever. I loved Brandon. His blue eyes, his blond hair, his crooked nose, his round ears. And his brain. I loved his brain. He remembered everything, even stupid details like your favorite cartoon from when you were a kid or that you didn't like coconut. He first asked me to the movies under the apple tree in Central Park on September 4. We had our first kiss on the day after Thanksgiving at the mall. We'd talked every day since then. He laughed at my jokes. He ran lines with inflection and improvised blocking. He said he believed in me and my talent.

"I'm not bored," I said. "I love you." I balled my hands into fists and willed myself to breathe slower, steady breaths. "You said you loved me, too. Every day. Until now," I said.

"I did. I *do*. But it's just not the same, Raina." His eyes pleaded. For what? Forgiveness? Understanding?

"But . . ." I said. My nose was starting to burn and my eyes to throb. I was standing next to a "Six Foods Teen Bodies Need to Thrive" poster. And the love of my life was shitting all over my heart.

I couldn't think of anything else to say.

"I'm sorry," Brandon said. How did he manage to sound like he actually meant it?

I stared into his crystal blue eyes, looking for the gag. The joke. The prank that this had to be. A tiny part of me grew pissed off that this asshole was ruining the color blue for me.

"If you see the pictures, I'm sorry."

I just stared. Mouth open. Comic, exaggerated features. Jagged little shards of my heart poked against my chest.

Brandon edged his way to the side, until he slipped outside of my reach. He straightened his sweater and ran a hand through his hair. He walked away and didn't look back.

I put one hand on the wall, another on the locker. Tears threatened. Tears of shock, rather than grief or sadness. I'd studied how my face felt when angry or sad or excited, so I could replicate the feelings needed in a given scene. But now—only shock.

Breathe in, breathe out, I told myself. From the diaphragm. Shallow breaths reduce vocal power. Brandon turned the corner. But I knew he heard my scream.

JANUARY 7: ANSWER AND NEW MATTER

I DIDN'T DO MUCH IN THE FEW DAYS AFTER Brandon stomped my heart into dust. Mom only let me stay home from school *one day*, saying that since life would continue on, I had to, too. Mom wasn't a sit-at-home-and-cry type. She was a night nurse at a retirement community and took care of a lot of people whose minds and bodies no longer did what they were supposed to. It gave her too much perspective to be able to put up with much from me. And since Dad was away most of the year hauling dairy freight, it wasn't like she had any backup in the daily-life department.

She patted me on the head before leaving for her shift. "There are plenty of other boys, Raina."

"We were together for five years," I said. He knew I collected teddy bears. He knew exactly when to put his arm around me at scary movies. I let him know everything about me, even things I wouldn't admit to Megan. He was another part of my body. A limb. An internal organ you couldn't just donate to some other girl without a thought.

"You are babies. You have nothing but time and chances. Use this in your art."

"Are you kidding?" I said.

"No. I know it hurts. But there are worse things. Find a new boy," she said. "Or a new whoever. Maybe we should get a pet. I've always thought having a cat would be nice."

She'd never liked Brandon much. She said that he was too pretty and that the pretty ones take what they want and then leave when they want. I hated how she might have been right about that.

Mom left to go work a double, and I buried my face in the old, overstuffed fuzz of the couch.

Still mourning? Megan's text buzzed my phone.

No one cares. No one understands, I texted back.

I care. I understand. Want company? she wrote.

Yes, I texted.

Megan brought chocolate-chip cookie dough ice cream and slightly more empathy than Mom.

"I saw them today," I told her. "Making out by the gym. You'd think he'd have some respect for me, in our shared space."

"Yes. Surely the dude who broke up with you for two weeks sophomore year so he was single for his spring-break trip to Cancún would have some consideration," said Megan.

Megan didn't like Brandon much, either.

"Was I this unsympathetic when you broke up with Todd? Or Kevin? Or Jack?"

"Jake. Most recent one was Jake," she said. "And mostly. But I was only with them for about a month each."

"I will never get over this," I said. "I feel like I'm going to barf if I even hear his laugh." I had, in fact, barfed twice just from hearing his laugh. I'd made it into the bathroom, but each time had been a close call. I didn't even know what I had to throw up, since I'd barely eaten.

"You know what I think you need? Professional advice," Megan said.

"Like a shrink?" I said.

"Oh, maybe. Your mom has health insurance, doesn't she? She's a nurse."

"Yeah. But it's super expensive. We have the probably-will-keep-you-from-dying plan. I don't know if it'd cover much. Maybe I could go to the guidance counselor."

"Oh. Maybe," said Megan.

"What do you have against him?" I asked.

"Oh, nothing. He's a nice guy. I went for my college-application stuff. It's just . . ." She chewed on her thumbnail. "Ruby is a student volunteer in that office."

I stared at her. "You aren't serious."

"I am. I saw her sitting at the desk, folding brochures."

"Well, forget that," I said. "I don't want to go anywhere near her."

"Yeah," said Megan. "Well, how about here?" she said, digging through her backpack. She unearthed an Oprah magazine.

"You think I should call Oprah?" I said. "A shrink would probably be cheaper, even without insurance."

"No! Well. I mean. If only. No—I think you should write for

advice. They have life coaches in here. And money coaches and relationship people. You don't have to do the Oprah staff. Write to that woman from the *Tribune Republican* who does the Two Hearts column. Bet she'd be all over this. She loves heartbreak."

I glared at Megan.

"You know what I mean," she said. "This is her job."

"What are her qualifications?" I said. I sniffed back tears that always lurked anytime we started talking about ~~Brandon~~ the dick.

"You are worried about the newspaper lady's credentials?" said Megan.

"I just don't want someone who is going to mess me up more," I said.

"Okay, okay, here," she said, picking up my phone. "I'll look at her blog online." She tapped on the screen. "Here's a good one. 'Dear Hearts, I have been with my boyfriend for two-and-a-half years. Recently, I flew to France with him to meet his family. I thought it went well. His sister and I really hit it off, and his mother and father were so sweet and kind. When we flew home, we talked about shopping for an engagement ring! Everything seemed perfect. But then fast-forward to a few months later, and things seem to have fallen apart. He barely calls, cancels plans, and asked for my key to his apartment back because "repair people" will be doing work in his place soon. When I asked what is wrong, he says it's "family stuff," and nothing more. I don't understand what is happening. Did I insult his parents? Am I missing signals I should understand? Help?! Sincerely, Confused Constance.'"

"Ouch," I said. "What's the answer?"

"'Dear Constance,'" Megan read. "'That sounds so hard. You think you are on one route, and then the plane turns in the middle of the sky and heads off into the clouds in another direction. I wouldn't read into the family visit—it sounds like that went well. It might be related, but since the behavior is more recent, it might be tied to something else. Perhaps your boyfriend was caught up in the excitement of the visit when he started the marriage conversation and is now pulling back.

I would encourage you to sit down and have an honest talk about where you both want your relationship to go and the pace at which you want to pursue that vision. Take heart, he could be acting this way for reasons completely separate from you. But the only way to find out is through open, honest communication. Readers—do you think the French family made her boyfriend want to say au revoir? Comment below!'"

"She didn't tell her that the boyfriend was probably banging Ruby since sophomore year spring break," I said. "So how could she help me?"

"Well, that wasn't what the question was about. There are others that are more related to your situation. Read those."

I flopped over onto her lap, knocking the phone out of her hand.

"Or you could continue to imitate a wounded orca," she said.

"Why does no one feel my *pain*?" I said. "This is the worst feeling in the world."

"I know," said Megan. "It sucks. It really does. I hate Brandon. I want to cut off his balls."

"Good," I said from her lap.

She stroked my hair for a second. "But it's still your senior year. You've lost the beginning of your last term to this dick. I don't want you to lose spring theater auditions. Or Carnegie Mellon auditions. None of it. Say it with me. Not because of the dick! Not because of the dick!"

"Not because of the dick," I mumbled.

"There you go. You are on your way toward healing. Which is good, because my mom is texting me to pick up groceries on the way home."

"Mmph," I said, rolling onto my furry throw pillows.

"Read the column, Raina. Write to this woman. It couldn't hurt, right?"

I lifted my head. "I guess not." I plopped back down onto the pillow.

Megan tried to give me a hug before she got up and went home, though I refused to stop lying prone on the bed.

I turned over and stared at the ceiling for a while. It was seven o'clock. Usually at seven, I'd text Brandon and he'd tell me all the latest gossip from Mock Trial, and I'd tell him what Claire had said that day, before our exchange devolved into eggplant and peach emojis.

I picked up my phone from the floor. The screen lit up with the Two Hearts column still open.

"'Dear Hearts,'" I read out loud. "'My fiancé of two years recently announced he no longer could live with my four cats . . .'"

They were all like that. Dudes changed their minds. Women got cold feet. Nonbinary partners decided that their person's crippling debt was too much to take on. Two Hearts really brought home the reality that love sucked for everyone and forever was a lie.

Two Hearts just tells people to keep going and honestly communicate their feelings. If I communicate my feelings in the way I would like, I think I'll be arrested, I texted Megan.

She didn't text back. She was probably getting ready for bed. She had the annoying habit of getting up for swim practice at five a.m., so she was never awake much past nine.

I got up to pee. I wandered around the quiet, dark house. I kept picking up my phone, expecting Brandon to live-text some video games or MSNBC on a really wild night.

But nothing came.

Around midnight, I sat down at my computer. My screen flashed to life, a picture of Brandon and I last homecoming. I went into my settings and changed it to a plain ~~blue~~ purple screen. I opened up a Word doc.

"Dear Two Hearts," I said, typing the letters.

What? I just turned eighteen and thought I'd marry the first boy I ever kissed? How pathetic that seemed. But it was true. I led with that.

I loved him, and he dumped me out of nowhere, I typed. *No explanation, other than he had moved on before even breaking up with me in the first place. And now I'm alone and I don't know what to do. I* finished with a flourish. I didn't reread it, I didn't edit it, I just copied and pasted it and emailed the remaining slices of my pride to the email address on the bottom of the Two Hearts page. I closed my computer, fell into bed, and dreamed of Ruby and Claire chasing me with giant knives.

JANUARY 8: RELEVANT PARTIES AND ENTITIES

I BARELY WOKE UP TO MY ALARM. I STEPPED into the shower and leaned my head against the freezing morning tile. The water ran over me, pointing out that my body still had nerves that fired and my brain still registered touch. Stupid brain. I half-heartedly blotted my hair with my towel and pulled on old jeans and a hoodie. There was no one to look cute for at school anymore, so why bother?

Megan tried to poke me into action before school and at lunch, but what was the point of laughing? Before drama, Brandon and Ruby passed me in the hall. Neither of them paid attention to anything other than each other, hand in hand, laughing at some joke only they knew. That joke was probably me.

I reached the drama room where Mr. Cooper stood in the front, deep in conversation with Claire and two sophomores I didn't know very well. They usually kept to the stage crew. I sat down in the front row of rickety chairs and folded my arms across my chest. *Breathe, Raina*. Diaphragm. In and out. I focused on the white board in front of me, the swaths of old marker arching like rainbows where an eraser just couldn't rid it all.

"Raina?" said a voice. I looked up. Claire stood over me.

I didn't answer.

"Did you hear us? Mr. Cooper called you."

I looked over and nodded at him.

"Are you okay?" she said. "Do you need to go to the nurse? You don't look so good." She backed away from me, as if significant-other abandonment was contagious.

"Fine," I mumbled. The story of Brandon dumping me by my locker was all over our small school within an hour. Claire had to know.

"Mr. Cooper asked you to come up to see him. Over there." She pointed to his desk.

I got up and walked over.

"Raina, did you hear anything I just said to the group?"

Mr. Cooper had been talking? Drama had started? It probably wasn't a great look that I hadn't been paying attention.

"No," I said. I tried to make eye contact with him. I'd blubbered in Mr. Cooper's office about Brandon more than once in our three-plus years of knowing each other. Three of those times had been in the last week alone.

He smiled.

"It's okay. Listen, we are voting on the spring production. Do you want to call people to order?" he said.

"Spring production?" I said. The words bounced around my head like a foreign language I used to understand. "Voting?"

"Yes, it's today. We determined the three selections on Tuesday and so we are going to vote—"

Tuesday. The day I sat at home hiding under my pillows after dick Brandon . . .

"As president," Mr. Cooper went on, interrupting my grief spiral, "it's your privilege to lead the process. Are you . . . are you feeling up to it?"

I glanced at the board. Even though I'd been concentrating hard enough on it to crack it, I hadn't notice the names of three plays written there: *Almost, Maine*; *Twelve Angry Jurors*; and fucking *Our Town*.

"*Our Town*?" I said. "These are our choices?" A small part of my brain registered *Twelve Angry Jurors*. I'd never been in that play, either. I'd seen a part of it at a festival once. That could be interesting.

"We had several members suggest that enthusiastically," said Mr. Cooper.

"I thought *Radium Girls . . .*" I said softly. But on Monday after Brandon broke up with me, I'd cried in the bathroom until Megan found me and persuaded me to go home. I skipped Tuesday and just zoned out in drama Wednesday and Thursday, and Mr. Cooper kindly let me. I'd never even suggested *Radium Girls* to anyone.

"All of these are by men," I said.

"So they are," said Mr. Cooper. He clapped his hands. "Okay, everyone, listen up!"

The twenty or so people in the room filed over to the folding chairs. Curious eyes stared up at me.

Mr. Cooper handed me the chalk. "Ready?"

I opened my mouth to speak, but nothing came out. I just walked over to the board.

"All for *Almost, Maine?*" he said. One hand went up.

"Yeah, it was a good run while it lasted," he said. "*Twelve Angry Jurors?*"

Claire's hand rose. Mine went up, too.

"Two for number two," said Mr. Cooper.

Claire and I exchanged a surprised glance. We never agreed on anything.

"So that leaves . . ." Mr. Cooper didn't even get a chance to finish. Everyone's hands shot up.

"*Our Town?*" Claire cried. "You can't actually be serious." She turned and glared at the group. "Everyone everywhere does this tired, old play. We should do something relevant. Something fresh."

Twelve Angry Jurors was from the 1950s, but I didn't have the energy to point that out. It *was* still more contemporary than something written in 1938.

"It's what we want," said Ben, a junior.

"It's a classic. It's time this department puts it on. Besides, maybe we can put our own spin on it," said Jane, a freshman.

Heads nodded around her.

Claire turned back to me. "Excuse me, new Drama Club leader? Are you really going to let this stand?"

The eyes turned back toward me.

"We voted," said a sophomore girl. "You could have said something before, but you didn't. This is what we want."

"Fair and square," said someone else.

The group cheered as Claire scowled. I tried to pay attention to it all, because fucking *Our Town*, but I kept flashing back to the beginning of the week, when everything seemed set and perfect.

"All right, then," said Mr. Cooper, clapping his hands and snapping me out of my daze. "I'll order the scripts tonight!"

The bell rang as I placed the chalk on the grooves next to the board. *Our Town*. God. My chest twinged with a weird burning sensation. I was either having a heart attack or being assigned this production felt like Brandon dumping me for Ruby again.

I drifted into the hallway without saying goodbye to Mr. Cooper. I felt an arm on my shoulder. I turned to find Claire looking over me.

"What the hell was that?" said Claire. "You just caved to fucking *Our Town*. Do you know how many schools are going to put that on in the greater Steelton area this semester alone? Probably, like, six. We could have done anything. But you let that happen, *Madam President*."

A familiar exercise-and-stress-induced asthmatic cough sounded next to Claire. Brandon, Ruby-free for a moment, stood next to her arm. A look of confusion crossed his face, as if his instincts were telling him he was meant to intervene with a sarcastic comment right at this very moment. But his dick brain also registered that I was no longer technically his concern.

"Uh. What? Hey," he managed.

Claire turned toward him. "Oh, don't think I don't know that this is your fault, you unfaithful dirtbag. *Everyone* knows that. I swear to God you better leave this hallway right now, and never let me see your stupid pimple-free face for the rest of the year. Because of you I have to compete to be Emily Webb or some shit. Leave. Now."

Because Claire was about two inches taller and a third more muscular than Brandon's skinny five-foot-seven frame, he listened. I watched him retreat down the hall as fast as regulation permitted him. Claire tried looming over me, as well. But all the fight I once held had just run toward the science wing.

"Look, I'm sorry about the moron. But this is bigger than him. Bigger than both of us. This is Drama Club. Don't you care?"

I nodded, but my face started the stupid burning thing. I closed my eyes, willing the tears to stay inside the ducts. Breathe. He wasn't worth it. Breathe. Diaphragm. I gave Claire a small wave that I hoped she interpreted as "thank you for being mean to dick Brandon." I headed to class. I didn't want to flunk out, though I didn't know if it mattered whether I did. It's not like I could bring myself to audition for fucking *Our Town*. I could hear Carnegie Mellon laughing at the joke my chances had become all the way from Pittsburgh.

Drama was my life. But so was Brandon. Now it seemed like both had slipped through my fingers, and I hadn't even realized I was losing my grasp.

EMILIA GOODWIN,	:	SUPREME(LY PISSED
	:	OFF) COURT OF
Plaintiff,	:	CAMBRIA COUNTY
	:	
v.	:	
	:	
THE STEELTON HIGH MOCK	:	Case No. NO2BOYSSSSS5
TRIAL TEAM,	:	
	:	
Defendant	:	

JANUARY 11:
MATERIAL WITNESSES

TODAY WAS THE DAY.

I looked in the mirror for the twentieth time. I smoothed the deep ocher and sienna folds of my skirt. I bent down and straightened my new knee-high socks. My faux suede Mary Janes completed this look. So what if it was 11 degrees outside?

I was ready.

"Millie, hurry up already or I'm not driving you to school. You can walk."

I couldn't walk. It was four miles, a mile of it through woodlands with poorly maintained paths covered in snow to get to school. But Dad might make me take the bus, the experience of which was on par with wildlife and avalanches.

"Coming," I yelled. One more look in the mirror. I turned and picked up my backpack next to my bathroom door and grabbed my coat hanging neatly on the hook just inside my room.

"Have a toaster pastry," said Dad. He shoved a piece of toast in his mouth, narrowly avoiding sticking the sleeve of his suit coat in the butter dish.

"Dad, look out. You don't have any other clean work clothes. Which reminds me, you need to go to the dry cleaner and pick up your work clothes."

"Yes. Right. Where is the ticket?"

"In your briefcase, in the little pocket on the front. Where it was, oh, I don't know, last week when we had this discussion."

"Right, right. Thanks, baby. Are you ready?"

Oh heck yes, was I ever. I smiled to myself as we headed to the Jeep.

We drove down our driveway and the long, winding woodland access road in silence. Traditionally, Dad didn't like conversation until we hit the highway. He needed to concentrate on not taking out a deer or raccoon or fox after hitting a patch of ice. Ever since Mom had left and then gotten remarried, the silence between him and me stretched the remaining miles and yards and feet until he stopped the car long enough for me to hop out in front of Steelton High.

I looked a lot like her, my mom. Same long dark hair, same dark eyes. I think that's why Dad had a hard time with me. Maybe I should have gone to live with her in Ohio. She kept offering. But she had a new baby, and cute as he was, I hadn't really felt like being live-in childcare or starting over in a new place my senior year of high school.

Besides, this was my year. Today I would gather my forces to make the most kick-butt Mock Trial team that Cambria County, the state of Pennsylvania, or our fine nation had ever seen. Mr. Darr, the Mock Trial teacher, had been at a conference last week when we got back from break, but now he had returned, and it was my time to take over. I didn't know if many people would join up. Most of the old team had graduated or defected to Model UN, since the field trips were better. But Jeffrey would still be there, of course, and Brandon. I'd be the third lawyer, but we'd need to find witnesses. Last year we'd almost taken state, so maybe that would generate some interest. I'd heard rumblings before winter break that the boys had a plan to recruit members, but no one new had shown up to meetings yet.

New-term energy still buzzed around me as people danced like honeybees communicating the directions their new schedules had taken.

"*Focus*," I said to myself. "*Only you can manifest your inner power*." My affirmation app always seemed to know what to say.

Or at least what to tell me to repeat to myself.

"Millie, over here!" Claire called.

"Hey," I said. The frenetic surge around me gave me life and made me nervous all at the same time.

"Look at you. You look *hot*," she said, eyeing me up and down. "I don't suppose . . ."

"Claire, we'd kill each other," I said.

Claire legitimately pouted. "We'd be good together," she said.

"No, you'd get sick of me in a week. Plus, as I have mentioned before about a hundred times when you bring this up, you like sex. A lot. You talk about that frequently. I do not. With anyone at all, maybe ever. It's nothing personal," I said.

"Yeah, yeah. I get it. Can't blame someone for trying. I haven't been on a date in a million years. And that really is an amazing skirt."

I beamed. "Thanks! Mom sent it. Mom guilt is really helping my wardrobe. I asked if she wanted to FaceTime on the first day of my last term. She burst out crying and then the Zara box arrived five days later."

"Wow. Uh . . ."

"It sucks," I said. "Kinda. But there are pros and cons to parents no matter where they are."

"Tell me about it," said Claire.

"What's up for you today? Spring play discussions, right? You'll be ruling VP style."

Claire sighed. "Yeah, Raina didn't choke on a strain of iambic pentameter in December, so I still have to deal with her. That girl has been bugging me in every play since *The Food Pyramid* almost a decade ago. She got to play the carrot, and I was stuck as the beet. And she was barely there last week so now I'm about to audition for fucking *Our Town*. *Our. Town*."

"Yes, you mentioned that a few times over the weekend. I'm sure you'll be great in it anyway. Break a leg!"

"I *will* be great in it," Claire mumbled. She looked up at me. "Same to you? Do you need luck?"

"A little," I said. "Let's hope I don't have to recruit people. I hate that."

"I believe," said Claire.

AFTER LUNCH, I MADE MY WAY DOWN TO Mr. Darr's classroom.

"Hello, Millie! Have a good break?" he greeted me.

"Yes!" I said. I looked around the room. I counted the people slumping into desks and chairs. Jeffrey and Brandon nodded to me.

"Wow," I said to Brandon. "Look at all these people. Who are these"—I strained my neck to look past him—"all these guys?"

"I emailed a few friends. So did Jeff. I knew we'd be short a few and didn't want to put the burden on you to solve our witness problem."

"Oh. Thanks!" I said encouragingly. Problem solved already. Perfect.

The bell rang, and Mr. Darr raised his hands to quiet us.

"Wow, there are a lot of you. How about we go around the room and introduce ourselves. I'll start. I'm Mr. Darr." All of us laughed.

"I'm Emilia," I said. "You can call me Millie."

"Chad."

"Mike."

They went around the room. I only really remembered Chad because he was the first. Or maybe that was Mike. I'd gotten them confused already. I made a mental note to study their faces.

Mr. Darr distributed the Mock Trial handbook, charter, and case materials for the district competition case. The papers burned fiery in my hands. This was the case that would send us to states in Harrisburg, and then the state case could send us to Pittsburgh for nationals. I'd committed 90 percent of my brain to knowing every inch of these documents (saving 10 percent for college applications, the rest of school, and talking Claire out of dating weird girls) since November. But this was the first time we would discuss it as a team, since the boys mostly kept to themselves or did other forensics competitions during the fall.

No one could want Mock Trial victories as much as I did.

No one.

None of the guys spoke or even looked up from their papers. I decided to take the lead. I stood and straightened my skirt. "Mr. Darr, if I may," I said.

He nodded.

"In any given trial, there are at least six people. There are three witnesses and three lawyers. Others can be on the team for research and consultation. Or we can rotate people for various competitions until we make it to states. And we *will* make it to states. Any questions so far?"

They shook their heads.

"Mm-hmm," murmured Jeffrey.

"Our season starts in about six weeks. We have one meet in February and one in March. Then districts are the week after that. Those are the three that we will focus on because we know for sure we'll be competing. We win our district, we go to states. After states—nationals."

"Thanks, Millie. Great summary. Everyone got it?"

More nodding.

Then Mr. Darr divided us into teams. Jeffrey, Brandon, two soph-omores, and one freshman and I formed the first. There were two other teams of six as well.

"Three lawyers and three witnesses," I said to Brandon. "This is great for the future of the program! We can rotate the sophomores and freshmen. And that one junior over there could be groomed for lawyer. Or, if you want to have a research team, those can be the guys who want lawyer next year."

"Yeah," said Brandon. He didn't look up from doodling in his notebook.

His flippant attitude annoyed me. They supposedly led this team. I was just the secretary of the group. (I didn't think the graduating seniors should have voted on the executive board officers of the club, since they wouldn't even be here this year. Why did they get a say in secretary and treasurer, let alone president or vice president? But I didn't have to be in charge. I'd learned freshman year that I could more effectively lead the team from behind the scenes, and Emilia Goodwin was nothing if not a team player.)

"Maybe we should swap out lawyers as well," I said. "One per competition. Two of us with experience could be at each trial, right? We'd only miss one each. I think it's important to get as many people participating as possible, because having this much interest in Mock Trial only bodes well for the future of government, don't you—"

"Millie," Jeffrey interrupted, "I've been meaning to address this issue."

I blinked at him. Oh, had he now? He could have mentioned this months ago, when I'd first asked about recruitment. Or last week. But this is how Jeffrey operated.

Jeffrey cleared his throat. "Excuse me, everyone?" He stood up and clapped his hands. "I have an announcement." Everyone turned to look at him. Mr. Darr glanced up from the papers he'd been grading.

"It's amazing that there are so many of us on the team this year.

But as you know, only six people can actually participate in a trial as a lawyer or a witness. So, we've decided to have a competition team, some understudies, and a research crew."

"What?" I said. "Why can't everyone get trial experience? We could make it work."

"No, this is the way it should be. We are going to audition for spots on the trial team," said Jeffrey.

"Audition?" Heat crept under my sweater and blouse to the buckles of the latest mom-guilt brand shoes. "How long did you know about this?" I looked up at Jeffrey, who was still standing over me.

He smiled. "We've been knocking around a few ideas."

"And who is this 'we,' exactly? Last I knew, I was still the secretary and had a say in these kinds of things."

"We didn't want to stress you out," said Brandon. "You have a lot going on."

I did? All I had going on was Mock Trial. I barely even saw my best friend anymore, as she was busy trying to take over the Drama Club from the president.

A gross feeling clawed its way up from my stomach. I fought it down. This might not be the end of the world. It sucked for the freshmen who'd be saddled with research. I'd been in that position. But preparation never killed anyone.

"Fine," I said. Best for a team player to keep the peace. "What are we having these guys do, exactly?"

"Oh. Well. We'll all be auditioning. Each one of us. Only the best people should be on the team, don't you agree?"

I frowned. Yes, I agreed. But I also knew that the chances of the Steelers winning the Super Bowl after an undefeated season were higher than Jeffrey's definition of "best" matching mine.

"So, Mr. Darr has found a case for us to argue, with some witness statements to practice and such. We'll audition Wednesday."

"One day to prepare?" I said. "*One. Day.* What? Mr. Darr, you knew about this?"

"I'm sorry, Millie. I thought you had agreed to this," he said. "I would say we could hold off a bit, but we really should have the team set. The first trial isn't that far away."

My mouth dropped open. Brandon didn't look surprised. Most of the other guys in the room didn't, either. Had they planned this? Why wouldn't they include me? Especially Mr. Darr? I was the hardest worker on this team. I'd single-handedly brought down the toughest witness Fogton Creek had to offer last spring. Was this some sort of horrible joke?

"You can grab the audition materials on the way out," said Brandon.

"Why don't we just use the actual case?" I said.

"It'll be fine," said Jeffrey. "I'm sure everything will work out the way it is supposed to."

The last time I'd heard that, Dad had been trying to talk us both into the fact that Mom didn't really want the divorce, that she'd leave her new contractor boyfriend and come home within the month.

She married the contractor exactly seven months later.

After the bell rang, I gathered my stuff and ripped the stupid audition case file out of Brandon's hand on my way out. I hoped I gave him a paper cut that would get infected and his arm would turn bright green or something. I glanced over the sheets.

"A death-penalty case? Are you serious? We would never see a death-penalty case in competition," I said.

"Talking to yourself?" said a voice.

I realized I'd walked straight to Claire's locker. "Get this. There was a boy coup d'état. I have to *audition* for the team."

"Welcome to my world," said Claire.

I glared at her.

"Sorry, sorry. It's just that ridiculous Raina is a mess. She isn't even trying at all."

"It was probably Brandon's fault. The Mock Trial VP. Apparently, he likes ruining things."

"Yeah," said Claire, unable to hide her disgust. "Clearly."

"I can help you run lines?" I said. That usually made her feel better.

"I don't know if I can bring myself to speak this shit out loud." She shook her script at the sky.

"Well, then maybe you can help me. Do you happen to know anything about lethal injection?"

Claire threw me a blank look.

"Yeah. Me either."

A stone sank from my brain to my throat and settled somewhere behind my appendix. Several more rolled out of my brain and wedged themselves around internal organs until I felt like they filled my body from head to toe. I barely managed to lift my feet to get in the car and go home.

"Good day, baby?" asked Dad.

"Yeah, Dad," I said. "Great."

"Mock Trial going well?" he said.

"It's going," I said.

I leaned against the cool glass as we bumped our way home. The silence filled the spaces between my stone insides, its heavy loneliness spilling out my ears and raining onto the floor until it filled up my room. I could drown in this, here at the bottom of a pool in my own head.

JANUARY 13: DISCOVERY CONTROL PLAN

"YOU'VE GOT THIS," SAID CLAIRE. "YOU live this."

"Yeah." I tried to say it confidently, but my voice cracked on even that one syllable word. Who could be ready in one freaking day? This was a set up for failure, and I didn't understand. Claire's face would have melted off if she'd had one day to rehearse a new play.

"These guys aren't going to get to you. You studied. You looked stuff up online. *I* ran lines with *you*. This is a complete role reversal, and I still don't know how I feel about it. But in my heart, I know you are going all the way to nationals. I believe in you."

I looked over at her. The soft tendrils of hair that escaped her headband floated up in the cold wind.

"Thanks," I said. "Wish me luck on the prosecution."

"Break a leg," she said, squeezing my arm.

All through morning classes, I kept going over anything I thought could help in my "audition." This whole thing seemed off, like Brandon and Jeffrey had a plan I just wasn't in on. I hadn't even known that Pennsylvania had reinstated the death penalty in 1976 and that three people had been executed since then. I didn't like what I'd learned. I always saw myself moving on to fight voter suppression or kids being taken away from their parents at the border or something.

Not this.

At tryouts, I watched two freshmen mumble their way through their arguments. Mr. Darr made notes. So did Jeffrey. Would he get to decide the team? How would that be fair? I didn't have too much time to ruminate because I heard my name.

"Millie," said Mr. Darr, "you're next." He smiled warmly, but he could have ended this whole fiasco before it started. I didn't know whose side he was on, but it didn't feel like mine.

"Um," I started. Dang. That was like rule one of public speaking. "Ever since the Supreme Court, uh." Double darn. I looked down at my notecards. Poop, card two was on top. I slid the back card onto the top. No, that was card nine. Where was card one? Did I leave it in my backpack? I should just wing it. I've been in more dire circumstances than these. Oh no. Had I been silent this whole time? Had it just been seconds? A minute? The freshmen dudes weren't this bad.

"Can I start again?" I said.

"Sure," said Mr. Darr.

Jeffrey and Brandon glanced at each other.

Focus on who you are. You are the best version of yourself right now, I thought.

"In 1995, punishment, um, arrived for a nearly fifteen-year-old murder in the form of lethal injection. I plan to argue . . . comment on the issues surrounding this form of execution."

I stumbled my way through the rest of the cards. It had to be the worst presentation I'd ever done in my life, including the time I'd accidentally lost Claire's pet rabbit at my fifth-grade talent show during my magician phase. (The bunny had been fine. We found him an hour later enjoying radishes in the sustainability garden.)

"What did you end up arguing, exactly?" asked Claire before our English class at the end of the day.

"I don't even remember." I put my hands against her locker and leaned my face into them. "I entered a fugue state."

"Surely it didn't go that badly."

"It did. It did, it did, it did."

"Would mozzarella sticks help?"

"Maybe," I said.

"And even if this bullshit was the worst ever, they'll make you a lawyer. They have to. You are a senior who has put in three years, and now it will be four. You've worked your ass off in everything I've ever seen you do. Especially this. They owe you."

"Okay," I said. "You mentioned fried cheese?" The thought of Pappy's restaurant, a mere two blocks away, made life feel a little more bearable.

"Yes, I did. I'll drive you home after."

"Thanks," I said. I texted Dad that he could stay at work as late as he wanted and that I'd bring him leftovers. I knew he'd love that.

I could get through the rest of this day. I could get through tomorrow if necessary. Eventually I'd find out that I was a lawyer, that Jeffrey, Brandon, and I could somehow work together to train the next generation of Steelton Mock Trial participants, and we could forget this messing around and get back on the path to winning.

Yes. I was sure of it.

Though I kind of dreaded whatever might be coming next.

RAINA PETREE,	:	IN THE COURT OF
	:	REVENGE OF CAMBRIA
Plaintiff,	:	COUNTY
	:	
v.	:	
	:	
BRANDON ROTH,	:	Case No. FUBRANDON444
	:	
	:	
Defendant	:	

JANUARY 15:
QUESTION PRESENTED

"'DEAR SHATTERED HEART,'" I READ OUT LOUD to myself in my empty living room.

"'Wow. I am so sorry. Not only was this your first love, the two of you were together for what amounts to about a third of your life. I can physically feel the sting through my computer screen. That's saying something because our wireless signal isn't that strong here at the *Tribune Republican*. If what you say is true, that your significant other dropped you for someone else with absolutely no warning . . . that just stinks. Plain and simple.

"'In your letter, I hear your anguish and grief and disbelief. But what I do not hear is a desire to get back together with him. Not that you should want to, only that it is notable that that isn't what you are asking. You only asked how you are supposed to keep going and believe in love again. This says to me that underneath all this crap, you have within you a strength and resilience that will serve you well. The question becomes—how do you access these resources? What will trigger them to kick in?

"I think you need something to distract you. You mentioned that you are some sort of artist, but that your art has suffered because of this break up. Your heart just isn't into it. It's okay to take a step back. One hobby or vocation (or relationship) does not define you. Can you start something new? Something physical, with your hands, that allows you to get into a new zone and make something? True story: Knitting saved my life after a particularly bad break up myself. What would you think about learning to knit? Readers—do you have stories of hobbies that helped you move on? (Or, possibly, sassy beginner patterns?) Comment below!'"

JANUARY 18: BRIEF ANSWER

I STOOD STARING UP AT A WALL OF YARN half an hour before school.

"Can I help you?" said a lady with a silver mohawk and impressive tattoo sleeves.

"You have a tattoo of a skull and crossbones with knitting needles," I said.

"Yes, I do."

"You are really into this?" I gestured toward the wall.

"I mean. I own a yarn store," she said.

"Gotcha," I said. I sniffed back a stray memory of dick Brandon. "I would like to learn. To knit. To cope with heartbreak," I said.

"You are the third one. A girl wrote a letter in the paper. Poor thing. I hope her ex drops dead. Good for business, though."

"I'm the third?" I asked.

"Yup. Here's what I'm recommending—long flat scarf. Great project to start, easy to correct mistakes, useful in the Pennsylvania winter, thoughtful gift, and can be used to choke someone. Perfect both practically and metaphorically."

"Yes, that does sound like what I need," I said.

"I'm going to set you up with some number tens and a pretty worsted weight. What is your favorite color?" she said.

"Blue? Actually, no. Any other color than blue. Green, maybe?"

"Great. I have some with gradient coloring. It will keep it interesting, watching the colors change without having to switch skeins."

Nothing she said made any sense to me.

"Awesome?" I said. "Is this the yarn I'm using?" I pointed to a section of wall with the most captivating rainbow of colors.

"Well . . . I would say to hold off on this stuff. It's hand-dyed Peruvian alpaca. It will set you back a pretty penny, and that particular kind is so fine it would take you forever to finish. If you devote yourself to becoming a full-fledged yarnie, I'll let you have your pick, twenty percent off. For now, use this." The woman walked over to another rack and pushed a puffy cylinder of green into my hands.

"Okay," I said.

"And take these." She handed me a pair of purple needles.

"Okay," I said.

She rang me up, and I surrendered the birthday money I'd been saving to buy Brandon a sixth-anniversary present.

"Take this, too," she said, slipping a flyer into the bag. "There's a beginner's group that meets upstairs every Tuesday. It's free but bringing snacks to share is recommended. Given my recent uptick in sales, it might also function as a 'newly single' support group."

"Thanks." I sighed.

"We've all been there, sweetheart. You'll cast it off soon enough. Roll the skein into a ball before you come to a meetup here at your LYS."

"LYS?" I said.

"Local yarn store. Actually, if you come early enough, you can use the yarn ball winder."

"Thanks," I said again.

I clinked the bell on the door on the way out. I passed a woman who could have been my mom's age coming in. Her face looked blotched and her eyes puffed. How many breakups had Steelton had lately? And who knew so many people read the paper?

Maybe she just had winter allergies.

JANUARY 19: DISCUSSION

"I NEED YOU TO COME WITH ME TONIGHT," I said to Megan.

"But I don't want to learn to knit. I'm not heartbroken." She turned the steering wheel and navigated her car into a parking space in the slush-filled Steelton High lot.

"You should do it for me," I said.

"I've come to every production you've ever been in. That's about three plays and maybe a musical a year. I hate sitting still. Why do I have to do this, too?"

"How many swim meets do you have in a year? Ten? *And* I came to the swim-camp mixer because that dude you liked stopped by."

"Michael Phelps is an Olympic world record holder. You got to hug him. I was doing you a favor."

"Ten meets a year. You've been swimming since third grade. I've helped you wax your legs. Tell me *one* knitting class is worse than that."

"Okay, okay, fine."

"Good," I said. I took a deep breath and got out of the car.

"All clear," said Megan.

A best friend who did a visual Brandon/Ruby sweep was a keeper.

"Great," I said.

"Are you sure you don't want to run lines or something at lunch? Usually by Presidents' Day you are forcing me to run lines for spring auditions."

"They're doing fucking *Our Town*."

"I know."

"I hate that play."

"You also made that pretty clear."

"So, what's the point?"

"Don't you have to audition for Carnegie Mellon soon? And Claire? Doesn't she want to go there, too? And they take about minus seven people into the program?"

I shrugged.

"Girl, forget tonight; obviously we need to go knit *now*." She looked at her watch. "At 9.30 a.m. I'll ditch school. I am seriously worried here."

"The group meets at seven."

"I'll pick you up."

"Okay." I waved as she walked into her homeroom. I moved through a sea of bodies toward my locker and there, of course, came Brandon and the new woman. Heads together. Happy.

Why were these assholes constantly walking down hallways, visible in public?

I ducked into the girls' room to do more breathing or possibly sobbing. The restroom wasn't a great place for this because the odor of pee and illicit strawberry vaping did not exactly create a calming atmosphere. I slid into my favorite stall, the one with the FEMINISTS WIPE THE SEAT graffiti. All my breakup grief had helped condition a pretty powerful new lung response. I bet I could project to the back of the auditorium without a mic now. Or maybe the entirety of the gym. In happier times, maybe this would have . . .

The sound of unmeasured gasps pulled me from my pity party. For a second, I thought I'd sat next to happy people getting it on in the girls' room, but no. I could recognize the sound of someone else sobbing, as well-acquainted I had become with my own. I weighed my options. Personally, I wanted to disappear when I hid in the bathroom. But this person sounded worse than I thought I ever felt, which was saying something.

I left my stall and looked at the closed door next to it. The sobs kept coming. I knocked gently. "Hello?" I said. "Are you okay?"

The sobs lessened a bit.

"Listen, I know this probably sounds weird, but I totally come in here to cry, too. Actually, I'm likely closing in on detention, I'm late for homeroom so much, but I think Mr. Plaza is just happy I'm not crying there. Are you hurt?"

"No," came a voice.

"Do you need a pad or something?"

"No," said the voice again, though it shook less than the first time. I heard shuffling and the door opened.

"Oh! Millie!" I said. I recognized her from Brandon's Mock Trial team. "What's wrong?"

She hung her head. "N-nothing," she said.

"Oh. Okay?" I said. She and I weren't exactly friends. I'd talked to her at a party once. She said her favorite musical was *Waitress*, and I could find no fault in that.

"No," she said. "It's awful. I've been kicked off Mock Trial! I think I was in shock before when I found out. Now that I've had some time for it to sink in, I couldn't keep it together in American Government class," she said.

"They can do that?" I'd never heard of such a thing.

"Since the team did so well last year, we had three times the number of people come out. So, they had tryouts. Made us go through old, weird case law that wasn't even related to this year's case! I usually have to spend way more time preparing my stuff, and they gave us no time to prepare. They picked a freshman whose dad went to Columbia to be the third lawyer. Who cares if he went to Columbia?"

"Yeah." I nodded. God, the poor girl. If drama actually kicked me out, fucking *Our Town* or not, my head might explode.

"The Mock Trial president is such an ass. *Jeffrey.* His dad went to Columbia, too. He thinks he's a sure thing for early decision. Dumped by that loser. I'm a huge reason the team made it as far as it did. I always made them do the extra research. It never hurts. But no. Some new person just swoops in. Brandon said I could be part of their research initiative. I'm not even an understudy."

Millie and I were starting to have a lot in common. She seemed to realize that at the same time I did.

"Oh, I mean, um . . . sorry . . ." she said.

"No, it's all right." I sighed. "The Mock Trial vice president sucks, too."

"Everyone who ran the group was boys. There were only three girls on the whole team. Two graduated last year, and I was the last one. Now it's all boys, even with all the new people. The rest of us can be understudies or fake paralegals, but eff that, you know?"

"Eff that," I agreed.

"This stinks. I love Mock Trial. I quit Model UN last year after it got weird because the secretary slept with the treasurer. Then Model Congress went downhill when they got gridlocked over the fake border-security bill, so I quit that, too. But I thought the mock judiciary branch was safe!" She hung her head and veered close to hyperventilating in under twenty seconds.

"Do you want a hug?" I said. It seemed the only logical thing to do with my sister-in-dumpedness, there in the middle of the girl's bathroom.

She either loudly nodded or hiccupped violently. I gingerly wrapped my arms around her shoulders. The bell indicating the end of homeroom rang.

"Listen. I can't be late to chem again. But I want you to know that I feel you on this. I feel you so hard it hurts. If you go rogue and form your own vigilante Mock Trial team, let me know. I could be a witness," I said.

She straightened up in my arms. I stepped back.

"What?" she said.

"What?" I said back.

"What did you say?"

"Uh. Only, you know. If you decided to form your own team, I could act. On it. The team. Not that you would." I had only been trying to make her feel better. I didn't think she'd actually been listening.

"Form my own team," she said, though it seemed mostly to herself.

"Well, I gotta go. Hang in there!" I called. I bumped out of the restroom and ran/walked to lab, which was blessedly close to the home-room I'd just avoided. On my way there I saw Mr. Plaza and let him know it'd been another case of potential early morning waterworks. He, as expected, seemed relieved he hadn't had to deal with me.

After lunch, I walked into drama ready to stare off into space, baffled at what my life had become. Or maybe ready to kick the wall. It could go either way with me in any second. Megan was right when she harassed me about my lack of participation in drama. Claire had become the de facto president, since I could barely get through club period without snapping a pencil I'd been doodling with and spent most of the time breathing deeply. I hadn't even looked at lines. Mr. Cooper had even tried calling Mom (though she slept through his calls and I was able to delete them from her cell before she detected anything).

I had started theater because Brandon said he thought I'd be good at it, and tween Raina had wanted to impress him. Ha! I had kept at it because it kept impressing him. Did I ever love it for myself? Even if I did, I hated being here because of Brandon.

The sophomores whispered to themselves and the freshman

scanned scripts. All the juniors and seniors circled around Claire. I couldn't bring myself to even go over to them.

"All right, everyone," said Mr. Cooper. "If you want to be onstage crew or tech, come over here. Otherwise, partner up and keep getting a feel for the roles you might like. Remember, there are no small parts!"

That was a lie. There were small parts. In theater and in life. Sometimes you were the leading lady, and sometimes you were a walk-on in someone's life. One sucked and the other didn't. What good did it do to pretend otherwise?

Three people took Mr. Cooper up on his offer for crew and tech. Usually we didn't have enough people in drama to run the board, so the AV Club stepped in to help. I imagined Claire would have to persuade them to do it again.

No, I would. Since I'm the president. That was my job.

"Raina?" a voice said. A junior minion of Claire's gestured me to the circle.

I noticed Mr. Cooper sneaking glances at me, so I heaved myself up and joined the group.

"Yup?" I said.

"Auditions are *this Friday*. As you know," said Claire.

Shit, really? I tried to keep my cool, but Claire could sniff out weakness. My brain fog lifted a bit, and I remembered Mr. Cooper saying something about that last week.

"Yeah. And you are running them. As *president* and all."

Brandon and I had only been broken up for two weeks. Two weeks of no arguing over what movie to watch, no hours-long text conversations, no *Sundays*. It felt like ten years.

"Raina, are you even here with us?" Claire said, scowling.

I thought about it. "Maybe not," I said.

This answer surprised us both.

"What does that mean?" she asked.

What did it mean? Had the center of my existence been a lie? If

I didn't care about this, what did I have left? What about the future? Could I really just go from the star of *Taming of the Shrew* to theater dropout in days? Over a boy?

Yes, I realized.

I could 100 percent do that.

But it was more than just the boy. This was about me figuring out what *I* wanted and why.

"Claire," I said weakly. I cleared my throat and projected with my well-worked diaphragm. "I've been thinking about it, and I've decided. I am resigning my position as president of the Drama Club. As vice president, it is now yours to run. I'm going to study hall with all the nonclub affiliates. Mr. Cooper, I'm sorry," I said.

Silence followed me to the doorway. I turned, because a small slice of who I thought I once was remained. "You could do a lot better than *Our Town*. God. It's so overdone."

I SPENT THE REST OF THE PERIOD ALONE IN the bathroom.

Megan had an away swim meet after school, so I didn't see her until she picked me up for our first knitting venture.

"You told who what now?" she said.

"I quit drama, and I might have volunteered to be on a rival Mock Trial team," I said. "Millie Goodwin was so upset. She got kicked off because a million boys joined up or something and she bombed her audition."

"You quit drama? That can't be for real. And too bad about Millie. Why didn't you invite her to *rows before bros* or whatever thing you are making me go to? I still smell like chlorine because I barely had time to shower."

"I did quit drama. And Millie—it didn't seem appropriate. It was a different form of angst. Also, she didn't seem ready to be handed spearlike objects. Speaking of which, are you going to buy needles?"

I wanted to change the subject before Megan got back onto the topic of me breaking up with my second great love before February.

"No need. Got some from my grandma a year or so ago. I've never heard that woman so happy as when I called and told her I'd be doing it again. I had to sit through a full hour with her FaceTiming from her yarn and quilting room. Which used to be my dad's, I'm told. He still seemed bitter about the changeover, and he hasn't lived there in twenty years."

"Knitting can stitch us back together, but sometimes you have to tear things apart to move forward," I said.

"You make that up yourself?"

"No, it was on the back of the flyer the yarn store lady gave me."

"Of course it was," said Megan.

We pulled up to the curb, since the tiny parking lot that served the yarn store and the bakery next door were full.

Megan shoved me in the door first. My friend from before looked up as the bell jingled.

"Hello!" she said warmly. "I was so hoping you'd come."

"Brought my ball of yarn and my needles!" I held up my Steelton Three Rivers Theater Festival tote bag.

"Excellent. And you brought a friend."

"You know my grandmother," said Megan.

"Oh. I bet she's thrilled to have another generation of knitter starting out."

"Yes. Yes, she is," said Megan, barely holding back a grimace.

I poked her with a knitting needle through the side of my tote bag.

"Well, head on upstairs, girls. We've got a full house tonight."

Megan hesitated at the base of the stairs. It was my turn to shove her. We hoofed it to the top, to a wide, open room with folding chairs formed into a circle in the middle. A long table sat covered in snacks. I hastily added my sad package of fig cookies to the pile. Most of the other stuff looked homemade. We helped ourselves to crackers and cheeseballs and fudgy brownies.

"I almost forgive you for this," said Megan.

"Mmphf," I answered, my mouth full of brownie.

After a few minutes, the store lady (who wore a name tag that read CARLA) whistled us to attention.

"Welcome, welcome! Lots of newcomers tonight. Thanks to you all, especially to the person who brought the crostini. Was that homemade?"

"You bet," said a tiny woman with purple hair.

"Fabulous. Okay, question. No need to go into detail here, but just out of curiosity, how many people are here because of the recent Two Hearts letter?"

Seven hands shot up, including mine.

"Got it. Okay, listen. We are going to get you casting on and stitching here, but I want to warn you that you can knit your emotions into your work. Tighter stitches could be harder for you noobs. Not as easy to get the needle in there and often a pain to fix if you aren't used to unraveling and trying again. Do a little finger flexing or some belly breathing before we start. That might be good for all of us."

"What Two Hearts letter?" the woman sitting directly next to Carla asked.

"Beatrice, dear, we don't need to talk about it. I told you . . ."

"She wrote it," Megan said, pointing to me.

I tried to kill her with my angry eyes of death.

"Wrote what?" said Beatrice.

"The letter," said Megan. She must not have gotten enough to eat after her meet. Too much exercise and too few calories made her hangry mean.

"Um. My boyfriend dumped me. The newspaper column lady told me to do something active to move on. Like knit."

"Oh my God, you really are in high school," said someone across the circle. "I thought the letter writer said that to hide their identity."

"Nope," I said. "Totally in high school."

"Wow," murmured the group. Apparently, these people all had to wait until after college to have their love stomped on. Was this what adulthood was? I thought life got better when you could vote and drink and gamble and rent cars with less insurance.

Carla cleared her throat. "Well, thank you for bringing us together, um . . ."

"Raina," I said.

"Yes. Raina. Knitting is a fantastic way to pass the time and make some beautiful art. It engages the fingers and the brain and, dare I say, the soul. Get out your balled yarn, please. Beatrice is going to lead us in some casting on. The pros here for fun or yarn winding, feel free to continue with your projects. I'll come around the circle for questions."

Megan and I watched Beatrice. I had trouble making a slipknot but caught on after a few tries. I breathed and flexed to avoid hate flowing through my needles to make extra-tight loops.

That took a few tries, too.

After an hour and a half, my back hurt, but I'd managed fifteen rows of green. Pride swelled through my whole body.

"I made something!" I said to Megan. I looked at her foot of scarf. "Well, I started something. How did you *do* that?"

"My grandma had me do this when I was little. It's been years. But it comes back to you. Muscle memory, you know?"

"You're holding out on me, woman."

"It's more fun than I remember. It's a lot easier now. I think it's probably because of my longer fingers and fine motor control."

"Yes. Sure. That," I said.

Megan was exhausted exercising all her motor control in a day, so she dropped me off right after knitting.

"There you are," Mom said. "It's ten on a school night."

"You are almost never home," I said.

"Are you out like this all the time?" she said.

"Well. No. Today was an exception. I went to The Dropped Stitch to join my first knitting circle."

"I . . . That is the lamest cover story I've ever heard."

"It's not a cover story. It's the truth. I'm trying to cope with my feelings through art."

"What about theater?"

I shrugged.

Mom stared at me.

"Look. I can prove it." I pulled out my tiny section of scarf. "See?"

Mom ran her fingers along the synthetic fibers. "Well. Shit."

"Exactly. I am a dangerous rebel, and you should fear for my future."

"I guess so." Mom yawned. "Did you eat dinner?"

"I had a lot of artichoke dip at my LYS."

"LYS . . ."

"My local yarn store, The Dropped Stitch, Mom. I told you."

"Right. Okay. I'm going to have some cereal and go to bed. I switched with someone because their baby was sick. I should know better. I'll probably toss and turn. Night, love." Mom yawned again and turned into the kitchen. "Oh, Daddy texted and said he missed you and to tell you hi," she said.

"Cool," I said. I had a cell phone and Dad could just have easily texted me, but he wasn't that great with technology. You'd think a guy who lived most of his life driving a truck would have a handle on keeping in touch with people long distance.

I threw my tote bag on the floor and collapsed on my bed. I was so over being awake and doing stuff and trying to be a functional human being in the world, but I still played on my phone for hours to wind down. "At least it's too late in the day for anything else to happen," I said out loud to my room.

Then my phone buzzed.

EMILIA GOODWIN,	:	SUPREME(LY PISSED
	:	OFF) COURT OF
Plaintiff,	:	CAMBRIA COUNTY
	:	
v.	:	
	:	
STEELTON HIGH MOCK TRIAL,	:	Case No. NO2BOYSSSSS5
	:	
	:	
Defendant	:	

JANUARY 20: PLANTIFF'S ORIGINAL PETITION

HEY, I TEXTED. IT WAS AFTER MIDNIGHT, and I shouldn't really be getting in touch with someone for the first time in the middle of the night, but I couldn't sit on the idea.

I stared at the phone. I should probably explain myself.

It's Millie. Got your number from Megan? I'm forming my own Mock Trial team. The idea is genius. Are you really in?

I stared at the screen again. Dots blinked in and out of existence.

Are you serious? she finally texted back.

I find being direct in these sorts of matters works best. I tapped the phone icon. It rang twice before Raina picked up.

"Yes," I said before Raina even had a chance to speak. "Mock Trial now has a 'varsity' team. Can you believe that? The dudes are calling themselves 'varsity.' Please. I checked with Mr. Darr, the Mock Trial adviser. He said starting a second team was fine. He didn't seem that happy about it, but he watched me look up the rules in front of him. We have to ask for an exception to have two different teams from the same school, but he said it's been done before. Only one team from a school can make it past states, though."

Raina said nothing, but I could hear her breathing on the other end of the line.

"And listen. This isn't just any team. It's going to be all girls. Or all nonguys. Whatever. There are words for this. I read them in *Teen Vogue*. Cis het. That's it. No cisgendered, heterosexual men, thank you very much. Because I am *sick* of being pushed around by guys. The boys on the team. Mr. Darr."

My dad. Especially him. But that seemed like a little TMI for someone I barely knew, who I was trying to sell on my idea.

"All the kids who have dismissed me or ignored me or said to my face that the team didn't need me. The boys who think they can just be done with you when they don't need you anymore without so much as a glance back at you. No one is going to feel like that when I'm in charge." I took a deep breath. "I need two other lawyers including me, and two other witnesses plus you, and maybe a backup or a timekeeper. I bet you know people who will want to be on this team. Brandon must go down with the rest of them. You were so good in *Taming of the Shrew*. Please?"

Surely Raina could respect a person smart enough to try to win her over by appealing to her vanity. Actresses loved that kind of thing, if Claire was any indication. Maybe this wasn't drama, exactly, but it *was* acting. And I had always believed Raina had been fascinated by Brandon's trials when she'd gone as a spectator. A guest?

A bystander? Actually, I didn't know what people who watched us pretend-to-be-lawyers were supposed to be called. It didn't matter. She needed to do this.

"Well . . ." she said.

"Think about it. Think about it tonight and then tell me yes tomorrow. Because when Mock Trial wasn't so popular, those guys still made me do all the work they didn't want to do and then took all the credit. NO MORE," I said.

I hung up.

Even though I had been tired before calling Raina, I was too amped to sleep now. I tangled myself up in the sheets trying to get comfortable. Then my foot would itch, or my brain would nag, or I'd wake up with a start, surprised that I wasn't in the middle of winning states. I got up and drank warm milk and listened to my meditation app, but the hours that crept by wrecked me more and more.

Wednesday morning edged its way from dark to light. I should have been making notecards on how to write an opening statement. Or watching videos of nationals past. Instead, I had to find an entirely new team in, what? Weeks. Days, really. We had to get going.

THE NEXT MORNING, DAD AND I DROVE TO school in customary silence. He glanced over at me twitching in my seat, but probably figured it had to do with my period and didn't want to ask. He thought everything had to do with my period. Claire was home sick, so I went to homeroom alone. I did all the things I normally did until after lunch when I gave myself a pep talk in the girls' room. Then I stood in the hallway, next to the second-floor water fountain, confused about where to go. I'd been forced out of Mock Trial. I could go to study hall, but the silence there would leave me alone with my thoughts. I could go to the bathroom again, but that had the same problem as study hall plus the pee smell.

"There you are," said Raina.

I practically jumped. Actresses could have a shockingly light step.

"I've been thinking about it. This Mock Trial thing. It'd be a new role for me." Her voice caught. "Not that I'm looking for a role . . ." She fidgeted with something shiny sticking out of her messenger bag.

"Do you have a knife?" I said. I could feel my eyes widen.

Raina laughed. "Close," she said, pulling a knitting needle out of the bag. It glinted under the flickering hallway lights.

"You . . . knit?" I said. This didn't seem to go with what I knew of her personality. Though, technically, all I really knew was that she annoyed the heck out of Claire (which was easy to do) and that she had loved Brandon.

"It's a newly acquired hobby," she said. "Anyway, I'm in. Goodbye theater; hello judicial branch. Give me the script. Er. The statement. Whatever."

"Yes," I said. I held my fist out for a bump.

Raina curled her fingers and let her knuckles meet mine.

"We have to find people. Do you know anyone?" I said.

The blank look on Raina's face offered zero encouragement.

A small shriek of panic suggested itself to the back of my throat. I fought it back. I had to focus. "Adversity is the first step to opportunity," I muttered.

"What?" said Raina.

"Nothing," I said. "Anyway, we need people—girls—who might be interested in the law, or acting maybe, but aren't already too committed to something else. Being a witness is kind of fun, if you like improvising. It's a lot of pressure when you are up there, under cross-examination. But there isn't too much writing or anything for prep work. The lawyers have to pick from an opening statement—I probably should do that—writing questions for the witnesses, closing statements. Maybe we could hit up the literary magazine. They don't have stuff on weekends for that club."

"Come to think of it, I might know somebody," said Raina. "One of the literary people."

"Oh! Fantastic. Who? Where is she? Can we find her now?"

"She's probably in the media lab for club period."

"Well, we technically aren't supposed to be just hanging out in the hallway right now. Lead the way."

I followed Raina down the stairs and into the shop wing, past whirring buzz saws to the end of the hall.

"I've only ever been down here once before," I said. Other than football, the shop kids probably were the pride of Steelton High. Half made beautiful chairs and armoires and chests and the other half fixed cars for the community. The people down here were artists. It helped that the media people made impressive commercials for them that aired with the televised announcements each morning.

"I had a brief poetry stint. It didn't last. But it got me some connections," said Raina.

We entered a long, narrow room filled with computers. On one end, several kids clustered around a dry-erase wall, intensely arguing over various displayed pictures of cats.

"Hey. Finally come back to the cool kids?" said a bored voice on the other end of the room.

Raina approached a girl with flawless brown skin and dark braids elegantly arranged on the top of her head. Her foot sat propped up on a chair, a white and bright orange cast covering most of the bottom of her leg.

"Nice scooter you got yourself, there," Raina said, pointing to a slender silver cart next to her.

"That's my sweet ride. I can kneel in it and roll right along. It's better than crutches. I hated the crutches." The girl glanced over to me. "Hello, new person," she said.

"I'm Millie," I said, sticking out my hand.

The girl raised an eyebrow at me but grinned. "Veronica. Pleasure to make your acquaintance. What brings you ladies down here?"

"We are recruiting," said Raina.

"What?"

"The boys of the Steelton High Mock Trial team recently decided they no longer require my competition-winning skills. I am forming my own team. Right now, it's just me and her," I said.

"Ohhhhh. Isn't your man on that team?" Veronica looked up at Raina.

Raina sunk into a chair. "He's still on the team. No longer my man," she said.

"Oh. Wow. That sucks. Sorry. I'm out of the loop these days. Sorry."

"Don't worry about it. I have decided to channel my feelings into the replica justice system," she said.

"Wait, what about the plays? You were all about those."

"I should probably text you more often," said Raina. "No more theater. It's a long story. Anyway—look. Mock Trial has everything that you like—writing stuff, winning stuff, and yelling at people."

"I don't know about—" I started, but Raina waved her hands.

"Imagine it. You in a real courtroom. Everyone listening to your brilliant arguments. You convince the judge that you know what you are talking about and the other team is a disgrace to the written word. Then we all win and high-five. It'll take up a few weekends with competition."

I watched Veronica's face as she considered this.

"Ronnie, we can't decide if we should go with the tabby or the Norwegian Forest for this month's back matter. Thoughts?" a voice called.

"The Norwegian Forest, obviously," she yelled. "I admit, now that I can't climb, I do have some free time. And my duties as assistant editor for *Puns of Steel* isn't taking as much time as I hoped it would. This annual Cattitude issue might destroy us all." She glanced over to her arguing editorial board.

"What did you climb?" I said.

"Walls, mostly. Rock walls."

"Veronica is one of the best competitive climbers in Pennsylvania. Maybe the country."

"Or I was, until I fell three months, two weeks, and one day ago. But who's counting? Shattered my ankle. The ol' climbing career is on hold for a while. I've been swimming, with my fiberglass cast here. Good for the arms. For cardio. But I'm slow so it's not like I can take on anyone with—wait." She stopped talking and pointed at me. "Wait. I'm sorry—did you say the dudes kicked you off the team?"

"Something like that." I sniffed. "A lot more people came out for the team this year. You can only have six people in a trial with speaking parts. I was an alternate. Or maybe they just wanted me to write everything for them. But since Raina and I both got dumped, I had this idea. Who needs those . . . those *jerkfaces*."

"Whoa, bringing the heat there, Millie. Careful you don't get us kicked out of here," said Raina, glancing around.

"Oh, I didn't mean to offend . . . ," I said.

"I will no longer be offended if you use my preferred term of 'dick assholes.' It is more accurate language," said Raina.

Veronica laughed. "Either works for me. That's just wrong, Millie who I just met. What year are you? You're a senior, too, aren't you?"

"Yes," I said. "Fourth year on the team."

"Jerkface asshole dicks," she said.

"What do you think? Are you in?" said Raina.

"Well, I don't know. I do like arguing with people. But it sounds like a lot of sitting around and talking."

"It is, but it's a lot more than that! It's debate! You have to listen to everything the other team says to find the holes in their argument. You have to be ready to jump on anything their witness might say to use it to your advantage. It's like—uh—looking for a handhold in a weird rock thing. You'd be perfect!" I said.

I didn't know much about climbing. The closest I'd ever gotten is Dad googling how much it would cost to take a trip to the Red River Gorge last summer.

"Well—" Veronica sounded unconvinced.

"We decided on a Chartreux!" said someone from the cluster at the other end of the room. "It's really the best. Now we can move on to my fifteen suggested quotes to go with it."

"Oh my God, would you at least look at the Birman!" said someone else. The group started arguing again.

Veronica sighed. "Yeah, okay," she said to us.

"What?" said Raina.

"I'm in. I'll do it. Lawyer it up with yinz. Send me a schedule. I have a date with the courts. Lord knows someone needs to reform it." She grimaced as she tried to shift her leg on its pillow in the chair.

"Fantastic!" I said. "You won't regret this! I'm really sorry you're in pain."

"I'm sorry the dicks dumped you," said Veronica.

"You wouldn't happen to know anyone else who might want to join up, would you?" I said. "I need another lawyer. And two witnesses. And a timekeeper. Actually, I need a lawyer to be our adviser. Do you know any lawyers?"

"No. I'm afraid not. My mom is a dentist, and my dad runs an online model-train supply store. I'm your girl if you need an HO- or N-scale caboose, though."

"Noted," I said.

You never knew. The Mock Trial cases could involve anything. I added Veronica's expert consultants to my mental database, vowing to remember teeth and trains.

The bell sounded, indicating the end of activities period.

"Pull me up, would you?" asked Veronica.

Raina and I each grabbed a hand. Veronica's muscles flexed under her sheer top as she righted herself into her kneeling scooter. She must lift, to be able to scale walls. I wouldn't want to take her on in any competition. The Steelton *varsity* Mock Trial team probably got winded walking up two flights of steps.

Today was a good day. Raina waved goodbye to me as we left the media lab and jogged off toward another wing. For the rest of classes I eyed everyone around me, sizing up their potential for the team. I left school and rode the bus home on top of the world. This was going to be easy! I was three people away from a team.

The affirmations really were true.

JANUARY 22: DISCOVERY CONTROL PLAN LEVEL

I SAT DOWN AT THE KITCHEN TABLE, IGNOR-ing the dishes still there from breakfast.

Recruitment was possibly not going to be as easy as I thought. It had slowed considerably after we got Veronica.

Technically, it had stopped entirely.

Claire, best friend in the world, I texted. *I am well on my way to Mock Trial domination. But I need more witnesses. Do any of your theater friends hate that play as much as you? Actors make good witnesses. No Mock Trial experience needed.*

I'm doing well, thanks, she texted back.

You had a bad cold. I figured you were still alive.

I waited a minute. Nothing.

How are you feeling, you poor, poor thing? Can I get you anything? Do you struggle for survival? You are so brave! I texted.

That's better. I had strep throat. I'm still coughing but I slept a bunch. And you have already taken up with my theater enemy, she wrote.

Raina needed something to do with her free period besides mourn lost love or whatever. And she found me another lawyer. This is good for everyone. Besides, you didn't even have to compete for the part you wanted.

IN FUCKING OUR TOWN.

Exactly.

She silenced her typing fingers again, so I called.

"I didn't think you'd pick up," I said.

Claire coughed.

"Oh stop it. I have a working relationship with your only acting rival in the school. Knock it off."

"Fine, fine," she said. She blew her nose. "Who is the new lawyer? Anyone cute?"

"Veronica, a literary magazine woman who also climbs stuff, only not anymore because she broke her foot."

"Oh, snap," said Claire. "She is *beautiful*. Is she single? Are you going to ask her out?"

"Yes. She's gorgeous." I rolled my eyes at her predictability since I knew she couldn't see. "And I think she's straight, but even if she weren't, you know my position on these things. Fortunately for me, she lives to compete and Mock Trial presents that in a seated format."

"Congrats," said Claire.

She did not sound nearly as enthusiastic as I would have liked.

"Are you really mad about Raina? This was her idea, and it gave me new life," I said.

Claire coughed for a while, but I think it was a cover, so she didn't have to respond.

"No, I'm not really mad," she said. "Jealous, maybe."

"Jealous of who?" I asked.

"Raina. Because she gets to hang out with you more. Possibly because she doesn't have to be in fucking *Our Town*, but I bet she also got a starring role as a lead witness."

"I mean, you can be on the team. Competition starts in February, and I am in a pinch here. You don't even need to quit the play."

"But then there's college auditions and summer stock to think about. And . . ."

"Well, I offered," I said. "Anyway, are you sure there isn't a junior I could borrow? One overly dramatic, angsty junior who could memorize seven pages of information? Surely there is *one*. You know what? I'm not even picky. I'd take a sophomore or freshman even."

"Hmm. Maybe. I'll think about it." Claire coughed again.

"Do you need something? Soup?"

"Nah, I'm fine. My aunt is bringing my grandma over with rum or something to heat up."

"That cures strep throat?"

"Or maybe it's whiskey. I don't know. You mix it with stuff. It sounded gross, but she swears it's kept her alive for eighty-five years, so I wasn't going to argue."

"Good move."

We hung up. Claire was still being fussy over Raina, but I knew she'd come around. Hopefully, she'd find me two reasonable people in the next week or two.

My gaze drifted up from my phone back to the kitchen table. My stomach rumbled, reminding me that it'd been a lot of hours between my ham sandwich and now.

The recycling hadn't been taken out in a few days.

Or the garbage.

And the counters never stopped being sticky.

I knew Dad's job kept the heat on, but honestly, he was still the adult in this equation. It wouldn't have killed him to clean something every now and then. When Mom left, it seemed he just assumed I'd fill all the roles she had filled. I realized day by day how many there had been. On top of cleaning and cooking, apparently Mom did all the doctors and dentist appointments for him because Dad had forgotten. Sometimes I'd peek in at him in his office, and he was just playing computer games, so how busy could the man be?

But sometimes you had to prioritize things in order to be a team player.

"Focus on the self that is the best self of all," I breathed.

I noticed that some daily affirmations made more sense than others.

I wondered if that is why she'd left. Maybe the new husband did more than mow the lawn.

I got a sponge and brushed the crumbs off the kitchen table into the last few centimeters left at the top of the garbage bag. I scrubbed at the strange stains on the plastic tablecloth and tried my best to make the counters shine. I unloaded the dishwasher, that I thankfully had remembered to turn on before I left for school. I reloaded it with all the stuff that hadn't fit before. I swept up and took out the garbage and recycling.

I'd been using a load of sheets and towels to play a game of chicken with Dad, to see how long it'd take him to notice them by the basement door. It'd been two weeks, so it occurred to me that maybe he'd gone laundry-blind and they'd just sit there and rot if I let them. I considered it, but the thought of work undone made me shudder. A girl had her limits. I picked up the dirty load and squashed it in our beautiful WashPro Elite, the last thing Mom demanded before she left.

Maybe she'd known I'd need it.

I vacuumed the living room, since I'd initiated the cleaning cycle and could never stop myself once it began. I had calc and English and history homework, not to mention plotting my Mock Trial team strategy. But my stomach rumbled again.

I parked the vacuum in the coat closet and started opening cabinets. I'd have to make Dad take me to the grocery store on Saturday, since we were low on all real food. There was fancy pizza dough that I'd snuck in the cart left in the fridge, with tomato sauce and cheese. Pizza night! This could all be salvaged. The lettuce, tomatoes, celery, and carrots were crisp (well, crisp-ish) and only a little brown. Salad! I could do this. I *was* making life work. When life gives you lemons, squeeze some juice on the counters to make them smell less weird, scrub them, and then use the rest to make lemonade.

Girl boss. That's what I was.

I listened to my Ruth Bader Ginsburg biography audiobook and got my lopsided homemade pizza into the oven. The kitchen warmed with the smell of garlic and onion.

Dad got home just as the timer went off. With great satisfaction,

I slid Mom's abandoned pizza stone out of the oven and sliced my creation into eight pieces. Next time, I should get some heirloom tomatoes or oregano to dress it up, like the fancy Italian restaurant up by the mall.

"Hi, honey," Dad said, sliding into his chair. "How was your day?"

"Great!" I said. "I am making progress with Mock Trial! You know, I actually am not on the same . . ."

Dad's phone rang.

"Sorry, baby, I have to take this. It's this nice, new lady my buddy from work introduced me to!"

Dad left the table.

I watched him retreat to the living room. I served myself pizza and salad, and then another helping of each before he came back.

"I never thought I could get back in the dating game, but it seems I'm there," Dad said.

"Oh. That's great, Dad," I said.

"It really is. Huh," Dad said, sliding a piece of pizza onto his plate. "Don't quite have your mom's technique down yet, do you?" He smiled sadly to himself.

I stopped chewing. Cheese and sauce lumped in my mouth. Part of me wanted to spit it out at him. I caught myself and choked it down instead. *This is not about you; this is about his own pain. He needs to do this to move on,* I reminded myself. I had read that in a *So Your Parents Are Getting a Divorce* pamphlet I'd found on the ground outside the guidance office.

It read a little like the same people wrote for the pamphlet company as my daily affirmation app.

Dad must have actually noticed the look on my face. "I'm sorry, honey," he said. "I just meant that I know this is hard on you, too. This all tastes wonderful."

We finished dinner in silence. I kept thinking of things I wanted to yell at him, but Dad got up and went to his tiny office next to the dining room when his phone rang again.

I surveyed the table. Clean up now, or clean up tomorrow? I sighed. *Why not both? Or why not take a flamethrower to it?* I thought. Sadly, I was all out of flamethrowers. I traced the same steps as I had after school (and before school and last night and . . .). The monotony broke a little when I transferred the sheets from the washer to the dryer. I watched blues and greens and purples rumble around one another in an endless chase. I felt like that sometimes—that everything I did was a blurred loop, repeating and repeating.

That was my excitement for the night. Identifying on an existential level with state-of-the-art appliances. Maybe Claire was right. Maybe I did need to get out more.

I waited a little longer to see if Dad would emerge from his cave, but by six thirty he still hid behind his closed door.

The dryer buzzer went off, and I slowly folded the sheet and towels. Surely, he wouldn't avoid me? What did I do except work as his maid?

I took the laundry basket upstairs with me and put everything away. I settled at my desk with my books. I heard Dad's door creak open.

"Don't worry, Dad," I said to my desk. "It's safe. You don't have to deal with me."

Stop! Focus instead on the positive, I thought. *Enough with the negative patterns. Dad is just tired and overwhelmed with work. And trying to date. And life. Stop it, Millie!*

"I forgive myself," I said out loud. "I have wants and needs, and I forgive myself for getting angry. I breathe in." I took a breath, held it, and exhaled. "I breathe out peace."

My chest felt more like it expelled barely contained garlic-scented rage, so I tried a few more times.

"Okay, time for homework," I said. "Because tomorrow is going to be another great day."

I didn't know if I believed that. But I wanted to believe it. And sometimes wanting it just had to be enough.

RAINA PETREE,	:	IN THE COURT OF
	:	REVENGE OF CAMBRIA
Plaintiff,	:	COUNTY
	:	
v.	:	
	:	
BRANDON ROTH,	:	Case No. OVERIT4SURE22
	:	
	:	
Defendant	:	

JANUARY 25: MOTION TO QUASH SUBPOENAS FOR DEPOSITION

BRANDON AND RUBY BROKE UP OVER THE weekend.

But then they got back together again today.

Not that I cared. *Obviously*, I didn't care, because I was totally moving on now, three weeks later. From his stupid blue eyes. And from the plaid shirt I noticed him wearing that brought back the memory of that time last year when we'd gone camping. It was just Brandon and me in a tent under a canopy of pine and spruce and twinkling stars. I'd been afraid of the too quiet, too dark night out there near Brandon's favorite fishing creek. But he'd made me laugh and held me close and that was the first time we'd . . .

But I didn't care anymore. *Obviously.*

Except when I did, which was more frequently than I wanted to admit to myself.

Then there was the *other* thing I totally didn't care about—Megan told me that Claire is really ruling on high in fucking *Our Town* rehearsals, because she overheard Judy from the band telling Kyle from Model Congress that Rebecca the freshman (who did commercials in middle school) was super impressed.

I wasn't smoldering over this when Mom interrupted my thoughts at the breakfast table.

"Are you working on college applications?" asked Mom.

"What?" I said. Mom had been talking for several minutes, but I hadn't been listening. I'd been wondering where Megan even saw Judy. They might have gym together.

"Applications are due soon, right? I know you turned in one or two already. I should have gone to that presentation with the guidance counselor. But they offered me an extra shift and property taxes were due. I'm sorry about that. But I want to support you. I really do. Did you hear from any yet?"

"Thanks, Mom. Not yet."

"What about NYU? Or Juilliard?"

"Juilliard, Mom? Are you serious?"

"Ah, so you are listening. Well, actors go there. New York is where actors go, isn't it?"

"I guess," I said. I made a chocolate star chase a marshmallow unicorn around in the milk at the bottom of my cereal bowl.

"Raina, look at me," Mom said.

I briefly flicked my eyes to hers.

"God, is this still about Brandon? *Raina.* Come on. Let's run lines for your play."

"Mom, I was with him for years, and we broke up less than a month ago. I'm trying here. Besides I don't have lines," I said before thinking.

"Okay, okay. A month or two for the boy. But he's not worth more. Does the spring show feature a bunch of mimes? Oh God, please not again."

Mom had never recovered from my "silent bodies in motion" performance two summers ago.

"No, I'm not in the show. I quit theater."

"You . . . what . . ." I knew I was in for it when Mom had trouble forming words. "Excuse me, young lady, I can't even begin to process . . ."

"I joined Mock Trial instead."

"You joined *Brandon's* team. That is even worse. I'm going to get your father on the phone, and we are going to . . ."

"No, I joined a rival team. All girls. It's kind of like the knitting. Therapeutic. Plus, they're doing *Our Town*. I will play a witness or two on this team and bring crushing defeat to my enemies. I needed something new, Mom."

Mom's face changed back from purple to red to its normal freckled, sandy color. I looked back down at my soggy breakfast, but I could feel her trying to bore into my brain for my thoughts.

"You joined Mock Trial for revenge?" she said.

"Kind of. Not really. It was an accident. This girl was on the team for years, and then the boys kicked her off. And I told her she should form her own team, and I'd join. I never thought she'd do it. But then she did, and *Our Town*, and here we are."

"Raina, uprooting your life for some guy is just not worth it. You need to live for *you*. Is this for you?"

I thought about that for a minute.

"Yes," I said finally. "It's still acting, Mom. But it's acting for *me*, not for Brandon. Trying something new has been helpful. It's a little easier to move on when you have something to move toward."

It was true. I was enjoying the idea that playing a witness was moving me toward something . . . else. Something meaningful. Not that acting wasn't meaningful, but this was different.

"Huh," Mom said, taking her time with her coffee. "Well, kid," she said. "You're eighteen. You've got a long time to figure it out. Just know that I'm not going to another two-hour 'speculative kinesthetic performance,' no matter how much it means to you."

"Got it, Mom," I said.

I escaped to school, where an already wound-up Millie greeted me before the first bell had even rung.

"It was going so well," she said.

"What was?" We hadn't even met as a team yet.

"Finding people. First you, then Veronica. But fifteen girls in a row have turned me down. Basketball, swimming, archeological dig—you name it. Everyone has an excuse." Millie shook her head.

"That sucks."

"Claire won't help find theater people," she said. She stepped toward me. Even though she was about five feet tall, the fire in her eyes made me take a step back.

"You. You know people. Find me a witness," she said.

"My best friend is a swimmer. Or spring musical people. Or Veronica."

The air went out of Millie like she was a popped balloon. "Yeah, you're right," she said. Her voice wavered dangerously close to tears.

"Hey, listen. We still have time. We got this," I said.

To sound confident, stand with your feet hip-width apart. Puff out your chest and breathe deep into the diaphragm. Push the air out with your words. Elevate the chin and look down at your speaker.

"Okay," said Millie. She closed her eyes for a second and moved her lips, as if in conversation with her own brain. When she looked up, I could tell she'd bought the act. "You're right. You did get us Veronica. And if we find people by next week, we will still have three weeks to prepare."

"Yes. And there are hundreds of girls here. Some of them are going to want in." I nodded for emphasis.

Satisfied, Millie left to go to the library or homeroom or maybe the intensity pod where she regained the energy it must take to live her life like that.

I'd given up my daily cry in favor of one good primal scream behind the gym.

"It actually gives you a bit of a glow," said Megan at lunch. "The scary yelling."

"Yes, it's part of my skin-care regimen now. Some moisturizer and a few broken blood vessels. I should market the technique," I said.

"I'd buy," said Megan.

"Can you come to The Dropped Stitch?" I asked Megan. "There's a special circle. Something about the past elections."

"Are you going to make sweaters for the poll workers?"

"No, Carla the owner said something about a local seat. I don't know. Come with me and you'll find out. I'm told there might be cake."

"Alas, I cannot. Away swim meet. I won't be back until late."

"All those competitions I've attended. *Does my devotion mean nothing to you?*" My head fell onto my curled arms.

"It means everything. But Coach will kill me if I don't show. You know people at YLS now. Fill me in later. I'll be on . . . wait for it"—I could feel Megan's grin—"pins and needles until you do. HA!"

"Wow, Dad. Thanks for that one. And using the yarn lingo."

"You are quite welcome," she said.

After lunch, I looked for Millie in the library, but she wasn't there. She'd probably cornered some poor soul to recruit and trapped her in a net of earnestness and fear.

Throughout my afternoon classes, I tried to spy on all the girls around me. Did anyone of them seen keen on pretending to bring truth and justice to fictional characters? Could any of them *believe* it? By junior year, most people really had their own thing going and didn't always want to try something new. Kelly was in track; Melissa babysat all the time; Ally, Connecticut, and Kathryn made movies; and Libby Dennison almost joined, but she made too much real money from painting miniature figures for some game that involved elves to sacrifice her free time. Millie was right. The rest of them were all year-long club, club, live-action role play, job, spring club, spring club, all of the above.

JANUARY 26:
MEMORANDUM IN SUPPORT

DAD HAD GOTTEN PAID, SO I HAD MY SMALL monthly cut of his automatic deposit that Mom had given me. I thought maybe new yarn would cheer me up. Mom had appreciated the hat I'd made her, even if it was lumpy, had two holes, and mysteriously expanded from the eighty stitches I'd cast on to end closer to ninety-five. I wanted to make Megan a fancy hat, but maybe I'd make Millie one first. Double-pointed needles and finer yarn still felt like too much of a challenge, even if hats were considered a beginner's project.

Millie's eyes were brown. Maybe a nice warm chestnut to match her eyes *and* her hair. Though she wore a lot of orange. Was this because it complemented her skin tone or because she just preferred it as a color? Megan would probably know this. I planned on using swimming-pool blue for her.

"Welcome back, Raina," said Carla as I walked into The Dropped Stitch. She carried handfuls of stitch counters and hung them on the rack next to the bargain yarn selections. "Can I help you with anything?"

"Just debating color choices for my next project. When you knit something as a gift, do people prefer you make it in their favorite color, or what you think would look good on them?" I said.

"I find people are touched if you make them anything at all," she said. "Go with the color that inspires you the most, I say. Or whatever reminds you of the lucky recipient."

"Yeah. Luuuuu-cky." I snorted. "I'll go with red. It's a power color. She'll like that."

"Oh, is this for your friend? The one who comes with your sometimes? What's her name? Mary?"

"Megan. No, this is for my Mock Trial teammate. I think I'll go with this nice bloodlike hue."

"Mock Trial! How appropriate for tonight. Blood it is. See you upstairs," she said.

I checked out with Carla's helper, Alex, and made my way upstairs to the meeting room. A few of the regulars were there, Beatrice and her crew, along with a few people I didn't recognize. I helped myself to cake, thinking I'd eat a piece for Megan since she chose chlorine over me.

"All right, folks, as I emailed, the Tuesday circle format is changing a bit going forward, although your penguin sweater is looking wonderful, Gretta dear. Your great-grandson is going to love it."

"Thanks!" said Gretta. "He turns five on March first, and he's excited to wear this to his party."

Carla beamed but then immediately turned all business.

"Okay, people, this is where we're at," she said. "There have been some court cases in the news lately that have me shook. The November elections did not go the way we wanted, so we have to focus on the statewide and municipal level. Like the new justice on the Supreme Court of Pennsylvania."

"That's a ten-year term," said Gretta.

"But the more immediate, pressing problem is a magisterial district judge we've got our eye on. Judge Herman T. Wise." Carla sounded like she was choking when she said his name.

Then Beatrice looked at me and another girl a few seats away who looked about my age. "A lot of things are determined at a local and statewide level, you know. I imagine you want access to legal pot, don't you?" she said.

"Not really?" I said. I'd tried it once after a cast party, but after it made me hear string cheese and taste colors, I'd vowed never to touch marijuana again. But there were lighting guys who swore by the stuff, and you always wanted the tech people on your side. I could fight for them. "He is against legal pot?"

I glanced over at the other girl. She had her hand over her mouth and shook slightly with silent laughter.

"Beatrice, for God's sake, you can go to your daughter's in Massachusetts for legal pot. They have bakeries for edibles on every corner up there. This is bigger than that!" said Carla.

"Easy for you to say," Beatrice mumbled, but then she winked at me, so clearly, she wasn't mad.

"Herman T. Wise has such a terrible record. He was accused of harassment by two of his aides. It was a shame, since his predecessor was a fierce supporter of a woman's right to choose, eliminating mandatory minimums, privacy laws. You name it," said Carla. "But then he had to go and retire."

"What could people have against privacy laws?" I asked.

"National security means the government should get to snoop whenever and wherever it wants, doesn't it? People could be texting terrorist bombing plans," said Gretta.

"Um . . ." I said. I had no idea. I thought about my midnight texts to Megan. I wasn't a national security threat, but the NSA might think I intended to hurt Brandon. I needed to bring Millie to this. I bet she watched the news. Some deep shit like Rachel Maddow. I'd have to ask her about all this.

"We are most concerned with Wise's record of judgments against women. In family-law cases, in civil cases . . . anything. He is a known misogynist. If we don't start letting our voices be heard, who knows what he will do. You think that smaller, local case judgments don't make a difference. But they can, they really can. Legal precedent can be set in the unlikeliest of places. One day you think women have the right to choose what's best for their bodies; the next the court determines it controls your uterus."

A murmur of agreement traveled around the circle. I stress-shoved more cake in my mouth. I didn't like the sound of *six years of woman-hating dude bro making law*. There was not enough Mock in this Trial for my comfort level. Maybe I could still do stage crew for fucking *Our Town*.

"What's the plan, boss?" asked Alex, the part-time store helper.

"I'm thinking we teach the noobs about anatomical yarning," said Carla. "And we do a bit of installation art. And door to door, for whoever has the time and hip flexibility."

"I finished physical therapy months ago, thank you very much," said Gretta, "if that was directed at me."

"Didn't your daughter forbid you from doing strangers' stairs?"

"I'll stay in my scooter and shout," said Gretta. She pointed a delicate, wrinkled finger at the center of the room. "Don't try to stop me, kid."

Carla held up her hands. "Fine. I just want everyone in the group to back me up when I tell your kids I wanted you on some stationary job. Like a direct-mail campaign."

"No one reads mail. You need to get on the apps," said Beatrice. "To reach the youth."

"How do you even . . . forget it. Bea, you do you. But I have print-outs of the anatomy patterns, and we will help anyone who wants to learn this for the remainder of tonight."

"Anatomical yarning?" the new girl and I said at the same time.

"Listen up, girls," said Carla. "I have a story to tell."

I sat up a little straighter. The other girl leaned forward, arms propped on her knees.

"Knitters have tacked and sewn liberty through the ages. There have been problematic elements—there are always are—but this tra-ditional women's work has forged nations."

"I . . ." started the other girl.

"Hush, Grace. For too long, maybe even today, it is believed that a woman's place is the home. Away from the public eye, out of view. But every person is capable of strength in the face of adversity, and that strength can't be contained by aprons or even legal subjugation," continued Carla.

"This is why we knit?" I said.

"Well, technically, I think people developed needlework and such because they needed clothing and mended socks and maybe just pretty things to look at. But in any art, there is a possibility to reach outside of yourself, outside the home or whatever cage you find yourself in. You can go out in public without anyone even thinking about what you are doing."

"And this is political how?" said the girl who must be named Grace.

"You ever hear of a thing called the American Revolution? About taxes driving the colonists batty? Maybe the men threw the tea in the bay—what a waste—but the women made their own cloth so they didn't have to pay exorbitant prices on British-made goods. And maybe knitting and sewing gave bored rich women something to do during the day, but it kept the working-class women alive. Today DIY throws a middle finger up to the corporations trying to sell you ease and crappy products made by mistreated workers."

One by one, the knitters put down their needles and clapped for Carla.

"Oh, stuff it," she said.

I grinned. "I'm still a little unclear about how this all will influence the judge?"

"Here is where you combine the proud activist roots of needlework with a little creative messaging," said Carla. "You have some options, here."

"I have a few great patterns for a sweater or a hat that looks like cardiograph. It represents the heartbeats of women who died at the hands of their abusers. Or you could read it as the imprint of those who died without access to affordable, appropriate medical care. Your choice," said Beatrice.

"Wow. That's deep," I said.

"And kind of dark," said Grace.

Carla nodded. "Understandable. You could also make little female reproductive organs. I have a bunch of extra cotton to stuff them."

"Why would . . ." I started.

"Complete with vulva, vagina, and uterus," said Carla.

"How would we . . ." said Grace.

"Fallopian tubes can be added if you wanted, but they are a bit floppy because they are slender, and I think the whole thing loses impact if you can't hold it firmly in your hand."

I could feel warmth rising involuntarily to my cheeks.

"Do you have the one with the labia majora, labia minora, and the clitoris? It's not difficult to change the colors on that," said Alex.

"The one I have had the uterus separate. Are yours together?" said Beatrice. "Is there something to be gained in attaching them? Truthfully, I haven't had half of those bits in twenty years. I don't even remember."

"Does the fuzz shed every twenty-eight days?" said Gretta.

Grace's face was far pinker than it had been earlier.

"Oh, don't mind them. Once you hit menopause, you really need to joke about it, or you just spend half your day angry about the lack of research into estrogen reduction and bone loss."

"What do you do with knit vulva?" I managed.

"You can also crochet it, too, dear," said Alex.

"Uh, or crocheted vulva?"

"Lots of things! I like sending vulvas to elected officials who try to exert legal control over my body. It's best to do that in bulk. Sometimes we show up and leave them in their office waiting rooms. Or they can be used in classrooms or doctors' offices. Models like these are useful for the very young who might need a speculum or vaginal exam, you know?"

"I also have a dick pattern!" called out Beatrice. "They make nice pin cushions."

The ladies roared. I worried Gretta would throw out her other hip.

Carla reached for her own knitting bag. She rummaged around for a second and handed Grace a uterus and me a vagina.

(Technically, she also handed me a vulva, clitoris, and some labia as well.)

"This is very soft yarn," I said, unable to come up with much else to comment on.

"That's alpaca. It's my display reproductive system, so I wanted it to be a higher quality. This is important, so you are welcome to use some."

"I don't even know if I can do this," I said. "My hats turned out all wrong."

"It's basically just a ball. And look, your vagina is a tube. They are like scarves that you just stich together. Don't worry. I believe in you. Have you been practicing reading patterns?"

"Yes," I said.

"Good. Use this one, then. It really is beginner. And it's pretty fast. You could make this set in a couple of days."

"This . . . dot in the middle?" I couldn't bring myself to call it by its name in front of the group. "It's only a few stiches of another color. How do I . . ."

"Your young fingers are nimble," said Alex.

"Just work it, honey."

"Knit that clit!" said Gretta.

Grace put her head into her hands.

"All of you are the worst," said Beatrice.

"Says the dick-pattern lady," Carla said.

Knitting circle at The Dropped Stitch could never be called boring.

At the end of the meeting I felt a little light-headed. I gathered my newly purchased, conveniently red yarn (with a small skein of purple for clitoral purposes, white for labia majora), and made my way to the parking lot as fast as humanly possible.

"Is it always this wild?" asked a voice behind me.

I turned and saw Grace heading out the door.

"This is only my second circle. This was the first mention of genitalia."

"Good to know."

"Have you never been here before?" I asked.

"We just moved here. Dad got a job running a lab at Penn State Steelton. I'm from Intercourse."

"Is this a knitting joke?"

"Intercourse, PA. It's a real place. I like leading with that. It either breaks the ice or scares people. You can tell a lot about a person by how they react."

I grinned. "Where is that?"

"It's not far from Lancaster."

I nodded like I knew anything about that side of the state. Everything east of State College might as well be a blank map with *Here There Be Dragons* scrawled on it. This was mostly owed to the fact that Philly schools crushed us at every state festival I'd attended, so I'd repressed the memory of them.

"Welcome to Steelton. We produce exceptional dairy products and fuzzy anatomy."

Grace laughed. "I actually start school tomorrow. I was going to wait until Monday, but I couldn't take another day at home unpacking with my dads. They take organization too seriously."

"Are you going to Steelton High?" I said.

"You got it."

I looked at her. She was on the heavier side like me, and had short blond hair, shaved on one side and the other swept into an artful wave on the other. Her lip and nose and ears were all pierced, and she wore several necklaces, long and short, over an explosion of colorful layers.

"Nice necklaces," I said.

"Oh, thanks!" she said. "I found this one in town today." She approached and held one up in The Dropped Stitch's porch light. "It's Ruth Bader Ginsburg's dissent collar."

"Ruth Bader Ginsburg," I said.

"Yes."

"The Supreme Court justice."

"Is there any other?"

Somewhere, I could sense Millie tense and psychically look in our direction.

"She's how I got into knitting, actually," said Grace. "Funny story. I wanted to go as her for Halloween, but I couldn't find any good costumes. They were all sexy lawyer and sexy judge, you know? And she has all these collars that always impressed me. Lace is hard and some of that sheer fabric is a bitch, but you can crochet something that gets close to a near replica. And it just went from there. I've even knit a few uteri in my day but never a vagina. And I've never heard them discussed at such great length." Grace glanced at Beatrice coming out of the door and grinned.

"Ruth Bader Ginsburg," I said again. "You really like her."

"Yes?" she said.

"Well, Grace," I said, "do I *ever* have an opportunity for *you*."

EMILIA GOODWIN,	:	SUPREME(LY PISSED OFF) COURT OF
	:	
Plaintiff,	:	CAMBRIA COUNTY
	:	
v.	:	
	:	
THE PATRIARCHY,	:	Case No. GRLPWR4US
	:	
	:	
Defendant	:	

JANUARY 29: NONPARTY'S VERIFIED MOTION

I BRUSHED THE SOFT PINK THREADS UNDER my fingers.

"This is so beautiful!" I said as I squeezed my anatomically correct heart (mostly—it had eyes and a mouth).

"My knitting group is getting political. I needed to practice before I could commit to their . . . other patterns. This heart is my first attempt at crochet. You'll note the valves in turquoise. Grace helped with those. This is Grace, by the way."

"Yes, I get it. I appreciate the happy face. It's really for me?" I said. I looked at Raina and the new Mock Trial recruit.

"I was going to make you a hat, too," said Raina. "But then needed to move to this."

"Would you like a set of lungs to go with it?" Grace asked. Her eyeliner sparkled silver. There was a magic to her there, even under the pale hallway lights.

I laughed. "I mean, if you want." The bell rang. "We are meeting Veronica in study hall after lunch. Don't forget," I said.

"How could we?" asked Raina.

Things were looking up again. It was pretty weird, and I didn't really understand why she was making such a thing, but a gift was a gift and Raina had found me another mock lawyer in Grace.

An incredibly attractive mock lawyer. Who was really into Ruth Bader Ginsburg?

That part made my heart feel like it was trying to do a little leap. I did my best to ignore whatever that was.

Focus, I thought. *Your goals will be yours.*

After third period, I stopped by my locker.

"What," said Claire, coming up the hall, "is that?"

"It's a heart," I said.

"Where did you get such a thing?"

I hesitated. "It was a gift."

"Oh?" Claire raised her eyebrows. "From whom?" From the tone in her voice, I guessed she already knew.

"Raina. And our new Mock Trial lawyer. Don't get all mad. She's knitting. Or crocheting. And they have to make body parts because activism, or something."

"You sure are spending a lot of time with Raina these days."

"She's nice. She's helping me. We have shared adversity, et cetera, et cetera. And may I mention again that we have another lawyer. A new girl who just moved here named Grace. Yes, she's cute."

That distracted Claire. It always did.

"Oh, really now? Tell me more, darling."

Claire had slipped into old-timey movie actress mode, which meant she had forgotten she was mad at me.

"Blond. Smart. Tall."

"You think everyone is tall."

"True. Still."

"Again with that girl *already*." Claire actually shuddered.

"Oh stop. You don't even really hate her, and you know it. Without her, you wouldn't have any competition. If my math is correct—which it always is—the two of you have split all the big parts in plays for years. She got Ginette in *Almost, Maine*, and you got to be the waitress. You got to be Sarah Brown in *Guys and Dolls*, and she got to be Miss Adelaide. The list goes on, here. Even last year when we all had lit together, you were that person with all the lines in the *Merry Wives of Windsor*, but then she got to be . . ."

"You are forgetting theater camp where I always get the best parts and she loathes me for it, and summer stock where she gets all the best parts and I *know* I'd be better. And that one time in ninth grade when I was in the chorus and she was the lead. Her competition is the most annoying thing in the world. Thinking she's better than me."

"Didn't you once tell me you thought you were better than everybody? And that competition kept you sharp?"

"Yes. You think I'd get up on that stage again and again if I didn't? You really gotta dig deep because this is a life of rejection. Actresses are like this."

"But isn't Raina also an actress? So, by logical extension, she would have to believe . . ."

"Don't bring logic into this," she said.

"Oh my God." I shook my head at her.

"Anyway, even though you are cruel and have taken up with that *hack*, I am kind and generous and have found you another witness."

We hurried into AP history, my favorite class.

"Oh!" I said as the bell rang. "Who? One of your theater friends?"

"Kind of. I'll bring them by study hall after lunch. There's a sub in for Mr. Cooper, and I am actively avoiding practicing my overdone lines."

"Fantastic!" I whispered to her back.

I could barely eat at lunch because I was too excited that we were close to forming a team and also because Dad's old debit card expired so I couldn't reload any lunch money. I was stuck with some strange cheeselike product on dry bread and a carton of milk that hadn't expired but probably should have. I should really get on him about taking me to get my license; then I could go shopping by myself.

Claire met me just outside of study hall, probably so she didn't have to spend any time with Raina without me there as a buffer, but when we got to the cafeteria, none of my other Mock Trial people were there yet.

"Over there," Claire said, nudging me toward the back wall. I followed her over to a red-haired girl hunched over a book.

"Hi," I said. She stood up. I could look her in the eye without straining my neck, which hadn't really happened since about sixth grade when I embraced the fact that I'd be petite forever.

"Hello," she said, looking to Claire.

"Millie, meet Izzy. Izzy, this is Millie."

"Please be on my team. You are welcome because of your height," I said. I recognized her from somewhere, but I couldn't put my finger on it. Probably around school or from one of Claire's plays.

Izzy gave a small smile. "That's all it takes?"

"I trust you inherently."

She laughed.

Just then Claire coughed, which I knew to be the universal sign that Raina had entered the room. I heard her laughing with Veronica and Grace. Izzy started fidgeting again, this time with her watch.

"Okay, well, I'm outta here," said Claire.

"You aren't staying?" said Izzy.

"Well. I mean . . ."

"Are you on the team now?" Raina looked at Claire. She put her stuff down next to a round stool at the end of the table.

"No," said Claire. "No, I'm not." She made a point of pursing her lips and cocking her head in her "eff you" stance before waving to Izzy and walking away.

Raina huffed. This was her universal sign that Claire stood within fifteen feet of her.

Those two really were a lot alike.

"Hello, everyone!" I said, maybe a little too brightly. "You all know my name. This is Izzy," I said, pointing to her. "And Raina and Veronica and Grace. Grace, Veronica, and I will be lawyers. Raina and Izzy will be witnesses. Well. Actually, I just sort of assumed Izzy is joining. No pressure!" I said.

Izzy looked like she was trying to figure out if we were all in our right minds.

"Hi, people," said Veronica. She propped her leg up on a chair.

"Hey," said Grace. "You represent the sum total of peers I know in this school. Please be my friends." She grinned directly at me. My heart did a strange little flip this time.

"Oh hi," Raina said directly to Izzy. "We've met, haven't we? Were we in a show together?"

"Uh. Well. Yes. Two summers ago. *Twelfth Night*," she said. "I do a lot of community stuff."

"Oh. Cool. That must be it," she said.

I could read the confusion on Raina's face, like she should be able to place Izzy but couldn't.

"Okay, so I made a few copies," I said. If there's one thing I've learned from Dad, it's that ignoring tension can lead to greater productivity. "Witnesses, here are a sample of your statements." My print allotment at Steelton High was dangerously low due to last term's senior project. Without Mr. Darr, I wasn't sure how to have enough paper for everyone, but I'd worry about that later.

"How do you pick who gets which part?" said Raina.

I thought about that for a second. A small realization wormed its way from the back of my brain that I'd never actually performed as a lawyer in competition. I'd spent three years in the background, researching. Witnesses didn't need research, just help memorizing and improvising.

"I guess pick the one you think you can"—What was that phrase Claire used?—"inhabit best?"

That satisfied both Raina and Izzy, who nodded at each other and started reading parts.

"I have a copy of the other case materials. It doesn't include the witness statements, but does have maps and pictures. I find this case pretty intricate and fascinating. Last year, by the luck of the draw, we played the defense in all our rounds, and it was tricky. After reading all this stuff, I thought the guy was guilty. We lost in the semifinals at states because the other team managed to make all the circumstantial evidence appear too compelling. Our team kind of lost our rhythm, and no one would listen to me when I said we should go after the prosecution's main witness. Their account had holes so big you could drive a cruise ship through. But noooooo. The guys didn't even remember to ask about it. So we lost."

A burning taste started in my nose and made its way toward the back of my mouth. I took a drink from my water bottle and tried to clear my throat. *Past failures bring present opportunities*, my inner affirmation app intoned. *You are at one with those who bring you harmony; you need not listen to those who bring you discord.*

Bitterness I thought I'd cleansed and released waved hello from my churning stomach. Darn it all.

"Hey," said Raina. "You are getting paler by the second, chief. I understand that the 'varsity' team is made up of dickwads. Don't worry. We'll listen to you. The powerful all-girl Steelton Mock Trial team is yours to command." She bowed a little.

"Seconded. Down with dudes. Do you know what they do to my

lit magazine? They boysplain em dashes to me daily." Veronica rolled her eyes.

"I barely know you, and I fear you," said Grace. "Ruth Bader Ginsburg is five foot one, for the record." Grace looked at Izzy. "You are both our RBGs."

"That might be one of the nicest things anyone has ever said to me," I said.

"Same," said Izzy. "You are already by far the most welcoming people here since I transferred this year from Cardinal Byrne High."

"Oh, you're new, too! Awesome!" said Grace. "Newish, anyway."

"Their trial team didn't even make it out of regionals. But it's okay. Their coach bailed midseason to take a job in Punxsutawney," I said.

"I wasn't on it; they were all huge snobs. You'd think they won everything. The theater people made fun of them."

Raina looked like a lightbulb went on over her head. "Wait, you were in Cardinal Byrne theater?"

"Yes," said Izzy, raising her eyebrows. "Listen. When I was in *Twelfth Night*, I had a different name last year. But now my name is Izzy. Only Izzy. I transitioned. She or they pronouns and stuff." Izzy smiled at all of us.

"Oh my God, yes! You played Maria!" Raina smacked the table. "Ha! I thought I was losing my mind. I totally remember. You were *transcendent*; do you know that? I hate when people are better than me. But I only had a small part in that and didn't get to know people because Mom thought we might have to move so I couldn't commit. But we didn't end up moving, so I was pissed I didn't go for a bigger part. But less pissed because you were so great. You carried the whole thing. Did you know that Robert, the director, ran off with the guy who played Antonio?"

"Shut *up*," said Izzy.

"I know, right? My camp friend played Fabian, and *he* said . . ."

"Raina," I interrupted, "I think Izzy might have been telling us something important?"

She stopped, ready to launch into the sordid details of summer-stock gossip. "Right, right. Sorry." She looked at me. "Don't tell Claire that, Millie."

"Claire knows," said Izzy.

"About Robert? Because I heard it was a complete secret. Which I am now telling all of you, but . . ."

"No, no, about *me*." Izzy's tone of exasperation matched the one I heard so often coming from my own mouth. "Listen, this 'all-girl' thing about the team seems important, and I would argue that I completely fit in, but we live in the Pennsylvania woods and you never know here."

Izzy slipped into silence, and the rest of us sat there in it with her.

I looked at Raina, who looked at Veronica, who looked at Grace, who looked back at me, while we managed a complicated four-way group glance.

Finally, Grace said, "What does it mean to be a girl, anyway?"

We considered that.

"I always felt most like a girl when I was climbing, and my fingers gripped handholds that no one else can see," said Veronica. "I'd be on top of the world, holding on to nothing. I am woman, hear me roar, and all that stuff. Then I got dumped by my coach. But there are other coaches out there. I'll get back to it. Being a girl means you are powerful."

"I thought I felt like a girl when Brandon dumped me." Raina looked at Izzy and Grace. "Brandon dumped me," she said, as if that would give the new people more context for her story. "My heart was smashed into pieces. But now I have this. I think I'm most a girl when I go after what I want. And I don't think that's Brandon."

"Yeah, now that you mention it, I felt like a girl when my girl-friend dumped me," said Grace.

Oh! I made a mental note to tell Claire.

"For not liking sex," said Grace.

Strike that.

Though, this meant Grace and I had something else in common other than Supreme Court justice appreciation. Something pretty huge. I could feel my face growing hot. I'd never met anyone who just came out and said it like that.

"But I moved on. Girls are survivors."

"I got dumped by Mock Trial," I said. "But I formed my own team. I'm a girl because I'm a boss. Or trying to be."

Izzy looked at all of us. "I've had my heart broken like three times this year. The whole other school sucked and kicked me out. Dumped me, I guess. But I came here. Girls take charge of their own fate."

"So, wait. Is the defining characteristic of girlness being dumped? A broken heart?" said Raina.

"No. Listen to what everyone said. It isn't the being dumped. Though, apparently you get crapped on more if you aren't a guy. The guys get better equipment and climbing time and press. I guess that *is* part of it. But being a girl is also what happens after all that. It's in how you stand up to all that stuff that's thrown at you and how you kick ass after," said Veronica.

"Life tries to knock you down, and then you kick its ass?" Grace said.

"Daily," said Izzy.

"Then it's settled. You are welcome here," I said. "I imagine you don't have trouble memorizing lines."

Izzy laughed. "Of course not! This doesn't even *have* lines. Just background."

"Yeah, what is that about? How much of this character can I make up, Millie? Exactly how far can I push things? Are costumes a part of this? Do we have a budget for that?" asked Raina.

A dark thought crossed my mind, that Mr. Darr was likely to want to keep all the funds for his "varsity" team. I quickly scrubbed it from my conscious, since it was surely more likely that he'd help a team player rather than an angry girl.

"A budget?" I asked. "Not for costumes, no. Now that you mention it, I have to ask Mr. Darr about that. They have money for travel and stuff. But I don't know if they'll give any to us."

"What?" said Grace. "Why?"

"I don't know," I said. "We've never had two separate teams before."

Grace had these super deep gray eyes. Were they gray? They weren't blue. Green? It depended on the light.

Focus, Millie, I thought. *Mock Trial, then college, then law school, then clerking*, I affirmed to myself.

"We need an adviser of our own. To . . . work with Mr. Darr? Advocate for us. And we need to find a lawyer to advise us. Anyone know a lawyer?"

Grace raised her hand. "I do. My aunt is one."

"Oh, thank heavens," I said. "Do you think your aunt would need a bribe or anything, or would she advise us out of the goodness of her heart?" I asked.

"I'll find out," she said.

"Wait, so does that mean I'm on the team?" said Izzy.

We all looked at her. "Do you want to be on the team?" I said.

Please, sweet universe, let her want to be on the team. Claire already liked her, which gave more of a buffer against her silly Raina animosity.

I didn't want to beg, but I was not above it.

"Yes, I do," said Izzy.

"Welcome aboard. The all-heartbroken-yet-triumphant Mock Trial team of Steelton High."

"I don't want to be heartbroken. Do you know how many times I stabbed myself casting on trying *not* to be heartbroken? Therapeutic fiber-art shit *hurts*," said Raina.

"Okay, not heartbroken, then. Too much heartbreak." I poked

around in my brain for how getting dumped by the other team felt. "How about angry?" I said. "Angry and triumphant."

"Pissed off. Accurate," said Raina.

"Works for me," said Izzy and Grace together.

"I'd prefer if you think of me as motivated. Motivated to burn down the patriarchy," said Veronica. "But I will consider myself angry in this one context."

"Great. We can be five motivated girls. Motivated by anger. Six, once we find one more teammate."

"It's like *Twelve Angry Men*, but with only six, because we're twice as powerful," said Raina.

"Twice as powerful," I agreed.

FEBRUARY 1: ADMINISTRATIVE ORDER ESTABLISHING STANDARD PROCEDURES

I HOVERED IN FRONT OF THE ROOM. I DIDN'T really want to go in. But it had to be done. I knew this was his only free period.

I pushed open the green metal door. "Hi, Mr. Darr," I said.

"Well, hello, Emilia. What brings you here?"

You are angry and triumphant and motivated, I thought in my self-made affirmation.

"I need the lawyer adviser form for my team," I said. "I looked online and I can't log in to the teacher section. Would you print one for me? The girls are seeking our own lawyer."

"Ah," Mr. Darr said. He got up and went over to a file cabinet. He shuffled around inside and pulled out the paper I needed. He handed it to me.

"Thanks," I said.

He turned back to his desk.

That was it? More than three years I knew the man and he really was just going to pretend this was no big deal?

"Mr. Darr?" I said.

"Something else you need?"

"Do you realize I did most of the work?"

"Pardon?" he said.

"I did the research. I planned our strategy. I coached the witnesses. I wrote most of the arguments. I sat there, and I let other people take the credit because I thought that was what the team needed. But I want to know—did you notice any of that?"

He opened his mouth to speak, but I wasn't done.

"And even if you didn't, you had to know I was in the room. That I showed up for every practice, every meeting, every trial. And then they just found a way to get rid of me. That's what that whole tryout thing was. You let that happen. Why? *Why?*"

He waited a beat to see if I would keep going, but I didn't.

"I know you were an asset to the team. I get how you may have streamlined the process. But there were a lot of people who wanted to join. Tryouts went the way they went, you know? I advise two other teams. There's only so much time in a day. I'm sorry it didn't work out the way you wanted, but maybe this is for the best."

He sat down at his desk and looked at the papers he'd been grading before I'd interrupted him.

I turned and walked out of the room. I figured asking about a budget wouldn't get anywhere.

What did he mean? Did he mean I was a nuisance, and he was glad to be rid of me? Or did he mean that I had a better chance of being happy or winning with my new team? Did he think the all-girls team was actually a good idea?

I would never ask, so I'd never know. Because in the end, they dumped me, and I didn't want to stick around someone who'd left me behind.

I remembered what Veronica said. It wasn't being dumped that defined you. It was what happened afterward. I had to complete my team.

Sometimes the best way to solve things is to pull out the yearbook. Each year, the seniors get their beautiful full-color entries, with their favorite inspirational quotes, life aspirations, titles voted on by their peers. The rest of us get crappy black-and-whites squashed in together like an old catalog, but it serves its purpose. Nowhere else can you get as comprehensive a list of people who attend the school, other than a roster from the office. (Ms. Ann, the school secretary, informed me that students were not allowed to have those. I doubted that was actual law and more negotiable school policy, but students aren't really in a position to argue with her. She controls the transcripts.)

AFTER SCHOOL, I SETTLED INTO MY COMFY pants and sweatshirt, pulled last year's edition of *The Beam* off my bookshelf, and opened it to the juniors, this year's seniors. Several of them already had checks by them from when I was looking for a junior formal date (as I viewed this document as an informational directory, rather than precious memories frozen in time). That effort went for naught. I ended up going with Claire since she'd broken up with her girlfriend and had sworn off dating that week. But this was more serious. This would be a semester-long commitment. I'd asked all my potential dates from last year, and all my friends, and all my friends' friends. I dropped to last year's sophomores. Only three possibilities stood out there, and four freshmen. There might be new kids in the mix, but I didn't know how to find them in the lower grades. I'd already managed to snag the new junior in Izzy and the new senior in Grace.

There'd be another prom this year. Maybe I should ask Grace. Lock that possibility in early so I didn't have to worry about it later. Would she wear a dress? She struck me as a vintage suit kind of girl. Or maybe something completely unprom like. I'd be wearing a formal gown, since there were so few real occasions for that in life. I wondered if she'd just wear what I requested.

Was my face burning? Here alone in my room?

When did I start getting even marginally interested in someone? This was not good timing to start.

Focus, Millie, I thought. *Goals.*

I texted a list of all my candidates to Claire, since she was my real social conduit in the world. I also texted one separately to Raina, who had equal but unique social connections. I needed one person. Two would be ideal.

Grace had texted me, so I'd have her number. I could text her. The new girl. Who only knew us. It made total sense. I had accidentally already added her to my favorites, for efficiency's sake. Why not just . . .

Just then a gavel banged over and over. I jumped and dropped my phone on the bed, my ringtone scaring me out of my thoughts of a certain teammate.

"Hello?" I said.

"There you are!" said my mother. "You are hard to get ahold of these days."

"Oh. Yeah. Sorry, Mom. Senior year and all."

A baby cooed in the background.

"Gavin wants to talk to you," she said. "Hang up so I can FaceTime you."

Before I could argue, Mom hung up. I clicked the screen when it lit up again. One chubby cheek took up the entire screen.

"Don't eat the phone, little man. Say hi to Sissy."

"Hi, Gavin," I said. Maybe the kid had my mom to himself now, but he certainly was cute.

"Maaaaaaa," he said to me. He held the phone out, a little too skilled at it for an infant. "Maaaaaa."

"Love you," I said without thinking. I didn't want to like him, this tiny stranger in my life. But he had golden ringlets framing his face and ridiculous eyelashes. Mom's contractor guy was super hot. He produced beautiful babies.

Gavin disappeared from the screen.

"Daddy has him," she said.

"Hi, Millie," said a deep voice from off camera.

"Hi, Matt," I said.

He even sounded hot. Poor Dad. He never had a chance.

"Let me look at you," said Mom. "Hold the phone away from your face."

I complied.

"You look tired. Are you getting enough sleep? Are you doing all the housework? Don't do all the housework, baby doll. You look taller, even the bit of you I can see here. I miss you so much," she said.

"Miss you, too, Mom," I said.

I did. Miss her. She and I had never been close, exactly. We didn't share secrets or gossip or go shopping or anything when she was here. But I liked having her around. In particular, there was that time sophomore year when I decided I should try to have sex with my boyfriend (because he was nice and it was something other girls had talked about) and came home sobbing because it hurt and I hated it; she didn't freak out. She said it could be better with someone else. And when I declared I never wanted to do it again, ever, she said that was fine, too. She said that she figured a lot of people felt that way, and one day she was sure I'd find my own someone who would rather obsess over obscure rulings than get naked anyway. Then she went back to harassing me to brush my teeth for two full minutes and that was that.

In a world that sometimes made me feel crappy about what my body wanted or did not want, Mom always made me feel normal.

But then she left.

"How is school?"

"Fine," I said.

"Mock Trial?"

I hesitated. She'd probably have something useful to say about the whole all-girl team idea.

But then. She had left.

"Good. Getting the team into shape," I said.

Mom studied my face. I could feel her sensing I just wasn't telling her anything on purpose.

"How goes the college applications? Ohio has a lot of schools, you know."

"Yeah, *in Ohio*," I said.

Mom laughed. "It's not so bad here. It's like Pennsylvania. Your vote toward the resistance will go just as far."

"Do you just want free childcare?" I said.

"That might help. It's more I think it'd be nice for Gavin to grow up knowing you. And Ohio State is known for its Mock Trial team."

"How do you know that?" I asked.

"I looked it up. Also, I'm pretty sure Miami University has a great program. They are up there in the rankings."

I could tell her that I'd applied to Ohio State for exactly the reasons she was saying now (even if I hadn't been able to visit them). I still had no desire to change diapers, but I'd always wanted a sibling. And maybe if I said my home base was with Mom, I could get in-state tuition.

"Oh. Thanks," I said instead. I had already visited colleges. The season for that was basically wrapped up. I figured it'd be a school close to Dad. He needed a team player around to make sure he'd be okay. Who knew if this new lady he kept talking about would work out. There were a lot of colleges in our wide state that could fit the bill. Also, *he* hadn't left me.

Mom smiled. "I see the wheels turning."

"I'll think about it," I said.

Just then a text came in from Claire.

"I should go, Mom. Homework and stuff."

"Good night, love."

"Night, Mom."

I should tell her I loved her, because she said it to me.

But then again, she left.

I tapped off the call. Mom's face froze for a second. She looked younger than I remembered.

Maybe she just looked happy.

I have no idea who these people are, read the text from Claire. *They go to our school?*

I sighed. *Yes,* I texted back.

Sorry, lady.

Also, I might kind of like the new girl, I texted before I thought about it.

Are you serious? Hell yesssss, she texted back. I muted my phone so I wouldn't have to go more in depth about that tonight. In fact, maybe I hadn't meant it. I needed to focus.

I abandoned any hope of doing work. We were so close to having a full team but still miles away. I heard Dad come home from whatever late meeting that had held him up. The ding of the microwave alerted me to the fact that he'd found the mac and cheese I'd left him in the fridge. I turned off my light and rolled over in my bed. I thought about Ohio State and baby Gavin. Did I want that? Had I really forgiven Mom for just up and getting herself a new life, even if she kept offering me a place in it?

I drifted off to sleep expecting to dream about missing Mom, but the last image I remembered was Grace handing me a corsage.

7

RAINA PETREE,	:	IN THE COURT OF
	:	REVENGE OF CAMBRIA
Plaintiff,	:	COUNTY
	:	
v.	:	
	:	
THE WORLD,	:	Case No. WHYYYYYYYYYY980
	:	
Defendant	:	

FEBRUARY 2: PROCEDURE APPLICABLE TO APPROPRIATE ACTIONS IN ALL COUNTIES

THE LOCAL MAGISTRATE JUDGE HERMAN T.

Wise had done something in a domestic violence and sexual assault case nobody agreed with. When I arrived at The Dropped Stitch, the knitters barely looked up. All knitting circles had become political.

Everyone looked haunted. Grace waved to me as I walked in the door and sat down next to her.

"What's up?" I whispered.

"The apocalypse, apparently," she said.

"You always think things will be different. Even when they are different, they are the same," said Beatrice.

"Do you know how many years I've been fighting for women's rights? Seventy years. More if you count the workers' rights meetings my mother took me to. And here we are with people in office, this guy on the bench. Saying rape isn't rape if you're married. And saying that he has rights to the baby since he got her pregnant. I . . ."

I'd missed the earlier context for whatever Herman T. Wise had done, and I was glad that I had.

"Gretta . . ."

"I have to live another six years to get that guy out," she said.

"What do we do?" asked Grace. "Can we knit our way out of this?"

The group sat quietly for a minute, needles clicking.

"There's always the pussy hats," said Alex. "Those are kind of relevant."

"Those were cute. Not without their problems, but a visible statement nonetheless. They made a point years ago. We need to knit something new," said Gretta.

"Yes. I have a plan," said Carla.

"Bring it on," said Gretta. "My grandkids say that. Or maybe it's the kids. Somebody."

"Your daughter is going to have my head," muttered Carla to herself. To us she said, "Okay, we need to focus on the sending of more body parts."

I raised my eyebrows at Grace.

"We tried it before on a small scale, but this time we go big. We each sent a uterus the last time they tried to take away abortion rights; this time, we send ten each. Last time, we sent a constructed penis when they tried to take away the rights of transgendered folks; this time, we send twenty. I would like as many people as possible to suspend their current projects and work on this, maybe by Valentine's Day. Yes. That's a good idea. This will be our love letter to justice."

No one said anything.

"Okay, good. We are agreed. We stitch body parts for the next few weeks. Let me know what patterns you want," said Carla.

I turned to Grace. "Will you help me? Everything I work on ends up with more stitches than I start with. How can that possibly happen?"

Grace laughed. "It's easy to do, even when you are paying attention. What happens with me is when the cheaper worsted weight yarn frays a little bit, it looks like one loop is really two. Gets me every time. Then once there is one extra stitch, there are four."

"Yeah," I said. I'd never noticed my yarn fraying. Though I usually tried to knit while binge-watching something on my computer. "Maybe I just need to watch what I'm doing. But I tend to think too much. I wonder if Millie would want a practice uterus." I surveyed my yarn options.

"You already made her a heart," said Grace.

"True."

"Are you two a thing?" said Grace.

I watched. She poked around in her bag, trying to seem casual. But clearly this was information the girl wanted.

I grinned. "No. Not at all. She just kind of saved me from a pit of despair, so I feel like I should show her gratitude. If I were really into her, I wouldn't give her my crappy first tries."

The Crappy First Tries. That'd be a good name for a band made up of Brandons. I made a mental note to tell that to Megan.

"Poor Millie," I went on. "She deserves better. *If there were a more experienced knitter who wanted to show her affection through expert fiber arts*, that opportunity remains available."

Grace put down her bag. "Oh, I see," she said, clearly blushing. "I can totally do that. Maybe I'll skip the uterus, though. With chunky yarn, a hat only takes a few hours. With a matching scarf even. How'd she save you from despair?"

"Good. I had wanted to make her a hat before and got distracted by anatomy. I sort of mentioned the boyfriend thing the other day.

My *ex*-boyfriend—" I tried to start. "Lead singer of the Crappy First Tries . . ."

"He's in a band? I've never heard of them," said Grace.

"Oh no. He's into Mock Trial and Model UN and girls named Ruby. He dumped me on the first day back at school after break *out of absolutely nowhere* and I fell apart." My heart started pounding. "Brandon decided he wanted another girl. Knitting helped, got that from an advice columnist—thanks Two Hearts!—but my life had been theater to that point. And I dropped it and didn't care nearly as much as I should have, and maybe I'd been doing a bunch of stuff because of Brandon all along. I was a mess. But Millie gave me a purpose. Or the beginnings of a new purpose, anyway." I looked at her. "It's been almost a month now. I'm still a work in progress. But I've stopped my daily crying. Now it's only twice a week. Three times, tops."

"Oh. Wow. That dick," she said.

"Yeah," I said. "Maybe I should make Millie one of those. A dick. But it'd probably send the wrong message."

"Let's go with the hat idea. Save the dicks for the elected officials," agreed Grace.

FEBRUARY 4: COMPLAINT COUNSEL'S RENEWED MOTION TO COMPEL

"RAINA, WHAT IS THIS?" ASKED MILLIE.

I'd managed to find her before we met to discuss the case materials she'd been obsessing over alone for weeks.

"It's a hat, *obviously*," I said. "It's just inside out. Look."

I took the hat from her and flipped the crisscross strands inward. "It matches this scarf, here."

"Oh, cool! You made this for me?"

"Grace made it for you, so that I could give it to you. I wanted to make something else, to thank you for getting me into this whole thing and partly out of my funk. Something other than an internal organ. The heart had been a practice project. But most of my stuff doesn't come out the way I want it. Grace was happy to do it, and that girl knits fast."

"Oh?" said Millie. She absentmindedly flipped the hat inside out again.

"Yes. Actually, she seemed concerned that you and I were a couple." I couldn't stop the grin from spreading across my face.

"What?"

"Yes, there might have been some jealousy there. She selected these alpaca yarns just for you. They are quite fancy."

Millie stared at the hat and scarf.

"Focus, Millie," she whispered, more to herself than to me. She looked up. "No time for love! Anger! War! Trial law!"

"Why not time for all of it?" I said. Someone should be happy in this life.

"Why are you telling me this now?" she said.

"Because you'll see her in a few minutes. I like to mix things up," I said.

"Great. Yeah. Thanks," she said.

"Anytime," I said.

We walked to the back corner of the library that Millie had declared our spot. We nodded to the school librarian, Ms. McClain.

"Hey," said Grace as we rounded the biography section.

Millie flushed a crimson similar to her new hat. "Is everyone ready to go?" She cleared her throat. "Ms. McClain said she downloaded everything from the district Mock Trial site and that everyone picked up their packets. Did you look through everything?"

"I did. And I brought Post-its," said Izzy. "This case. Wow. Who knew there was so much to these things? I should have been in Mock Trial at my old school."

"Right? I was supposed to watch the boyfriend's game, but I got caught up in all the witness statements. I was sure the defendant was guilty, but now I'm not so sure," said Veronica. "Boyfriend was pissed I didn't pay attention. But like he can do better than me."

"You thought they were innocent?" I said. I'd been hoping to play the defendant. "They are so guilty!"

"Did you read the rest of the case materials? It's ambiguous at best," said Veronica.

"Post-its will solve this conflict. A rainbow of Post-its. To annotate," said Izzy.

"Do we get to pick?" said Veronica. She glanced up at Millie. "Whether we are defense or prosecution?"

"We are assigned," said Millie.

The rules calmed her. Then she sat next to Grace and her face immediately turned bright red.

The rules calmed her *a little*.

"When do we find out? Do we practice both sides?" said Izzy.

"Yes. Since we are lacking in members, witnesses will have to learn two parts—one for the defense, and one for the prosecution. We'll have to prep arguments for both. Outlines are acceptable at this point. Any luck on another witness?"

All of us shook our heads.

"Grace, did you ask your aunt about being an adviser?" Millie asked.

"Yup," said Grace.

Millie perked up. "Really?"

"She said she'd think about it, but I am almost certain she is going to come through. She was a big intellectual property lawyer in Pittsburgh but got burned out or something. Now she teaches yoga somewhere here in town."

"Is she . . . still a member of the Pennsylvania Bar Association?" said Millie.

"Uh . . ." said Grace.

"Does she really need to be?" I said. "I mean, I doubt the legal knowledge just falls out of your head in downward dog."

"Probably not," said Millie. "The boys' team just has this guy from the city, too. He's never lost a case. He bills at a stupid amount of money per hour. He is absolutely brilliant. But he's also super busy and only gives them a couple of hours. He never once went to one of our trials. Even states. If we have someone who could be available, bar or no bar, that could give us an edge."

"If she burned out, will she *want* to do it?" said Veronica.

"Mom seemed to think she kind of missed it. Not enough to go back to being a partner someplace, but maybe just enough to help a group of girls triumph," said Grace. "I emailed her about it."

"Nice," said Veronica.

"My mom came up with the pitch," said Grace. "Millie, I have her card for you to call. I figured you could sell the cause best."

The blood rushed back into every capillary in Millie's upper body. "Me? But you are her flesh and blood."

"Yeah, but she's super competitive with my mom," said Grace. "It will go over better if you are also involved. Besides, she said that Aunt Kay was interested. That's her name. Kay Elliot. Esquire. Although that's not on her card anymore." Grace held the card out to Millie. "My mom said that she won't be able to say no to you. I told her you were charming."

"I'm not very flexible," said Millie. "I mean. Yoga. I mean . . ."

"I doubt she'll make you sign up for a class. You got this. We can role play," I said. "But what about the issue of the final person? We have a few days, but . . ."

"About that," said Millie, again snapping back into herself. "We need someone yesterday. We've been challenged to a scrimmage next week before the first real trial."

"What's that?" I said. "They have those in Mock Trial?"

"Yes," said Millie. "And since we are a school with two teams, Mr.

Darr decided it would be a good idea. I think he just wants to prove to the principal that they shouldn't split the funding, so he thinks this will end our team before it starts."

"Oh, the *hell* it will," I said.

"We have to find a witness, learn our parts, write arguments, persuade a lawyer to work with us, and fully prepare. Fantastic. Not a problem," said Veronica.

I couldn't tell if she was being sarcastic or was just that driven. It was hard to tell with lit-mag people.

"We also need a faculty adviser."

"What?" we all said together.

"Isn't Grace's aunt enough? How many adults do we really *need*?" I threw my hands in the air. In theater, Mr. Cooper just left us mostly to our own devices. Claire and I wouldn't even let him direct. And the stage-crew people were practically a cult. No one messed with them.

"A teacher is needed for us to travel places from the school. We can't just go on our own," said Millie.

"Can't we have a parent do it?" I said. Not that I knew a parent who could, but they seemed as likely as finding a teacher who wanted to do still more stuff on the weekends.

"Not unless the parent is employed by Steelton High."

All of us sat there silently. Izzy chewed her lip; Veronica looked at the ceiling tiles, lost in thought; Grace and Millie tried to pretend they weren't both stealing glances at each other.

"Why does this have to be *hard*," I said. "It's more injustice," I said at the bookshelves, more loudly than I had intended. "Millie should be leading the stupid varsity law squad. WE NEED AN ADVISER TO JUST DROP OUT OF THE SKY!"

"But then we wouldn't have a team," Izzy pointed out.

"We're almost there," said Veronica.

Wheels squeaked behind us. A red cart filled with books turned from the aisle.

"What on earth is going on back here?" said Ms. McClain. "Are you causing a riot?"

"Something like that," I mumbled.

"We are trying to form a Mock Trial team to compete with the other Steelton faction," said Veronica. "But we need all these advisers and another witness, and what seemed like a good idea is now crumbling."

Miss McClain rubbed her chin. "You need a lawyer?"

"We probably have one of those," I said.

"You need a teacher?" said Ms. McClain.

"Yes," said Grace.

"For Mock Trial?"

"Yes," said Grace again.

Ms. McClain looked thoughtful. "The team almost took states last year. Everyone knows that, Ms. Goodwin. Mr. Darr talks about your research skills all the time. I heard your senior project wowed."

Millie gave a tiny smile. "Thanks," she said.

"You know," said Ms. McClain slowly. "I almost went to law school. Law school or library school. I'm glad I got my Master of Library Science, don't get me wrong. This is the best job in the world." She glanced around at her neatly kept nonfiction sections. "But I'm still a bit of a legal wonk. I watch a lot of old lawyer shows. I just love that stuff. And I gave up Ski Club because of my back. I have some free time . . ." She trailed off.

"Wait, are you saying you might be interested in advising us?" I said.

"That is what I'm saying, Ms. Petree."

"They want to have a scrimmage next week. They want an excuse not to give us any money to get to competitions," said Millie.

"Who? Mr. Darr? The principal? Please. If there's one thing a librarian knows how to do, it's make something out of nothing. And to find funding where there is none. Plus, Darr isn't going to take me on. Or if he decides to get plucky, I can out pluck him. Don't you worry about it, girls. I'll go get the paperwork and fill it in after the final bell."

"Wow, so you'll really do it?" asked Veronica.

"I really will," said Ms. McClain. "But only if you quiet down back here. This is a library, thank you very much. We have standards."

The squeaky red cart retreated into the depths of the current periodicals section.

"That was oddly serendipitous," said Izzy. "So much so it could be an SAT question. 'Is this word used correctly: It was oddly *serendipitous* that the librarian appeared at the exact moment the Mock Trial team needed an adviser.'"

"I'll take it," sighed Millie.

The bell rang and we all gathered our stuff. I thought about anyone I'd ever met who would consider helping us out. In the hallway I had an idea. "WE NEED ANOTHER TEAM MEMBER TO JUST DROP OUT OF THE SKY," I called into the hallway.

No one even looked over at me, the din drowning out my plea.

Nobody appeared interested in both the judiciary and theater.

Grace raised an eyebrow.

I shrugged. "It worked a few minutes ago," I said.

"Yeah," she said. "But that was the power of the library. You can summon librarians in there. Out here, it's just these people." Grace pointed to a dude sticking his tongue down a girl's throat over by the sophomore bank of lockers.

"True," I said. "If I tried it again in there, Ms. McClain would probably kick me out." I waved to Grace and the others as we parted ways to get to class.

It was probably for the best. A person didn't want to use all the library magic too quickly. It might melt the books or something.

FEBRUARY 5: COMPLAINT COUNSEL'S OPPOSITION TO RESPONDENT'S MOTION

I WAS HAVING THE STRANGEST MORNING. I had become pregnant with Brandon's baby, but I didn't know how that was possible because I was pretty diligent about taking birth control. Also, as far as I could tell, I hadn't been with Brandon because . . . we'd broken up? I guess we hadn't. I wondered why I was standing in the middle of Steelton High. Oh. Didn't I have to get to biology class? The rest of my eighth-grade class rushed around me. Then the baby was born somehow, and it was made of socks. I could hear my cell ringing because the sock baby wanted to talk, but I couldn't find the phone. My body felt stuck in quicksand, and I must have lost the sock baby, but my ringtone just kept belting lyrics from *Wicked*. What the . . .

I opened my eyes and squinted against the early morning sun. *Wicked* played next to my face, over and over. I breathed in, taking in for a second that I had never been pregnant and that there was no sock baby.

I picked up my phone. "Hello?" I said. I still wasn't 100 percent sure I was awake.

"Raina!" Megan's voice burst from the other end. "Raina, are you awake?"

"I don't have a sock baby," I said.

"What?" she said.

"I . . . never mind. Are you okay? What's going on?" Waking reality stumbled clumsily into my brain.

"Yes, I'm great, oh my God. I had to tell you," she said.

I sat up and yawned. "Tell me what?" I said.

"I got into Syracuse University! I think I'm going to get to go to

France for their Discovery Program for my first semester. Decisions aren't usually until March, but Coach went there—the cross-country coach not the swim one—and I am going to run and probably swim, let's be honest, and I. Am. So. Happy."

"Wait, you got into your first-choice school?" I said.

"Yes!"

"That's fantastic," I said. I realized that it was, in fact, over-the-world fantastic as my fog completely cleared. "I'm so proud of you!"

"Thank you! I wanted to tell you first."

"Of course you were going to get in everywhere. You are a swim and running goddess," I said. "I will miss you!"

"Well, you didn't hear yet. You never know. I know you didn't apply to Syracuse, but there's still NYU! Same state, at least!"

"You bet," I said. The strange sock-baby mood returned. When I thought about college—studying theater in particular—I wondered if it could be real. Did I want that life? Competition and constant practice and auditions and who knew what. But if I got into some-place, I doubted I could say no. I didn't know how Mom intended to pay for a school, even with aid, but she always made things work.

Since Megan had woken me up so early, I had time to kill. I sat down at my computer and logged into my CMU admissions portal. I clicked on a message in my inbox, a small, secret part of me hoping that I'd somehow been accepted early as well.

Audition dates, the subject line read.

"Oh. Shit," I said. I scrolled through the list. After all the drama in my own life, it'd slipped my mind that this was something I had to do. NYU and most schools allowed digital acting portfolios, and since Mom couldn't miss work to go to New York, I'd done that in December for their early decision II process. There were two Pittsburgh weekends in February, one of which didn't overlap with a trial. I clicked through the registration process and prayed Mom would be able to take me. I logged on to my NYU account just for good measure, and then the others. No decisions were out. I knew that, but sometimes I just logged on in case of a glitch. Or because my best friend achieved superstar athlete status and got treated as such.

I showered and got dressed and ate breakfast alone. Mom had just gotten home from her double but was already asleep on the couch. My knitting bag sat on the couch across from Mom, so I sat down to get in a few rows before I left for school. I pulled my vagina out and surveyed the clit and vulva. The lips were pretty even, and I didn't think switching colors for the uterus would be too complicated. Carla had suggested I try to crochet the lady bits, saying that one dull hook might suit me better than two sharp ones for this particular endeavor. The round opening actually looked realistic, insofar as any yarned body orifice could. Grace and the circle would be so proud.

It felt good to do something with my hands. To *make* something tangible that I could hold, even if most everything didn't turn out the way I had expected. Sometimes it still looked good enough. A little thrill of accomplishment zipped through me each time I finished even a small project.

I got the rest of the vagina sorted out. I wanted a red for the uterus. It needed its own color, different from the tube's long pink. The fallopian tubes could be something fun, like indigo or lilac. The rate I was going, I could finish two or three of these before Carla wanted them in the mail. Satisfied with all that I'd accomplished before school, I gathered up my yarn on the couch. I found my coat and boots and gave Mom a peck on the check.

"What are you doing, baby?" Mom said.

I surveyed my project one last time. "Just checking out my reproductive organs, Mom," I said.

"Okay. Have a good day at school," she said.

You couldn't shock a nurse. It just wasn't a thing.

I set off toward the bus stop with more hope than I'd had in a while. Megan had gotten into her dream school. I hadn't blown my chances at CMU even though I'd had my head up my ass. And maybe I could be a crochet prodigy while I got up to speed with knitting. I could start making hats or little fidget octopi for preemie babies. Or sweaters for creatures in wild fires or oil spills or victims of climate change. There was no end to how fiber could heal the world.

My boots crunched through the ash-colored snow, flecks of road debris making it appear like old newsprint. The chilly air dug into my eyes and nose, the only parts exposed. The bus pulled up before too long, and I shivered inside. Once I was seated on the sticky plastic seat, I pulled out my phone to play on the ride to school. I noticed I'd missed a text from Millie last night.

We have the final witness was all it said.

Maybe I still dreamed of Brandon, so at least part of my brain wondered and cared about him. I wanted to be over him faster. But other things were starting to grow slowly where my love for him had been uprooted. I smiled under my scarf. Today the slate strands of the world knit together with silver and shadow, instead of bland winter gray.

EMILIA GOODWIN,	:	SUPREME(LY PISSED
	:	OFF) COURT OF
Plaintiff,	:	CAMBRIA COUNTY
	:	
v.	:	
	:	
KAY ELLIOT, ESQUIRE,	:	Case No. YESUCN1313
	:	
	:	
Defendant	:	

::

FEBRUARY 7: PLANTIFF'S FIRST SET OF REQUESTS FOR PROTECTION

I WILLED MYSELF NOT TO LOOK IN THE mirror.

I wanted to look again. The last time I had, my pale skin seemed paler, my hair limper, even though I'd exfoliated and primed and conditioned and blow dried.

"Beauty is within. I see that beauty without." I breathed in a deep breath and held it for four seconds. I exhaled. "I see everything I need within myself."

Maybe I should put on a different shade of eyeliner.

Or change my outfit.

"For goodness sake, Emilia, get it together," I said to myself.

My brain almost never listened to my affirmations' advice. I should stop paying three dollars a month for the app.

Even if Grace was like me and knew she wasn't interested in . . . things, I wondered if she still also sometimes got butterflies around certain people and wanted to get closer to them.

Like, say, me.

My phone buzzed. *Outside!* the text read.

A feeling that almost resembled relief flooded through me. I'd have to go with the blue eyeliner and the green corduroy pants with a silky white tunic. The hair would stay in the ponytail.

I grabbed my coat and bag and yelled to Dad in his office. "Off for a school-related project. Back by dinner!"

"Okay," he called back.

At least he acknowledged me.

A nervous lump settled in my throat in the ten feet from my door to the driveway.

"Focus, Millie." I breathed in. "Your destiny awaits at the crossroads of desire and dedication."

"Hey," I managed to speak out loud, slipping into the idling SUV. The winter chill immediately melted from my body. "This seat is really warm. Is that on purpose?"

"We are a full-service operation here." Grace grinned. "My dad insisted on the butt warmers."

"Nice," I said. I remembered to be nervous again. I tried to breathe in cosmic strength from the butt warmers.

"Aunt Kay might have breakfast for us. She's taken up baking in retirement."

"Yoga and baking. Great combo."

"Yes. And fishing. Her hero Rachel Maddow fishes."

"The news anchor?"

"Yes. Totally loves fishing, I'm told. Maybe that's where the baking comes from, too. Who knows?"

We pulled onto the main road from my driveway.

"If we get the lawyer, we only need the last teammate," said Grace.

"Oh!" I said. "I forgot I only told Raina. We have our final teammate."

"Seriously?" said Grace. "Way to bury the lede there."

"Ms. McClain kind of found her."

Found her was a smidge inaccurate. *Ms. McClain forced Nikita Varman to join as a punishment in lieu of payment for too many late books* was much more precise.

But sometimes details like that got in the way.

"Well, don't keep me hanging. Who is it?"

"Do you know Nikita? Former gymnast? Current dancer and cheerleader?"

"No. But I'm new."

"Oh. Well. She's got spirit, yes she does."

"What?" said Grace.

"You know, like at pep rallies? The cheerleaders shout, 'We've got spirit, yes we do, we've got spirit, how 'bout you?' Then you answer them, presumably, with enthusiasm."

"I see. We didn't have cheerleaders at my old school. They were hippies who wove baskets and stuff. Competition was discouraged."

"That's horrifying," I said.

Competition was life. What did you possibly do for fun if you didn't compete? Knit, I guessed.

Grace laughed. "So, *do* you?"

"Do I what?"

"Have spirit?"

"Not really," I said. "I respect cheerleading. It's very athletic. But football never made sense to me, and that's really the only thing they cheer for."

"What a waste. We need some Mock Trial cheerleaders," said Grace.

"Well. We now have at least one," I said.

We turned off the highway and bumped down a smaller road much like mine.

"Almost there. She's number thirty-three."

Over the hill filled with bare trees rose a powder-blue house surrounded by a white fence. Grace expertly pulled the SUV up against the berm and shifted into park. I followed her to the front door, where she rang the bell.

"Gracie! You don't have to ring the bell. Just come in!" said the woman standing in the doorway. The woman who must have been Grace's aunt looked at me. "And who might you be?"

I stuck out my hand. "Emilia Goodwin, ma'am."

She shook it, with a nice, firm grip. She wore yoga pants and a loose-fitting, long-sleeved top with a llama captioned LLAMASTE.

"Just call me Kay. Do you two want any tea?"

"No, thank you," we said.

"Muffins?"

We both took her up on the baked goods. Her kitchen smelled like vanilla and cinnamon. The sun poured into her breakfast nook, warming the cushioned benches that surrounded the table.

"Your mom tells me you need help with a school project," Kay said to Grace.

"It's a bit longer term," I said. I told her the whole sordid tale of being dumped and starting my own team. "We have a practice scrimmage that you wouldn't really need to attend. Then the competitions are three weekends total in February and March. Maybe states, maybe nationals. I really want to go to nationals."

Kay looked into my eyes for a long moment. "You want to go to nationals to beat the other team that kicked you off?"

"No." I thought about it. "Or if so, only a little. If I could have anything, honestly, it would be to lead the team I had to nationals, the dude bro team, because that has been my goal for years. That's what I thought we were all working toward. But it turns out we weren't really a team. I'm not going to get that back. I want this new group to really be a team and to be the best. Because who doesn't want to be the best?"

I took a breath. If the calming energy of the universe were anywhere, it was in that breakfast nook with these whole-grain blueberry muffins.

"I see," said Kay. She glanced over at Grace. "You want to win, too?"

"I am doing it for Ruth Bader Ginsburg," said Grace. "And the women of the court. And I was new, but they welcomed me with open dockets."

Kay carefully peeled back a baking cup, contemplating the organic crumbs that fell onto her lap. "This kind of thing can get to you, you know," she said. "Winning. Losing. Trying to get ahead. Is it really fun to set yourself up to fail?"

"Who says we'll fail?" I said.

"No one," said Kay. "But if you love the law, why not just study it? Why not observe real-life trials? Even the thrill of the work wears off, on a long enough time line. Disappointments and glass ceilings, why do that to yourself . . ."

I waited for her to say more, but she stayed silent. I glanced at Grace, whose face clearly read, *I know my aunt is being kind of weird and you only just met her.*

"I mean. It's my life," I said. "I love it. I've poured myself into it. And I've already been disappointed in it, since my team turned out to be a bunch of jerkfaces. Maybe you are right and Mock Trial and the court system and the world are filled with jerkfaces. It would explain a lot about judicial backlog and unjust sentencing. But why not try to change it? Why not start here? You have to start somewhere."

"What if trying to change it just wears you down, with little discernable reward?"

Kay was awfully full of questions for someone who may or may not be active with the Pennsylvania Bar Association.

"Because I'd get too bored not trying," I said.

"Same for you?" Kay cocked her head at Grace.

"Supreme Court justices. I'm a fan. Or maybe it's just the dissent. I don't know. Did I mention the instant new friends part?" said Grace.

Kay raised her eyebrows at us, and small chills ran inexplicably down my spine. This lady must have terrified the other side in sidebars.

"I have a lot of time on my hands," said Kay. "Lots and lots of time. My Śīrṣāsana is by far the strongest in my training program. I should probably just do the full one-thousand hours at Kripalu at this point. But I'd have to move away from all of you."

"That's great?" Grace said. "That sounds . . . relaxing?"

"No. Yoga school is hard. I'm fifty, you know? The two-hundred hours was enough. It's fantastic for you, yoga. I thought of studying Sanskrit. Like I said, I have the time. But I'll stick to Hebrew. More local teachers. And a lifetime of practice there. It all feeds the soul, really."

I was pretty sure at this point Kay had forgotten she was talking to Grace and me.

"And the baking is going well. I thought about opening a little pop-up. Scones and tea. Maybe grow some fun herbs in the garden and make my own blends. And there's no end of causes to get involved in."

"Do you want to learn to knit? There's some local judge who needs some vaginas," said Grace.

"Knitting? What? You think I need a hobby like the heartbroken girl in some love advice column?" said Kay.

"Oh! We know her!" I said.

Grace sniffed. "Don't knock it until you've tried it. Yarning is for everyone. Unlike, I guess, baking or tea brewing. I didn't hear you complaining when Mom made you all those toeless socks."

Kay laughed. "Fine, fine. I guess you got this from your mother.

It was my job as a big sister to make fun of her for anything she was good at that I wasn't."

"We have spent a fair amount of my life together," said Grace.

"It would probably annoy your mom if I said yes."

Grace shrugged. "It was her idea in the first place. Said you might have—time—for it."

"Yes. Time. I used to work eighty, ninety hours a week. Now I work twenty. Maybe thirty if people want extra classes picked up. Leaves a lot of time for studying. And baking."

"And tea," I said.

She pursed her lips. "If I help you, it's because I have family loyalty."

"Yes," said Grace. "I appreciate that."

"And maybe I like the law. Seems a shame to waste the UC Berkeley degree. It cost enough."

"It really does," I said. I knew that from the spreadsheet I'd started in fourth grade of law-school tuitions across the country.

"Fine. You've got yourself a legal consultant. Forward me whatever it is Mock Trial uses these days."

"Fantastic," I said, rising out of my seat. "I consider this a binding verbal agreement."

"You need two witnesses for that," Kay said.

"And we are leaving right now before you can change your mind," I said. "Come on, Grace."

Grace and Kay followed me to the coatrack by the front door.

I stuck my hand out again for Kay to shake it. "You won't regret this," I said.

"We'll see," she said.

As we drove home, I forwarded the documents I had saved in my cloud drive from my phone.

You have a real future in this, kid, she emailed back almost immediately.

I grinned the entire way home.

FEBRUARY 8: THE PARTIES

I WENT STRAIGHT TO THE LIBRARY AFTER lunch. Ms. McClain gestured to one Nikita Varman to distribute file folders to Grace, Veronica, Izzy, and Raina. Nikita wore brushed gold on her eyelids and fingernails and everything about her, including her evident apathy, was radiant. I was by far the least adventurous dresser out of anyone on this team, including Ms. McClain and the fifty-year-old ex-lawyer yoga teacher baker adviser.

"Welcome, Nikita. Glad to have you on board."

"Glad to be here," she said flatly.

She and I took the remaining seats around the table. Ms. McClain handed me the remaining folder.

"I took the liberty of printing everything for you," she said. "I know you've seen the case before, but I thought it might be helpful for each of you to have all the materials for reference. Let me know if you need anything else."

"Thank you!" I said. I loved librarians. "Okay, everyone, here's the deal. We talked Grace's aunt into being our adviser. Grace, Veronica, and I are the lawyers. We are going to develop a strategy for both defense and prosecution. Raina, Izzy, and Nikita—you will each be playing two witnesses. One for the defense and one for the prosecution. Look through the files and see if any part calls to you. Nikita, I don't suppose you have any experience with this sort of thing? Acting? Or law?"

"I'm a cheerleader," she said.

"Fantastic," I said. "Close enough." I had no other options but to affirm her for what she could bring to the table.

"Our season starts too soon for my comfort, but it is what it is. Our first trial is on February twentieth, our second is on March sixth, and districts is on March thirteenth—unless it snows, but it has never been postponed before so we should be fine. States is April tenth and then nationals is in May. We will get there. One trial at a time."

I had the witnesses move their chairs into a semicircle away from us lawyers. I looked at Veronica and Grace. "Let's read the documents again, and then we can start talking about what we need to do to get started." The other two nodded. All of us sat reading. After everyone finished, we reconvened.

"Okay, so tell me what we've got," I said. That's how Mr. Darr always started us out on the other team.

"As I understand it," Veronica said, "the plaintiff, Jane Marsh, met her best friend at a party celebrating some sort of corporate milestone. Jane's partner, Jess, was there as well. The two of them talked to the defendant, Chris Banks, about a patent they were going to file for a product they developed as a pet project, a robot that scrubs floors, in their home makerspace. Chris had been a big part of the development of the robot and the three of them got into an argument at the party over whose intellectual property the Scrub-Bot really was. A few weeks later, Jess the partner is dead, and Jane is convinced Chris is at fault because of the particular circumstances surrounding their unfortunate demise. But the evidence is circumstantial. Maybe. If that's the word."

"Great summary. I don't suppose you picked parts?" I asked the witnesses.

"They let me be the defendant," said Raina.

"I want to be the mean friend," said Nikita.

"There's a mean friend?" said Izzy.

"The one who thinks Chris is guilty. The one who was at the party and the after-party. Reminds me of pretty much everyone in dance troupe," said Nikita.

"Oh, that's a prosecution witness. I can be Jane for prosecution and Beth from their development team for the defense," said Izzy.

"And I can be snarky boss for the defense," said Nikita. "If we do that side."

"That leaves the other person from their development team who thinks I'm guilty on prosecution. I'm fine with that," said Raina.

"That makes you the tech expert who says Chris rigged . . ." Izzy looked at her notes. "Jess's car to explode. Can you be a tech expert?"

"I just have to memorize these five pages?" Raina asked. "I don't have to study explosives, do I?"

"No, you just need to know what's in your part, and maybe the case documents," I said.

"Then I'm an expert."

That was almost too easy. The guys always fought over the parts. There were dude tears. Eventually, Mr. Darr made them pull parts out of a hat and then everyone silently resented one another for the rest of the year.

"You could rotate parts if you wanted, in case you get sick of your character," I said. That was always Mr. Darr's suggestion, which no one took.

"There are only, what, five shows? Six? Surely we can do it for a short run like that," said Raina.

"It'll take me at least one to even figure out my motivation," said Izzy.

"Isn't it prison or no prison?" said Nikita.

"No, my internal motivation," said Izzy.

Raina nodded in solemn agreement. Nikita just threw them a blank stare.

"Great, well, that's settled, then." The surprise at the instant teamwork made my voice go up an octave or two. "We can assign parts for the lawyers."

"You do opening and the first witness, I'll do second and third witness, and Veronica can close for defense. I'll do opening, Veronica first and second witness, and you do the third and close. You tell us how to order the witnesses," said Grace.

"Works for me," said Veronica. "All the prosecution skills!"

I grinned. Angry (or motivated) girls were several orders of magnitude more efficient than the calmest of men. They were already team players.

"Well then," I said. "What's next?"

RAINA PETREE,	:	IN THE COURT OF
	:	REVENGE OF CAMBRIA
Plaintiff,	:	COUNTY
	:	
v.	:	
	:	
VARSITY LEVEL MEN,	:	Case No. KNIT4GUD15901
	:	
	:	
Defendant	:	

FEBRUARY 9:
REQUEST FOR RELIEF

"YOU'RE MUMBLING TO YOURSELF," MY mom said.

"I'm running lines," I said.

"Oh? You're in *Our Town* all of a sudden? You told me not to reserve tickets. Those shows sell out early, you know. Not much else to do in this town."

"No! God no, Mom. It's for Mock Trial. I'm the defendant. I'm memorizing all of my information. Although, to be honest, I think I did it."

"What?"

"Millie says these cases are meant to be ambiguous. But I've read everything, and I feel like I murdered Jane's partner. Or maybe I just meant to hurt them and ended up killing them. I don't know. I'm awfully good at this remote detonation stuff. Well, it wasn't actually a detonator. It was more of a robotic prank thing that was too close to the engine so the whole thing exploded. Then again, I'm pretty savvy with these sorts of devices, so wouldn't I have known what would happen when I put the exploding thing close to something so flammable? Anyone who pumps gas knows you turn the car off because any kind of spark could blow everybody up."

Mom squinted at me. "I don't know if I should be frightened or happy that you are getting back into your acting groove."

"The answer here is frightened," I said. "Hey, speaking of my acting groove, can you ask off February twenty-seventh?"

"Why?" she said.

"That's the last weekend for CMU auditions. Could you take me?" I *could* drive, technically, but I'd never gone more than a few miles from home.

"Um . . . I'm really, really sorry, Raina. But I don't think I can. We have one girl out on maternity leave, and the new guy just threw out his back. I can see what I can do, but it's not looking good. I would probably need the car. Can you get a ride from someone else?"

"Maybe?" I said.

Just then, Mom's phone burst to life.

"Oh, it's Daddy," said Mom. "I forgot he said he was going to call. He's even FaceTiming us. Wonder who taught him to do that."

"At seven in the morning on a Tuesday? Are you kidding?" I said.

"He wanted to get us when we'd both be home."

Dad's face popped up on Mom's screen. "How's my girls?"

"Russel?" my mom said, almost like she didn't believe it was him even though she knew he was supposed to call. So much time away did that.

"You were expecting another man?" he said.

"Never," said my mom.

"What are you up to, kiddo?"

"Not much, Dad." That wasn't true. Even a little. But this is what it felt like to talk to Dad—off-balance. I knew Mom was happy, but she and I had a system when he was gone. A routine. I did whatever I wanted, and Mom let me because she didn't have time or energy to do much more than pray that I was as boring as I seemed to be. But since Dad was home so infrequently, even a call threw me. It was nice to know he was still alive, and he loved us, but it was never enough interaction to fully get me, because I'd grown since the last time he'd tried to fit into my life.

"How's the boy? Benjamin, was it?"

Case in point.

"No boy. Boy gone," I said.

"Really? You were with him for at least a year!"

It'd been almost four. But who was counting?

"He dumped me for another girl," I said.

"What? Well, he's an idiot, then," he said.

"Thanks, Dad."

"What play are you in now?"

The man was trying, but this is what happened when you didn't bother to spend more than five minutes on the phone once every few months.

"No play. I'm in Mock Trial now. Law."

"Seriously?"

"I'm playing a witness."

"Oh." He rubbed his beard. "That's neat. I've heard of that. Your grandfather did that in college."

"What?" I'd never heard that.

"Yeah, Pap wanted to be a lawyer, you know. What was it he did . . . Moot Court? It's where you argue constitutional law. It's not a trial. More like a speech competition. He did real good in that.

'Course he was drafted right out of school. Vietnam wasn't good to him, and he always said he couldn't think like he used to when he got back. Went to work in the mills here instead. It's a shame you probably don't remember him."

I didn't. There was a picture of him having a tea party with me when I was about two years old. And another of him letting me cover him in stickers and me laughing hysterically. Sometimes I felt like I remembered him, flashes of his soft skin and green eyes. But that might just be me reading into the pictures or reconstructing stories my grandma told before she died. Dad looked more like the Pap in the pictures each time he came home from the latest run. Dad had wanted to be a fighter pilot, but his eyesight prevented him from even enlisting. Mom mentioned that he might have wanted to be a writer at some point, too, but talked himself out of it before he even tried.

"I think I do," I said. It was true enough, and I knew it would be better for Dad to hear.

"Well, he'd have been tickled pink to know you might be taking up where he left off."

"Thanks, Dad. I should go to school."

"Yes, study hard," he said to me. He turned back to Mom. "Are you off to work?" he asked.

"Not till three," she answered. "We have some time to get reacquainted."

My feet could not carry me out of there fast enough. I didn't even want to imagine them "getting reacquainted" over FaceTime, lest I never be able to close my eyes again.

I SWITCHED BOOKS AT MY LOCKER AND made for my homeroom. I slammed the door shut and nearly screamed to see Claire standing inches from my face.

I jumped back three inches, knocking into the dude at the next locker.

"What are you doing here?" I said.

"Wanted to know if you had auditioned yet," she said.

"For what?"

"Carnegie Mellon," she said.

"No. I signed up for the last date." Normally I wouldn't give her this kind of information, but she'd nearly scared the ever-living shit out of me, so I was more forthcoming. Maybe that was her plan all along. I made a mental note to ask Millie if this would be a useful strategy in court.

"Yeah, me too. Are you driving there?" said Claire.

"I don't know. I don't think I'm allowed to drive that far by myself."

"Me either. My mom has to watch my cousins because my uncle got hit by a car riding his bike."

"Oh my God, is he okay?"

"He broke his sacrum. He's alive, but he isn't taking it well and will go to rehab and stuff. His partner is a known horrible narcissist. We have his five- and seven-year-old in the house, and Mom almost started crying when she thought of driving them to the city and hanging around all day. They aren't taking this well, either. She said it's fine if I take my dad's car, since he'll be out of town on a business trip. But she doesn't want me to go alone. So, I wondered if you wanted to."

"Wanted to what?" I said.

"Wanted to ride down with me?"

Was Claire offering me the ride I now so desperately needed? She really was. I'd been thinking about taking the train, but I hadn't bothered to look at the schedules since I had a mental block against all things future and theater related and just found out Mom couldn't take me. I probably owed Claire a little bit for bringing this to my attention, though she certainly didn't need to know that.

"Maybe? Let me talk to my mom and get back to you? I need to check on her plan." I didn't. But I couldn't bring myself to be grateful to Claire just yet.

"Okay. Uh. Then text me? Right. Great. Right. See you," she said.

I could knit the entire reproductive *and* digestive system with the strands of awkward weaving themselves around the hallway after that.

Team Millie had the witnesses partner with lawyers during Mock Trial practice. Veronica grilled me over my knowledge of electronics and then she grilled me over why I could ever think peaceful protestor Chris could do such a thing to Jane's partner. It was a little odd, playing opposite sides all within an hour. On the other hand, it was different. Exhilarating, even. And apparently the law ran in my veins.

Or at least dramatic arguing did. What's the difference, really?

As I waited for the bus after school, I felt a tap on my shoulder.

"Hey," said Brandon.

I stared at him.

"Here," he said, reaching out his hand. He handed me a silver chain with a delicate letter *R* dangling from it. "You left this at my house a while ago. I thought you might want it."

I took it from him almost by instinct. A tiny diamond sparkled at the top of my initial. Brandon had bought this for me just this past summer. I'd worn it every day. I think it had gotten snagged once when I was trying to get his shirt off. I'd asked him for it back a half a dozen times.

I searched his face for sadness. For remorse. For anything. He looked a little like he wanted to throw up.

"Why are you giving this back to me now?" I said.

He shrugged. "I don't know. I found it. It's yours."

I considered chucking it into a pile of snow. Instead I grasped it tightly for a second and then held it out to him.

"Here," I said.

He didn't move.

"*Here*," I said again.

He held out his hand.

"I loved you, asshole." I planted my feet. Drew my breath from the diaphragm. "And you didn't care. Give this to Ruby. She won't even know it was mine."

The bus pulled up then. I turned and walked up the steps without looking back to see what he had done.

My fingers burned where I'd held his stupid gift. Maybe it was just from the cold.

Once the bus dropped me off, I didn't want to be home alone with my thoughts, so I texted Grace and suggested we head over to The Dropped Stitch early.

Parents making kale smoothies for dinner. I'm already on my way to get you, she texted back.

She pulled up in front of my house less than five minutes later. She rolled down the window.

"What are you doing?" Grace asked.

"I'm kicking this pile of snow," I said. I imagined Brandon's head in the block of ice sitting there, dirty and frozen.

"Uh, okay?" she said.

"You shouldn't text and drive, you know. It's dangerous," I said. I tapped the remains of ice-Brandon off my heel before getting into her SUV.

"I wasn't texting. I can talk to my phone through the car, and it types it for me. Besides, I was at a red light. I have to be careful, because if you are listening to music it will insert the lyrics in your message. You want to have an awkward conversation, try explaining Drake to your dad."

"Wow."

"That's what I'm saying," she said as we pulled into the parking lot.

I sniffed a little.

"You okay?" said Grace.

"Stupid . . . boys. Stupid . . . Brandon. Do you know what he did?" I wanted to scream into the wind after his stunt today, but I'd already spent enough energy on imagining his face exploding. I took a breath in and held it for a couple of seconds before letting it out. "You know what, he's not even worth talking about." I was surprised to realize that I might have been beginning to mean that. "I'm feeling good about vaginas and fallopian tubes," I said. "It's good they aren't that big. There is something to be said for crocheting, with its one hook and no stabby points. Did you get Carla's email?"

"I did. I knit the squares in the pattern she sent. They look clitoral. Is that a word?" said Grace.

"Uh. What?" I said.

"The squares we were supposed to knit in the 'assignment' she sent. They look like reproductive bits only—you know—flatter?"

"I didn't get patterns. She just told me to knit brown and beige squares. Or crochet or whatever. Which is what I did. But I am still not great with the patterns without a lot of practice, so maybe we had separate assignments. Do you know what this is for? Are we going to make a blanket and mail it to the Pennsylvania legislature or something?"

"Beats me," she said. The parking lot looked too narrow with freshly plowed snow blocking half of the entryway, so Grace parked next to the curb.

The bells over the door jingled as we pushed out of the cold night.

"Keep your coats on, girls; we are going on a field trip," said Carla. "Bring your knitting bag. I trust you did your practice assignment."

We nodded.

"There's no artichoke dip?" I said.

Carla chuckled at the obvious horror in my voice. "It's in the mini fridge upstairs. This will be an hour, tops."

Several of the regular under-seventy crew joined us after a few minutes.

"Gretta wanted to come, but the hip is acting up," said someone.

"That's for the best. It's icy out. Don't tell her I said that, or she'll kill me."

We followed Carla back outside. We walked down the block toward the main part of downtown.

"Where are we going?"

"Secret mission. It's on a need-to-know basis," said Alex.

"It seems like we'd need to know," I said. My feet felt seconds from sliding out from under me. I kept grabbing on to Grace to keep from falling.

"Sorry, sorry, sorry," I said.

"It's all right. I have traction cleats. I anticipated the ice."

"You can drive in those?" I said. I managed to grab her coat before I wiped out on at the end of a slick driveway.

"You *can*. Arguably my dad said I maybe *shouldn't*. I brought shoes to change at the store. But I'm saving lives here."

Grace stopped Alex from sliding into a mailbox shaped like a dachshund.

"Haven't all of you lived here for a long time? Why no cleats?"

"I never tend to be out in the elements," I said. "And the one time I wore them, they just fell off."

"We're here!" said Carla.

We'd stopped in front of the city courthouse, looming gray and morally imposing in the moonlight. Icicles reflected flickering streetlights, casting an eerie glow on the other knitters' faces.

"Okay, here's the plan, everyone. We are yarn bombing the joint."

"We're what now?" I said.

"Yarn bombing. Peaceful. Warm. Cozy. But still makes a statement. Get out your squares."

All of us shuffled through our bags. I'd gotten eight or nine done, as I'd really gotten the hang of the uterus gig. I'd been diligently mailing them to the list of addresses Carla had provided. But this was next-level spy-knit shit.

"Okay, first the flesh tones. Alex will stitch them together onto the railings. Grace, dear, maybe you can help. I have the squares from Gretta and the others," said Carla.

My nose already had begun to tingle. I rewrapped my scarf and unearthed my gloves from the bottom of my deep coat pockets. I stomped around a little to thaw my toes. I still wasn't sure what was going on.

"Raina, do something useful over there. Keep watch," said Carla.

"For what?" I said.

"The fuzz."

"What?"

"That was a yarning civil-disobedience joke. I meant the police. Or security or anyone wandering by. We need to keep this stealth for the time being, if you know what I mean."

"Sure, Carla." I doubted that the Steelton Police Department would be on the lookout for rogue knitters on a random freezing Tuesday, but I did as I was told.

Grace and company diligently stitched together everyone's separate work over the wide stone railings in front of the courthouse entrance. The pieces curved around and under each part perfectly.

I stomped back and forth, alternating between gazing down the empty street to watching the knitters at work.

"It's amazing how it just seems to fit," I said. "All the pieces together."

Carla directed the group to move to the railing on the other side.

"Oh, I cased the place weeks ago. The key to a good yarn bomb is to sketch and measure and plan. I tried doing it in the day, but there were too many witnesses. Literally—there was a huge trial, and they must have called half of Cambria County to testify. I found that not long after everyone left work in the downtown, the places get awfully quiet. Sad in a way. It used to be busy with restaurants and shops."

The crew finished the other side more quickly than the first. Diverse yarn textures and weights made the patches uneven. The cool marble beneath peeked out from the looser woven patches. Was it a multi-skin-toned flower? There weren't petals, exactly. It looked more like a Georgia O'Keeffe painting.

Oh.

Oh my God.

"You made the courthouse banister into a *vagina*?" I said. A good six-foot vagina.

"Shhhh, you are the lookout!" said Carla.

"Why all the vaginas? Vaginas everywhere! What kind of social movement are you running here?" I tried to whisper. I kind of understood the whole "mailing body parts to people who make the laws." But was this illegal?

"The other side are breasts," said Grace matter-of-factly.

"They are meant to appear lactating, but you probably can't see it in the dark," said someone.

I could just make out one of the nipples from my vantage point, pink and red against what I thought was probably peach and umber and sand. Each yarn bomb looked regal in its way.

Honestly, a dick on a banister would have just looked stupid.

Just then something moved out of the corner of my eye.

"There's a car headed this way," I said. I squinted into the night.

No sirens blared as the car crawled down the poorly plowed street, seemingly in no real hurry.

"I think we're good," I said.

No sooner had the words left my mouth that the front door of the courthouse opened. Silhouetted by dim backlighting stood a man I recognized from the news. The Honorable Herman T. Wise stared at us.

"What the . . ." he said.

"Run!" Carla yelled in a half whisper-half shout.

No one could run, with the ice and snow.

"Come back here. Don't think I don't know who you are," yelled Judge Wise.

We marginally hustled one street over and hung on to Grace in a knitter choo-choo back up the hill to The Dropped Stitch. No one pursued us, but you'd have thought there was a (slow but) deadly force hot on our heels. A few minutes later, we all got back inside and shook off our hats and coats and boots into a heap next to the door.

"That was close!" said another fellow Justice Yarner.

It wasn't. Close. The judge had barely breached the doorjamb by the time we were well on our way to safety.

"The courthouse doesn't have cameras, do they?" asked someone.

"They do. But they haven't worked for years. We're good."

"Did we break the law?" I said. "He seemed to indicate he knew who we were."

"Well . . ." Carla said. "That's always been a little hazy. I mean, it's vandalism, though most people probably wouldn't call it that. It's going onto other people's property and putting something there they didn't ask for. We didn't get permission. We *wouldn't* get permission. But then again, I'm a taxpayer. I own a piece of that place. I would knit blind justice a sweater if I wouldn't dislocate my shoulder trying to get on top of the building."

"So that's a maybe, then?" Grace said.

Carla ignored us and opened the mini fridge. "Anyone want dip?"

FEBRUARY 10: RELIEF IN THE FORM OF MANDAMUS

WHEN I GOT UP FOR SCHOOL IN THE MORN-ing, I found Mom asleep on the couch. I poked her.

She opened her eyes right away.

"Hey there," she said.

"I was checking to make sure you were alive," I said.

"Mighty thoughtful of you," she said. "I don't suppose you made coffee?"

"You know I don't drink coffee. But I know how to push the button on the machine," I said.

"Glad to see I might be raising you right," she said. She got up and went upstairs.

I changed the filter and started coffee. I helped myself to some cereal.

"Can you for sure not take me to Pittsburgh? I had an offer of a ride from . . . uh . . ."

What? A friend? A complete rival who could be left in the dust at home and not be my competition?

". . . A classmate who also needed a companion," I finished.

"Honey, I'm sorry. I really am. But the car isn't that reliable even if I could. It'd be great if you could get a ride with someone."

"Yeah, I figured." My heart sank at the thought of taking Claire up on her generous offer, even if she kind of needed me to go. "It's okay. I understand."

"Thanks, hon," she said. Even after the coffee, she still looked exhausted.

At school, I sought out Claire on purpose for perhaps the first time in our lives. She was standing next to Millie at her locker, whispering something to her.

"Oh hey," I said.

"Hi," Millie said. "Looking for me?"

"Actually, I'm here to see Claire," I said. I cleared my throat. "I would like to ride with you. To Pittsburgh. In a few weeks. Together."

I wanted to communicate that maybe I'd be riding in the trunk to avoid interacting with her, but that might have been implied.

"Yes. Great. That's amazing. A ride. To Pittsburgh," she said.

Millie stared at us. "The two of you are going to auditions together?" she said.

"It is a matter of necessity," I said. "Carnegie Mellon has a prelaw program in addition to theater. Maybe we can walk by some of those buildings while we are there."

"Yes. Sure," said Claire.

"It's a two-hour ride to Pittsburgh," said Millie. "With the two of you. Together." She didn't even bother to hide her grin.

"Well, I have to go. See you. Later. In two weeks or so, at least. Millie. I will see you at Mock Trial." I walked away. The less time we had to talk, the better we got along.

Millie snickered when she saw me in the library after lunch but wisely didn't bring up the universe throwing me and Claire together as the team assembled in our usual spot.

"Okay, team, we have a few days before the scrimmage. We are going to practice," said Millie.

"How, exactly?" I asked.

"We can have our opening and closing statements. Both of which are a work in progress." She glanced at the lawyers. "And maybe try to question the witnesses. We only have an hour at the moment, but let's see what we can do."

"Okay," everyone agreed.

"I have the opening. Sort of. Do you want to hear it?"

Nods went around the group.

Millie shuffled back and forth, from foot to foot. She flexed her fingers. She murmured something to herself and took some big breaths. Theater people had similar rituals—vocal exercises, stretches, visualizations to get into character. Maybe the courtroom wasn't so far off from the stage. I didn't know what that said about the criminal justice system but *probably* nothing good.

"Good afternoon, Your Honor," Millie began. "And ladies, gentlemen, and nonbinary members of the jury. I stand before you today representing Chris Banks, a woman wrongly accused of killing not just an acquaintance, but one who could have been viewed as a friend and colleague. The prosecution will try to sway you, but we intend to prove that any evidence they present is at best circumstantial, and at worst a partial picture devoid of essential context. The defense's case, presented as a whole, will leave far more than a reasonable doubt in your minds about the prosecution's claims against our client."

Millie paused, and someone sneezed.

"Bless you," said Izzy to me.

"I didn't sneeze," I said. Though the sneeze sounded oddly familiar.

Izzy had turned her chair around to face Millie but craned her neck to look at me. "Sorry. Bless you, Nikita."

"I didn't sneeze, either."

Another familiar sneeze echoed from the aisle of books next to us. Millie looked annoyed.

"As I was saying. Our case . . ."

"Wait a second. I know that nose. *I know that nose very well*," I said. I jumped up and nearly knocked Millie over taking the turn next to the *World Book* encyclopedias.

"Goddamn it, *Brandon*," I said.

"Oh, hey, I was just looking for something. Reference material. Yeah, here it is," he said.

He pulled an ancient dust-covered book off the shelf. Most of the books worth reading were either part of the digital collection or up front. The only thing back here were the sets I think Ms. McClain kept out of some sort of nostalgia.

"You were *not*. You were spying."

Brandon tried his hurt face. Then his surprised face. Then his puppy-dog eyes. All in rapid succession with absolutely no thought to preparation or transition or motivation. He was always a terrible actor, with no real appreciation of the craft.

To think I had, until very recently, thought his cluelessness was cute.

"What is going on?" said Millie from behind me.

"We have a spy," I said.

"Honestly, Brandon. Are you serious?" she said.

"Who is this dude?" said Grace.

"The ex," said Millie.

"You went out with this guy?" said Grace.

"Not my ex. Raina's," she said.

"Ohhh." Grace looked Brandon up and down. "If there is any argument that supports the fact that you can't choose your sexuality, it's straight girls." Grace shook her head and went back to our table.

"Hey," Brandon said. "Listen, I don't know what you are talking about. The library is public space. I was just here researching an assignment. It's not my fault yinz all happen to be meeting here."

"You're doing homework during activities period? Since when was that a thing?" I said.

"I got permission," said Brandon.

He looked at his feet when he lied. Damned if this guy wasn't the worst actor in the world.

"You didn't. You're here to try to gather intel or whatever. I get you are intimidated, but I don't know why your team would send *you*."

"Come on now, Rain." Puppy-dog eyes. And his pet name for me. "Your hair shines even in this weird light. I remember every day how beautiful you are."

This had worked on me?

I held up my hands, lest my heart tried to drag me toward him, ridiculous as it was. "No. You. Leave. Now."

"Is there a problem here?" said Veronica. She rolled around behind Brandon.

"Oh look, a boy wasting my time. Typical," said Nikita beside her.

"They could have at least sent someone who knew what they were doing," said Izzy.

"I know, right?" said Grace.

The all-girl Steelton High Mock Trial team gathered at each end of the reference aisle. Books on either side of him, girls blocking any means of escape, he turned slowly in a circle, realizing he was trapped.

"Brandon! There you are," said another dude voice behind me.

"How shocking, it's the president of the other team," said Millie. "Come to collect your inept minion, Jeff?"

"Brandon needed to do research or something. I don't know what you are talking about," said Jeff.

"Astonishing," said Nikita.

"Just leave," I said. "Both of you. We'll see you at the scrimmage."

A slow smile crept from one edge of Jeff's face to the other.

"Yup. That you will. Come on, Bran. Nothing we need here."

Brandon kept looking at his feet as Nikita and Millie parted to let him through.

The bell rang, ending the period.

I sighed. "That was the last thing we needed."

"We still have a few days," said Millie.

"Yeah," I said.

There is an often-repeated myth in the theater that everything comes together at the last minute. That a show will somehow magically become great, even if people are still missing lines and sets are half-painted and four of the lights are out. But I've been in more than one show where it didn't come together. Where that dress rehearsal was a hot mess and opening night was a flaming pile of shit. Maybe that was the boys' game. Limit how much time we had to practice. Psych us all out before the scrimmage so we just gave up.

But that just meant they were underestimating their opponent.

There was a show in two days. Or trial. Whatever. I hoped Brandon would be the one to cross-examine me, that he'd be the guy to try to trip me up. Again.

Just let him try.

EMILIA GOODWIN,   :   SUPREME(LY PISSED
                                   :   OFF) COURT OF
Plaintiff,   :   CAMBRIA COUNTY
                                   :
v.   :
                                   :
THE STEELTON HIGH MOCK   :   Case No. WiNNR4NW
TRIAL TEAM,   :
                                   :
Defendant   :

FEBRUARY 12: SUMMARY OF THE ACTION

I AM ONE WITH THE UNIVERSE.

I breathed in.

"Millie, where are my loafers?" Dad called.

There are only good things surrounding me. The energy I put out, I receive threefold.

I breathed out.

"Millie, have you seen a green folder? Maybe it's blue. One of each, green and blue."

"My potential is limitless," I said to my reflection. It stared back skeptically, though it looked great in a black turtleneck, if I did say so myself. Mom really wanted me to go to college in Ohio and darned if she didn't want me to be fashionable while doing it.

"Hey," said Dad from my doorway. "Did you hear me?"

"I was affirming myself. Big day. Scrimmage. I'll be home late. It's after school," I said.

"What?" he said.

"Mock Trial, Dad," I said.

"Oh. Right. Have you seen any of my stuff?"

"Your loafers are by the door. Probably under your scarf and hat if they fell off the hook."

They didn't fall. He just never bothered to hang them up.

"Your folders are probably on your desk under stuff, too."

"Thanks, babes," he said.

"I hate when you call me that," I said. But he was already downstairs.

"Found the shoes," he said.

I knew he'd find the folders. They were always on his desk, whatever it was that he was looking for. Mom used to say, "It's wherever you left it." Eventually it didn't matter what Dad said. Even if it was an "I love you; you're so amazing for doing everything," Mom would say, "It's wherever you left it."

Mom was always angry, in the end. Sick of taking care of a grown man.

Maybe that was just me.

I gathered my stuff and grabbed Dad's keys to warm up the car. He kept saying he would teach me to drive, but I wasn't really in a hurry to learn in the winter. It gave me an excuse to ask Grace for rides.

I wondered if she'd pick me up for school.

Or, say, prom.

I shook the thought out of my head.

"Focus." I breathed. *"The universe is with me."*

At least Dad didn't think of anything to ask from me on the drive to school. He just rambled on about Sheila, the woman he was dating. And after lunch, my trial girls were focused, at least. Brandon's little stunt had galvanized them. Raina and Izzy knew their parts, and even if we'd only had a chance to go over a few questions, I knew I could count on them. Nikita on the other hand . . . I didn't know. I couldn't tell if she cared. Veronica was smart and could think on her feet. Or foot. Grace . . . she loved Ruth Bader Ginsburg. That meant something. She was probably incredibly competent, but I kept getting distracted thinking about cuddling by some fireplace in a ski chalet my brain invented.

Bet she'd look darn good in a fuzzy sweater. That she knit.

"Darn it, focus, Emilia!" I hit my clipboard.

"What?" said Izzy.

I hadn't noticed she hadn't left the library after our practice yet.

"Uh. Nothing. Nothing."

"You nervous about this afternoon?"

"Something like that," I said.

"You seem like you are hard on yourself," she said.

I snorted. "I am easily distracted."

"Not a vibe I'm picking up from you," said Izzy.

I didn't say anything. Actresses were annoying with their accurate observations and exploration of human emotion.

On my way out, I nodded to Ms. McClain, who was busy updating her Black History Month display. In honor of Mock Trial, she had a full bulletin board devoted to Charlotte E. Ray, the first Black female lawyer in the United States.

"Ready for this afternoon?" she said.

"Totally." I breathed in optimism and breathed out confidence.

Ms. McClain had offered to host the scrimmage in the library, but Mr. Darr felt it would be "more realistic" to hold it in his classroom. Neither one was much like a courtroom. Whereas the library was open and airy and smelled of dust jackets and paper and ink, Mr. Darr's room smelled like the recycling bin across the hall. It also was one floor above the gym, so you could hear the faint din of some team warming up downstairs.

"Probably lacrosse," said Nikita, without anyone even having asked.

So, all of us—my huge, twelve-person, ex-team and my new small team and Mr. Darr and Ms. McClain—sat in his dank, gray classroom. Even the maps of the world scattered over boards and walls did little to cheer up the place. Why had I ever loved it in here?

Ms. McClain and Mr. Darr arranged chairs as per Mr. Darr's instructions. I shuffled my notes, glancing over at Grace and Veronica. Grace smiled at me, and I could feel peace and serenity and confidence burst into flames and turn themselves into scarlet heat shooting across my neck and face. Veronica, for her part, sat looking flawless in matching black pants and blazer.

"Hey," I said to her, "you look great."

Veronica grinned. "It was a pain getting into skinny pants with the boot and all. But I feel half of the battle in any event is to look the part. I talked my mother into buying me opposition-eating clothes."

"You look very formidable," said Raina.

"All right, everyone," said Mr. Darr. "We flipped a coin. I'm going to be the bailiff. And Ms. McClain will be the judge. We start when I start. Got it?"

Everyone snapped to attention. My stomach fluttered.

"All rise," he said.

We all rose.

"The Court of Westmoreland County is now in session, the Honorable Judge Connie McClain presiding."

Ms. McClain swept up to Mr. Darr's desk. Even without a robe or gavel, she appeared dignified.

"Thank you, bailiff. I want to welcome you young people here today. This is a great thing you are learning to do. Are there any questions before we begin?"

No one said anything.

"Very well. Let's get right into it with opening arguments, then, shall we?"

The boys had won the coin toss, so Jeffrey rose to their podium. It used to be the defense would always go first, or they'd leave it up to the teams to decide. But ever since the Parent Observer Incident of 2017, a coin toss now determined who started.

Grace and Veronica took notes. I tried to mentally go over my statement once more as Jeffrey laid out their case. When he finished, I stood and grabbed the podium to steady myself.

"Good morning, Your Honor." I looked up at Ms. McClain and gave her my best winning smile. "Fellow humans of the court."

I looked around the room. The guys had gone the "ladies and gentlemen" route, but Izzy pointed out that we should be more inclusive.

"Advisers, parents, and students. We are here today because our client, Chris Banks, stands accused of a serious crime that she did not commit. You will hear many things about her, and her possible involvement in a tragic, heinous crime. But what you hear must convince you beyond a reasonable doubt of her guilt, and we are confident that the circumstantial evidence the prosecution will bring forward will not move you to this end. The burden of proof lies with them, and we will demonstrate that there simply is not enough to determine Dr. Banks guilty."

I took a deep breath. Courage, wisdom, justice—into the lungs. Sneaking suspicions that Jeffrey was more prepared (not that that mattered)—out.

"On November 4, 2019, our client, Dr. Banks, attended a happy hour sponsored by Warren Tower Technology. WTT was celebrating its recent transition to becoming a publicly traded company. Dr. Banks, a former employee and current WTT contract consultant, attended the party to network with new contacts and catch up with old friends. While at the party, she ran into current WTT staff Dr. Jane Marsh and Jess King. Through the course of their conversation, Dr. Banks learned that Marsh and King had continued to work on a pet project named Scrub-Bot that my client had helped conceive and begun developing during her time at WTT. The project did not belong to the company, as it falls outside their niche concern with information systems. Marsh and King had taken our client's work without her knowledge, continued development, and submitted two patents on proprietary systems. Also unbeknownst to my client, Marsh and King recently received a seven-figure offer for this technology, as it seemed poised to revolutionize robotic cleaning systems."

I could feel the boys and Mr. Darr staring intently at me. I could hear the boys then scribble as I spoke. I tried to breathe in as much calm as humanly possible.

"My client grew angry in front of several people, and words she has come to regret left her mouth. They were not threatening, as the prosecution might lead you to believe, but hurt and angry. Two people she thought were friends had betrayed her for . . . what? Money? Acclaim? Would it have been so hard to alert our client—who still was affiliated with WTT—and cut her into her rightful share? Anyone would have been upset about that—it is only human in the face of such duplicity. That is the subject of other pending litigation outside the scope of this trial. What is at stake here is what happened next. The week following this event and unfortunate exchange, Jess King was killed in an accident involving their car. The circumstances around that accident were indeed suspicious and unfortunate—but my client had nothing to do with them. As righteous as her anger may have been over the Scrub-Bot situation, my client still cared about both King and Marsh and would never have hurt either of them. She would never hurt anyone. She is known as a gentle pacifist and nature-lover. My client knew that she would eventually get her rightful claim of the money from Scrub-Bot. She had nothing to gain and everything to lose in circumventing the law. Finally, on the night in question, my client was otherwise engaged across town from the scene of the crime and could not have been involved. We will present evidence that demonstrates not only reasonable doubt that our client could have committed this crime, but also a compelling argument that there was no way she could have done it at all. Thank you, Your Honor."

I grabbed my notes and turned back to my seat. Veronica nudged into my side and Grace into the other. I noticed Grace's light gray blazer and low-cut white tank underneath and art-appreciation adrenaline mixed with the opening-arguments rush.

We'd either win this case, or I'd pass out trying.

At least the boys appeared rattled, and Mr. Darr kept shifting uncomfortably in his seat. I knew from experience that was a tell that he didn't think things were going well for his team.

Good.

Because his team should have been my team.

Veronica's cross-examination of Randy from the Scrub-Bot development team made my team fist bump triumphantly and Jeff scowl. Then Izzy gave a tearjerker of a testimony, and Raina threw herself so righteously into a dramatic portrayal of Chris, the accused. Then Grace's cross-examination (and blazer) . . . all great.

But then it seemed like Nikita had not studied her part or she went off script on purpose. She kept saying things during my questioning of her that the boys wrote down and then made her backtrack during cross-examination. And then I could tell the boys' closings impressed Ms. McClain. And the new kid (Chad? Mike? I never did sort them out) gave a performance equal to Raina's.

"Who's that kid, and why hasn't he been in theater?" she whispered to me.

That was practically a standing ovation coming from her.

After we were done, Ms. McClain and Mr. Darr left the room.

"That was . . . something," said Brandon.

Raina's face got red, but she didn't say anything.

"Fear doesn't look good on you, boys," said Veronica.

Jeffrey glanced over. "You know, it's really a waste of resources to have two teams." He stretched out in his seat. "You could come back, Millie."

I blinked.

"Come back to the team?" I said. "Your team?"

I had to admit, it wasn't an unattractive offer. Sure, they'd dumped me and treated me like crap. But it would be a lot easier to bring my girls over and join forces.

Brandon yawned. Jeffrey rolled his head back on the desk behind him. It reminded me of all the other practices where they were all bored out of their minds and I did everything to make us successful.

"No, thanks," I said. "No, thank you, ever."

Jeffrey didn't even bother to look up.

Ms. McClain and Mr. Darr came back into the room.

"We consulted, the bailiff and me. And there were strong points on either side. And places that can be improved. Which we will be discussing."

"We have decided to declare a mistrial," said Ms. McClain.

Everyone groaned.

"You just don't want to determine a winner!" said Mike or Chad.

"Maybe there was no winner, teams. You both clearly have work to do. But the burden of proof lies with the prosecution to convince me beyond a reasonable doubt that the defendant was guilty. Can't say *we* had that. Reasonable doubt." Ms. McClain winked at me.

Mr. Darr grimaced and my heart soared.

No one was dumping on these angry (or motivated) girls today.

FEBRUARY 18: NATURE OF ACTION

THE HIGH FROM OUR WIN (OR AT LEAST OUR nonloss) in the scrimmage kept me calm and happy for the first half of the week. But we were facing Squirrel Hill Prep in two days for the first trial, and I knew they'd come prepared. They lived and breathed this stuff, and most of their team members graduated and went prelaw to an Ivy. It'd be an uphill battle under the best of circumstances, and I felt our witnesses were underrehearsed and our arguments underprepared.

No amount of breathing could calm the fear of humiliation at the feet of Squirrel Hill, so I decided to try to download some new affirmations. When I opened up my computer, a screen popped up, alerting me to new messages in my inbox. My breath caught in my chest. It was from Ohio State. Decisions were to go out before the end of March, and it was only the beginning of February.

Another box popped up. And another. I might have overdone it with the alert settings. My hand hovered over the touch pad. Maybe I should just leave it alone. Better not to know. Stay mindful of the here and now, as the therapist and apps and affirmations and meditations and sleep stories often advised.

But how could you keep your mind in the here and now when tomorrow was freaking out all over your lock screen?

I tapped on Ohio State. I didn't really want to go there anyway. That one was a reach. It was for Mom. Who cared if they were always in the top ten college Mock Trial power rankings? Rankings didn't matter. Best to forge ahead with a calm and cool . . .

Wait, the first line preview said *Congratulations*.

I called Claire immediately.

"Oh my gosh, Claire, oh my gosh!"

"Did you win a competition I didn't know about?" she said.

"No. I GOT INTO OHIO STATE. RANKINGS MATTER. WHO ARE WE KIDDING?"

"I . . . What?"

"Ohio State. I was accepted. Mom lives in Columbus now, you know."

"Wow! Holy shit! Congratulations."

"Yeah, actually . . ." I opened my other notifications. I clicked over to my applicant portals and all three of them had switched statuses. Instead of *pending*, they read *accepted*.

"HOLY GOODNESS, I GOT INTO ALL THE SCHOOLS!" I was yelling now.

"OF COURSE YOU DID. OF COURSE." Claire could always match the energy of any given situation.

"But this means I have to choose someplace," I said. "I didn't really think that would be a thing."

"You didn't think you'd get in? Are you kidding? You're, like, number eight in our class."

"Yeah, but our school isn't that big. And I'm out of state. I don't know. I honestly didn't think it would be on the radar. Mom had been talking about it, so I just . . . kind of did it."

"Listen. You're sitting for your Supreme Court confirmation hearings, and I haven't even auditioned for my top school yet. Do you have to sign a legal thing that says you'll go to one of these schools?"

"No. It's not binding. You just find out sooner."

"Oh. When do you have to decide?"

"I have a month or two. I've been saving birthday money in case I have to deposit at more than one school," I said.

"Wow," she said. "Okay, Your Honor. I gotta go. My mom is calling for dinner."

We hung up.

It was kind of true, what I'd said. I'd really been saving it in case I got into a school I didn't want to tell my dad about. Which was pretty much all of them. His vision, which he laid to me out every month or so now, was that I'd live at home. Go to Penn State Steelton or maybe Pitt Fogton. He thought it was a waste of money or dangerous to send me off on my own. Dad would never dream of depositing at more than one school until I decided. He would think that was irresponsible.

He'd also freak if he thought I wouldn't be commuting. But as far as I knew, his dream schools didn't even have a Mock Trial team. The main campuses in State College or Pittsburgh did. I'd applied to those. Penn State was in the top fifty in the power rankings. And they had a creamery that made the best known ice cream in the universe.

But Penn State was still too far. I wouldn't be home for meal prep and to do laundry.

Possibly to find his shoes and blue and green folders.

Because Dad lived in 1950.

A shudder shook me right then, just a little. Poor Dad. I loved him. He hadn't left me. And he held down a job and paid for my braces and made sure I had a credit card for Schwan's deliveries. But for an adult, he required a lot of . . . something. What? What had Mom called it?

Nurture. Dad needed nurturing.

It wasn't a good look.

I wouldn't have to nurture anyone but myself if I moved. Though, I didn't know how I'd pay for school, either. I'd be giving up a lot if I didn't follow Dad's plan.

A part of me knew that I'd be giving up more if I *did* follow it.

Just then, I heard Dad open the front door. I snapped my laptop closed out of instinct. Dad wouldn't look at it, even if he came into my room. But I felt guilty for all the less-than-nice things I'd just been thinking. I went downstairs.

"Hi, Dad," I said.

"Hey, babes. Any dinner going?"

"No, sorry. School stuff. But why don't I make a quick pasta salad?"

"That'd be great. I'm going to get in a quick run and shower. Think it will be done in a half an hour or so?"

"Yeah," I said.

He was already on his way to his room to change into his workout clothes.

I opened the cabinet and unearthed the pasta I'd bought on my last trip to Giant Eagle. Then I unwrapped the vegetables and the chicken I'd broiled over the weekend in case this exact situation arose.

I filled a pot with water and heavy as it was, I slammed it down on the burner hard enough for water to splash all over the stovetop and drip onto the floor. I should probably clean it up. Someone could slip and fall. That's what a team player would do.

But then again, maybe everyone in this house could just look out for themselves for a change.

11

RAINA PETREE,	:	IN THE COURT OF
	:	REVENGE OF CAMBRIA
Plaintiff,	:	COUNTY
	:	
v.	:	
	:	
CLAIRE FOWLER,	:	Case No. CMURBST2025
	:	
	:	
Defendant	:	

FEBRUARY 20: DISCUSSION SECTION

I WAS USUALLY NERVOUS BEFORE A SHOW. I had rituals. I made sure to be prepared. But this felt different, our first official meet. Sure, we'd faced off with the boys' team and Brandon had been there, but that wasn't real. That wasn't *competition*. I hadn't tried something new in forever and now I had knitting *and* Mock Trial. Every time I'd seen Brandon question a witness or a witness give a compelling performance, I'd tingled with want. Why hadn't I done this before?

What else had my single-mindedness about Brandon kept me from doing?

Mom dropped me off at the downtown courthouse on her way to work.

Grace arrived at the same time.

"Morning." She yawned. "Didn't feel like carpooling from the school?"

"Had a rare ride today. Hope they have coffee," I sympathized.

Grace held the door open for me. We were both early, so only a few others from other teams milled around inside.

"I am so ready," I said.

"We're prepped. I feel our win just sitting here waiting for us. It's just Steelton and the nearby borough schools. I doubt anything that interesting will happen."

"Pardon me, girls," said a male voice just then. "Mind if I sweep past you here?" Grace and I turned and moved out of the way of the courtroom door we'd been blocking.

"Here for Mock Trial?" said the man. He looked familiar.

Grace's eyes widened. "Um. Yes, sir. We're assigned to this room and waiting for everyone."

The man winked. "Splendid. I'll see you in there. I'll be the one on the bench."

The man opened the door and went inside the courtroom.

"Do I recognize him?" I said. "He's been on TV?"

"Judge Herman T. Wise of Dropped Stitch infamy."

"Yup." The situation took a second to sink in. "Well," I said, staring at the door with Grace. "Let's hope Carla doesn't show up with some vaginas to throw at him."

"Agreed."

FEBRUARY 23: FIRST SET OF REQUESTS FOR PRODUCTION

AS IT TURNED OUT, I KILLED IT AS DEFEN-
dant Chris Banks on Saturday. I was *born* to be fake sworn in and
embody Chris-the-embittered-inventor, if I did say so myself.

And I did. Say so. To Megan about forty times and everyone else
within a twenty-foot radius.

"That's nice, dear," said Gretta, tying off the last strings of her
uncircumcised penises. "Were you out on bail this whole time?"

"What? No?" I said.

Gretta looked at Grace. "You seem a little young to be a lawyer."

"I'm in high school," she said.

"Yes, that's what I thought. Did you get an online degree?"

"This is Mock Trial. Emphasis on the *Mock*," I said. "I was never
really accused of killing anyone. Grace was just acting as my lawyer.
Pretending, if you will. The laws and things are real. We could win
or lose. But we won."

Brandon's team had been there, too, of course. They went up
against Fogton Creek High and won. They were up against Squirrel
Hill, and we were up against Fogton Creek for the second trial on
March sixth. After our scrimmage, I knew we could take them. But
we didn't get to find out in the real competition.

"Your performance was inspired," said Grace.

"And you were brilliant. You all were," I said. I glanced at her,
seeing the moment to reveal a secret between us to the group. "Even
the Honorable Herman T. Wise said so."

The whole room stopped after I spoke his name aloud. A few
people glanced up from knitting ambiguous genitalia. Carla and the
rest of the crew stared at us.

"What did you just say?" said Carla.

"We won at Mock Trial," I said.

"After that."

"The judge thought we were good?" I was hoping she'd missed that part. Grace and I had expected him to eat us or at least tell us off, but he'd been nothing but kind and fair.

"Judge . . . Wise . . . thought you were good?"

"Yes," I said.

Carla considered that. "He's not all bad. I heard he volunteers most of his free time, a lot of it with schools and at-risk youth. I just wish his guiding legal beliefs weren't so archaic."

"We aren't going to see him again," Grace said.

"I found his courtroom barely tolerable," I said.

Carla grumbled something under her breath. Louder she said, "He came over here after the yarn bombing, you know."

"What?" I said.

"After the courthouse. We yarn bombed it because of him, and he knew it. He's always in the paper these days. Didn't even take the bench long ago but has had enough time to make people's lives difficult. *Women's* lives difficult. Delays hearings. Suppresses evidence. Heaven forbid you're a mother who commits a crime. He sets bail higher or denies it all together. There are any number of indignities that you can inflict on a family. And he finds a way to do that. And the burden of proof in assaults. The list goes on."

"He didn't do that at the trial. He was friendly," said Grace. "It wasn't real."

"He came here the day after the yarn bomb and said if he caught wind of any more 'vandalism,' we'd be 'in for it.' He didn't say what 'it' he meant, but it was probably the business end of his misogyny. Did he recognize either of you?" said Carla.

"Nope," I said.

"No," said Grace.

Carla grumbled again. But she didn't say anything else about it after that, so I thought we were likely in the clear with her.

After knitting, Grace gave me a ride home.

"Are we consorting with the enemy in our resume-building activity?" I said.

"We didn't know he'd be there. And even if we did know, what choice did we have? Besides, he was neutral up there."

"True. There were three separate courtrooms. Three judges who could have gotten our trial. Funny we had him of all people."

"Yeah. Maybe the guys will have him next," said Grace.

"Megan overheard Brandon bragging about it. He probably did it near her on purpose. Their judge loved them and praised their witnesses' acting. I *know* he was talking loudly on purpose." I hadn't said Brandon's name out loud in a while. It felt strange. Lips together, rolling the consonant cluster *br* that isn't softened at all by the harsh short *an*. The *don* is softer, almost delicate. I used to love saying his name, much to Megan's chagrin. I wrote it in little hearts in the margins of my script. I thought It constantly. But now it just felt wrong in all contexts.

"I was kind of hoping they'd lose, mostly for Millie's sake," said Grace.

I rolled my eyes. "Assholes," I said. "I should knit them colons."

"Do it! We could put them on their lockers!"

"They probably wouldn't get it. Why waste the yarn?"

"Agreed."

Grace dropped me off at home, and I was greeted by a sleeping mother in front of the television. I turned it off and tried to cover her with an afghan. It only had enough material to cover half of her. I resolved to crochet a blanket big enough to cover her, once I could do more than make a fallopian tube with my crochet hook. Unless I knitted her one made out of square vulvas.

That I could start making today.

FEBRUARY 27: MINOR TALENT RELEASE AGREEMENT

MOM WAS UP BRIGHT AND EARLY THE DAY OF my Carnegie Mellon audition.

"How are you like this at five o'clock in the morning?" I asked.

"I have to go into work anyway. I might as well see you off since I can't take you. Have you kissed your bears?"

"Maybe," I said. I had a preshow ritual where I kissed all the bears Dad had gotten me over the years. I hadn't played with them since I was about ten, but you could never mess with something that brought you luck.

"I thought you had to get them all or else it would go wrong. Snowy. Bear Bear. Pinky. Binky. Bunky Wunky . . ."

"Why do you remember their names?"

"Smile Face. Cutie Butt. Pepper. Jakey. Ice Cream Cone . . ."

"All right, *enough*. I keep them because Dad bought them."

"Uh-huh. Sure."

I rolled my eyes at her. "I hear a car out front. Must be Claire. Gotta go."

"Wait, not *the* Claire? Can I meet her?"

"Bye, Mom!"

I checked my bag for the twelfth time to make sure I had my pieces printed and prepped to practice for the car.

"Hey," I said to her as I slid into the front seat.

I'm in a car with Claire Fowler right now, I texted Megan.

Break a leg today! And not Claire's! she texted back.

Claire and I sat in the front seat pretending we were not ignoring each other. I studied my newly painted nails, and she mumbled her monologue to herself.

I cleared my throat. It would be a long ride if we sat in silence the whole time.

"So. What piece are you doing?" I said.

"Scene from *Twelfth Night* and one from *Arsenic and Old Lace*," she said. "You?"

"Also, *Twelfth Night*. And *Arsenic and Old Lace*," I said.

"Funny," she said.

"Yeah."

"Drama teacher suggest that?" she said.

"Well. Kind of. He mentioned it last year when I started looking at schools. I hadn't thought about it in a while, so . . ." I trailed off. I looked out the window. "I *do* still care about getting into CMU. It's all I've wanted since I was a kid. But I think I wanted it at least partly because of Brandon. That idiot always encouraged me to just focus, focus, focus. Once I had some space to breathe, I realized there's other stuff I like. Law. Knitting. Activism. And now I don't know if I should spend all this money on one path if I really want to do something else. Or more than one thing, you know? I loved Brandon so much. *So much.* When he left it felt like he took part of me with him. But now, a couple of months out, I think maybe that there were some things I didn't really like about myself when I was with him. I was too dependent on him. So it still sucks, having someone you loved crap on you, but on the other hand, I have this freedom to do whatever I want."

I saw Claire glancing over at me, unsure of what to do with this way too honest information.

"Uh. Yeah. Anyway. Is CMU still your first choice?" I said.

"Yeah," she said automatically, gracefully ignoring my overshare. "It's close to home. It's so good. I love Pittsburgh. It's just the right fit. New York seems too big. I guess you go there eventually, to act. Or LA. And that seems even *more* overwhelming. It might be super competitive, but at least I'd still feel like I had some kind of home-stage advantage here, you know?"

"I do," I said. Those were all the same reasons I had wanted to go to Carnegie Mellon. Since when had Claire and I had so much in common? Had we always?

We fell into silence again.

"I think it's cool you've branched out. You might as well do your best at your audition. It's good to have options."

"Oh man, my mother says that to me all the time," I said.

"Mine too. I just channeled her right there."

We both laughed.

Another thing we had in common. If these kept coming, I'd have to rethink yet another motivating factor for my theater career.

Eventually we made it into the city, driving along the Allegheny River. It never got old, leaving the winding brown and gray hillsides behind for the towering steel and glass skyline. Most people probably thought Pittsburgh was pretty dinky for a city. It wasn't New York or Los Angeles. But it was my first taste of professional theater, with lights and sets and costumes worthy of Broadway. CMU had a beautiful campus, with a wide, snow-covered lawn and tall buildings with windows sticking out in places I didn't expect.

"This is the business school," I said. "Do we know where we're going?"

"No," said Claire. "But those people look like they do. Let's follow them."

"How do we know they aren't business students?" I said.

"All five of them are in all black. That one's wearing a beret. And that dude"—she lowered her voice—"is wearing *an ascot*. These are our people. Follow them."

I couldn't argue with her logic.

We crossed a good portion of the campus. I shivered, wondering why Claire hadn't parked closer to our actual destination, but I realized she'd probably just gone into the first lot she'd seen. Hopefully we were allowed to be there and wouldn't be towed or something. We followed Ascot and Beret into the most impressive walkway I've ever seen. I heard Claire gasp as we entered. The white stone columns and walls rose up to a vaulted ceiling painted as a tribute to a multitude of artistic expression.

Inside, we found more actors clad in black, along with the more colorful types with the dyed hair and multiple piercings. My stomach kept doing little flips. But it wasn't the kind of nervous I expected to feel before an audition. The audition of my *life*. Instead, I looked around and wondered if I belonged there. Sure, I practiced. Sure, I loved the craft. But *why* did I love it? Did I want this for me? Or did a version of myself I'd molded after someone else want this? Was I that girl anymore?

After Claire and I checked in, things passed in a blur. I went to the bathroom, but despite the fact that CMU's facilities were a lot nicer than Steelton High's, I couldn't hide there, because rows of girls applied makeup, brayed vocal warm-ups, and tamed their hair. Outside, people clung nervously to the people they brought with them or stood in corners practicing. I spotted Claire behind a pillar, reaching up to the sky in her preshow warm-up.

I just scrolled through my phone.

Eventually, it was my turn. I entered the room where a lady I recognized from the website sat at a table with two others. I ran her face through my mind and realized that she was the head of the whole program.

"Welcome, Ms. Petree," she said.

"Thank you, ma'am."

I never called anyone "ma'am." Would theater people hate that? Oh God . . .

"What have you prepared for your classical and contemporary piece?"

"Um. *Twelfth Night?*" I should have warmed up. I should have practiced more. I shouldn't have just thrown this whole thing away to pretend to be a witness. "And *Arsenic and Old Lace.*"

"When you're ready."

I cleared my throat (which is terrible for the vocal cords). I remembered the time I played Viola, and after Brandon had kissed me in the gazebo in Stackhouse Park.

"I left no ring with her. What means this lady?

Fortune forbid my outside have not charmed her.

She made good view of me; indeed, so much . . ."

Somehow the asshole hadn't ruined Viola, at least.

I tried to give *Arsenic* all that I could as well. When I was done, the three people watched me. I looked at my feet.

Maybe I should have bowed? It was probably too late.

"Interesting choices," said the program director.

They weren't. They were probably what the least original candidates did.

"Why did you pick them?" she asked.

"They were only ones my mom ever wanted to hear again," I said. "She loves both plays. She works night shifts and often falls asleep during my shows. Sometimes to escape, if it involves miming. These kept her awake through the show. I figured if I could do that, it must be worth doing."

The people behind the table chuckled.

"What would you say about mixing this up a little bit. I read in the supplementary materials you recently submitted that you also like Mock Trial. What would these look like if Viola was a witness?"

I blinked.

"What?" I said.

"I want you to imagine that this speech is taking place in a contemporary courtroom. You are arguing here."

I tried to channel Millie in her opening statement.

"Now I want you to do your second monologue again, only gobble this time," a man behind the table said.

"Pardon me?" I said.

"Do it again, only as a turkey."

I stood there for a good thirty seconds, wondering if they were mocking me.

I didn't know if these people were out of their minds or geniuses. Maybe both.

Maybe they just really hated Joseph Kesselring.

When it was all over, I went back to the quieter bathroom and threw up.

I found Claire next to the same pillar as before, almost hyperventilating.

"You okay?" I said.

"I'm trying to do Millie's affirmations, but they aren't working. They were really kind people, but the program director kept trying to *direct* me. Everywhere else they just said, 'Thanks, bye.' No, that woman wanted me to *embody* the piece. I had to *use* the *space*. Lord." She looked at me. "You okay? You look a little green."

"I had to gobble."

"What?"

"I had to do my contemp piece as fowl."

"Are you kidding me?"

"I am not." I leaned my back against the pillar and sunk to the ground. "That must mean they hated me so much they needed something to liven it up."

Claire sat down next to me.

"No," she said. "They made some dude in front of me be a robot. Another kid had to do it while making snow angels. I think it's just their thing."

I glanced over at her. "Really?"

"Totally."

So often I was hyped up after a performance, but today exhaustion oozed from every pore. I should love this. Why didn't I love this?

"You ready to go?" said Claire

"Yeah," I said.

"Want to go Eat'n Park? There are two on the way home. Three if I take the creative route," she said.

"Always," I said. I was as hungry as I was tired. "Hey, Claire?"

"Yes?"

"Thanks," I said. "Really."

"Welcome." She smiled at me.

Maybe I'd blown my chance at my dream. But maybe I hadn't. Because I had a lot of different dreams now. And I realized I'd had more fun at that audition than I'd had in so long.

Besides, any life path worth choosing veered next to a place selling smiley cookies.

MARCH 2: RESPONSES TO PLANTIFFS' INTERROGATORIES

"WE SHOULD ROLL ON THE IDES OF MARCH," a newcomer to the circle said to Carla.

"This is wonderful pound cake, dear," said Gretta.

"Thank you. It's the ex's favorite. He'll never eat it again," she said.

"His loss," said Megan. We hadn't had a chance to hang out in a while, so I'd dragged her to knitting.

The woman's husband had left her for his personal assistant two weeks prior. Two Hearts had apparently started emailing the newly dumped who wrote in to give out the addresses to their LYS. You got 50 percent off your first purchase if you brought in the email. A lot of burned women were making scarves these days.

"Anyway, I'm invested in this. I used to embroider with my grandma. Got pretty good at it. Gave it up in med school. Just seemed like there was no time. That's when I met him. Only had time to jog and geocache because that's what *he* liked. No more! No, I'm going to clothe elephants!" she said.

"What?" said Beatrice.

"I read an article that they knit massive sweaters for elephants to keep them warm. That's my goal. Make something grand. Only for the female elephants, though."

"You do that, dear."

"March fifteenth is the Meet the Officials town meeting. We need to go and meet this Wise guy and his other minions and give them the what-for."

"They haven't had a town meeting in years," said Alex. "Maybe this Judge Wise will try to be better."

"Yes, maybe," said Carla. "But this is the same as helping the kids out with their Mock Trial. Maybe you are a decent human being, but behind closed doors you do harm on a policy level."

"Aren't trials usually public?" said Grace.

"Criminal trials are," I said.

"You know what I'm saying. It's about his underlying beliefs," said Carla.

"People can be more than one thing," said Alex. "You can have some misogyny floating around in there with your faithful civil service. It's almost like people are complicated."

Carla glared at her. "Maybe he's a great guy. It doesn't matter in this case. We are acting against what he *does*. Not who he *is*. Because if we can change what he does, we might make lives better."

Alex crossed her needles in front of her chest in what seemed to be a sign of yarning acquiescence.

"What exactly are we doing when we roll later this month?" asked Beatrice.

"I haven't figured that out quite yet," said Carla. "Since this is the first I'm learning about this *Meet the Officials* town hall. But I'll let you know."

"You going to go up against your friend?" Carla looked at Grace and me.

"I don't know him!" I said. "It was one extracurricular activity!"

"Good. I'll expect to see you there."

Knew that drill. I made a note in my phone to keep the evening of March fifteenth open. Maybe Millie could be on a need-to-know basis about my Judge Wise interactions. Hopefully, we wouldn't meet him again for Mock Trial and it wouldn't matter.

After knitting, Grace, Megan, and I got wings. "Ready for the second trial? This Saturday, right?" said Megan.

"Yeah. First one was okay. But Aunt Kay helped me with my close for prosecution for the one this week," said Grace.

"What do you mean?" said Megan.

"She gave me a two-paged typed list of pointers for the closing and for your questioning. She either wants to win, or she's just pissed at not lawyering anymore."

"This works out for you," I said.

"Yeah." She chewed for a while. "How did your audition go?"

"Eh," I said. "I guess it could have gone worse."

"Do you always say that? So you don't jinx it?" said Grace.

"No. I would tell you if I were God's gift to Shakespeare. Because sometimes I am."

"Believe her. She'd tell you if it went well," said Megan.

"Okay then." Grace laughed. "Well, I hope you get in."

"Where are you going to school?" I asked.

"Ohio State. Early action, right there. Three generations of the fam went there, and I will be continuing the proud tradition. I signed on the dotted line and at least don't have to think about it until August."

"Cool. For what?" I said.

"Not sure. Maybe political science. Maybe English. Undeclared."

MEGAN DROVE ME HOME AFTER THAT. MOM wasn't there, so I just curled into bed. I wished I had a life plan. Surely *somewhere* would take me for theater. I'd done my audition clips for the virtual portfolios before I'd lost track of my lifelong goals. What could I see myself doing for the rest of my life? Knitting. I wanted to knit. There might be room for two Steelton yarn stores, the way people got dumped in this town. I also liked being in the courtroom. Listening to each side build a case, trying to come to the truth. But I couldn't do what Millie or Grace or Veronica did. I never thought of myself as much of a writer. Though I *did* like to argue. And if I was being honest with myself, a small part of me *still* hoped that maybe the past two months had been a bad dream. That I might wake up at any moment with ten texts from Brandon telling me he missed me and couldn't live without me. We'd both end up in Pittsburgh somehow and be those high school sweethearts who beat the odds and end up together. But then again, I wouldn't want to give up Mock Trial, since I had a feeling Brandon wouldn't want me to compete with him. Going back to him would be comfortable, but maybe being too comfortable held you back from something better. Now that I'd glimpsed that possibility, I wanted to find out what that *something better* was more than I had ever wanted Brandon.

I drifted off to sleep fantasizing about watching Millie convict Brandon of crimes against humanity, sentencing him to a solitary prison camp far, far away. It was the most peaceful I'd felt in ages.

12

EMILIA GOODWIN,	:	SUPREME(LY PISSED
	:	OFF) COURT OF
Plaintiff,	:	CAMBRIA COUNTY
	:	
v.	:	
	:	
EMILIA GOODWIN,	:	Case No. WWRBGD2025
	:	
	:	
Defendant	:	

MARCH 8: DEFENDANT'S PRETRIAL PRELIMINARY STATEMENT

SEVERAL THINGS ABOUT THE MOCK TRIAL team concerned the heck out of me.

We did well in the scrimmage against the boys. Then we won our first trial, mostly because I think the judge was impressed by the acting on our team. I was pretty sure we won the second trial two days ago because the other team didn't know what it was doing and seemed to have forgotten which side they were assigned.

For the district meet this coming weekend, we were the prosecution again, which wasn't great. But we were up against the school that had won states last year, which was bad. The team would get to practice more, which was good. But Nikita kept having to leave for dance practice, Veronica had to keep putting out fires at the lit magazine, and Grace . . .

Grace was walking up to me that very second.

"Hey," she said.

"I was just thinking about you," I said. Blood rushed to my head when I realized how that sounded.

"Oh?" she said.

"Yeah. Mock Trial. You were really good. Kay's notes helped."

"Agreed. Listen—question: I know that districts are this week. And we all need to concentrate. But I was wondering if you wanted to do something on Thursday. Get your mind off it. Unwind. But still let you obsess about it the night before. I'm all about balance."

Wait. Grace was asking me out?

On a date.

With her.

Which should be good. I liked Grace. I *really* liked Grace. Her hair and eyes and clothes and her weird hobby of knitting body parts with Raina for social-activist reasons I didn't quite understand. But college was coming up. I had to make a decision, and whatever that was, it would surely lead to heartbreak. People didn't stay together when they went to college. Those were just the facts. People barely even stayed married, obviously. And what if things went wrong before states? Or nationals?

It made focusing on the "now" difficult.

Especially because Grace's confidence matched her persistence.

Focus, Millie. You steer the ship in the river of dreams.

"What do you think?" said Grace.

"Yes," I said, suddenly very warm.

"Yes, you want to do something?"

"I don't like sex," I said.

I tried to suck in more oxygen to my brain because clearly it wasn't getting enough to properly communicate as people did.

Grace laughed. "Listen, I feel you there. I really do. But all I wanted to do was go to a movie. Do you eat popcorn?"

"Um," I said. "I do."

"Candy?"

"Yes."

"Soda?"

"That stuff is terrible for you."

"Noted. Do you want to make out if the movie is boring? Making out is not sex. It's fine if you don't want to, but I can get a ballpark of what you'd enjoy."

Actually, I felt kind of cold. Clammy. Some sort of stasis should soon start to spread over me due to the obviously extreme temperature swings I currently experienced.

"I mean. Like, kissing?" I said.

"We can go back to the popcorn if that is more comfortable."

"I do like kissing."

"Millie. Honest, it's just a movie. We can watch it. That's it. You can pick. There's some documentary about the Constitution playing at the hipster place up on the hill on Thursday."

The woman had done her homework.

"Okay. Yes. That would be useful." *Breathe*, I willed myself. Neurons immolated themselves to escape the awkward.

"The documentary would be useful to you?" Grace grinned again and shook her head. "And I'm allowed to join the two of you?"

"I don't have a lot of dating experience," I said. "I'm sorry about this. Mock Trial is usually my boyfriend. Or girlfriend. My significant other."

"How's that working out for you?" she said.

"It's complicated," I said.

Now Grace *really* laughed.

Maybe she was into absurdity.

Fortunately for me, Raina returned. She easily accepted all the attention in a room if you offered it to her. She launched into a monologue about auditioning as a turkey.

When the bell rang, Grace handed Raina a ball of bright yellow yarn from her backpack.

"Knit something sunny," she said.

"Okay," Raina said.

To me, Grace leaned over and whispered, "See you Thursday."

The chills down my spine counteracted my internal combustion enough so that I didn't incinerate everyone right there in the hallway. That was partly a shame because Mock Trial president Jeffrey brushed past me.

"Pardon me," he said.

"It's fine," I managed to say. The sensation of Grace's lips close to my ear still tingled in my neck.

"Oh. That's good. Wouldn't want you getting hurt or anything, keeping you and your team out of competition."

I turned to look him full in the face.

"I helped you for years," I said.

"I—"

"I was never mean to you. I laughed at your jokes. I got you that girl's number at the Mansfield meet. I spoke up on your behalf when that senior, Zack whatshisface, tried to kick you off closing arguments because you were a sophomore. You were better than him. You are better than most, Jeff. But then you decided I was beneath you, and now you are acting like this? Why?"

"Well . . . I mean . . . you are the competition now," he stammered.

"And whose fault is that? I'd still be there, on the team, doing my part. Helping, again, to get us to the championship. I was never a weak link. And now you are trying to trash talk me in the hallway."

"We did work, too, you know. You just never liked how we wanted to do things. You had your own plan, and if anyone wanted to go against you, you'd quit contributing."

"That's *not* true," I said. "You barely listened to me as it was."

"Like six generations of guys in my family are lawyers. Same with Brandon. Same with Mike this year. We know what we're doing. I knew you wouldn't listen to us, and you would have demanded to do your own thing."

"That's what this is about? I don't have the right family? The right background?" I said.

"No. It's about you being a know-it-all. You thinking you did everything and that you deserved all the credit when other people actually went up there and won the trial." Jeffrey looked around, not liking the scene we were making in the middle of the hallway. "You never stopped talking about your ideas."

"Like you are any different."

"I let other people talk."

"Whatever, Jeff. You know what? You did me a favor kicking me out. The boys were way more vocal than me *and* claimed too much of the credit for the work. You never had a problem with any of them. What do you have to say about *that*?"

He just stared at me.

The thing is, Jeffrey wasn't a horrible person. I knew that. None of them were. But here he was, being kind of horrible. Because I talked too much? Because I shouldn't have tried to take credit when it was due?

"Better work on that argument, counsel."

I left him standing there, still seemingly unable to think of a comeback.

Toxic masculinity didn't make you any cleverer, it seemed.

Though, this *did* give me a little hope for winning a place at states after districts.

MARCH 11: OPPOSITION TO THE STATE'S MOTION FOR A JOINT TRIAL

"DAD, I'M GOING OUT TONIGHT," I CALLED to the office.

He might have made a sound.

"Dad?" I yelled.

Nothing.

I knocked on his door. "Dad?" I said, pushing it open.

He wasn't in there.

There was money and a note on the table. *Gone out to dinner with Sheila! Order pizza?*

This was a new one, him leaving.

I sighed and shoved the twenty dollars he left into my purse. *Also went out. Thanks for the cash,* I wrote underneath his scrawl.

I counted this as an "uninvolved parent" tax. He owed it to me.

I went upstairs to survey my wardrobe choices. Mom had sent the cutest maroon turtleneck dress (with pockets!) and a pair of silver leggings last week, and I hadn't gotten a chance to wear them yet. I might as well go big for this. Maybe if Grace got distracted looking at me, she wouldn't hear the nonsense sure to come out of my mouth.

The thought of Grace looking at me made the dress feel clingier than I remember.

At exactly seven o'clock, I heard someone pull up in front of the house. I breathed for a minute with my smart watch, grabbed my bag, and headed out into the wild unknown.

"Hi," she said. "You are wearing a dress."

"Yes, it has pockets!" I said.

"Do you always wear dresses?"

"No. I often wear skirts," I said. "Do you have something against dresses?"

"Not at all. I love them on you. I mean. Not to objectify you or anything. You are smart and powerful. In a dress. With pockets."

Grace was a mess, too! That was amazing news to me.

I grinned. "When does the movie start?"

"Seven thirty."

"Just enough time to get popcorn!" I said.

We had more than enough time, as it turned out. And the entire theater to ourselves.

"Why isn't this more popular?" I said. I twisted around to make sure I hadn't missed any freedom-and-justice-loving moviegoers in the back.

"The new *Spider-Man* is opening," said Grace.

"There's one of those every month," I said.

"I think there's that new one where stuff blows up. I forget the name, but that guy is in it. It made a lot of money already."

"You are really selling me on that one. Maybe we should go to that instead," I said. "But this empty theater has benefits."

I meant that I could put my feet up on the seat in front of me and our coats on the chair next to us. But even in the darkish theater, I could see Grace's face get pinker.

"Oh. Yeah," she said.

I was pretty sure it was the dress pockets that were making me bold. They held limitless potential. And extra napkins.

I stuffed popcorn in my mouth before I proposed to Grace or something.

The lights grew darker and the screen moved from the preshow entertainment to the actual movie. That was the sad part about documentaries—you usually didn't get the fun previews.

The movie traced the history of the Supreme Court to its current iteration. Grace's presence was never out of my mind, even if they interviewed every living justice. I tried to commit every one of Ruth

Bader Ginsburg's words to memory, for my own personal use and also because I knew Grace worshipped her like me.

As the credits started to roll, I turned to her. "That was amazing. Thank you."

"Anytime," she said. "They have another showing. We could stay."

She was joking. This registered in my brain. But the offer tempted.

"We could also go find more food."

"Even better idea," Grace said.

We debated between several places but ended up at the big Sheetz with the tables.

"We are classy, classy people," I said.

"Whatever. You know what this place has? Gas. I promised I'd fill up the tank. But I can also find made-to-order hot dogs. And Galliker's chocolate milk. *And* Tastycakes, thank you very much. Can you get that somewhere else? No, you can't."

"I want a sub."

We entered our order into the computer kiosk and took our stuff to a table by the window.

"This is romance," I said.

Grace's face got pinker again. "You want romance?" she said.

The dress pockets had room in them for wild chances as well, clearly.

"I mean. I wouldn't say no to it. Only I probably should. Because I need to focus," I said.

"Yeah, you mentioned that. Focus on winning?"

"Mostly. Life. Goals."

"What other goals do you have?"

"Winning mostly," I said.

We laughed. Being with her was easier than I imagined. I could feel the tension I generally carried like armor ease out of my shoulders.

"But we are just going to leave in a few months. To college and stuff."

"True." She looked out the window for a while. "But not for a few months. A lot can happen in that time. Like, you know, prom, for example."

I dug my hands deep into the dress pockets.

"Are you . . ." *Breathe, Millie, breathe.* "Do you want . . . Um . . . Should we go to the prom together?" I said.

My mother would freak and send me fifteen dresses if she heard about this.

"Yes, that's kind of what I was getting at," she said.

"Shouldn't this be bigger?" I said. "Signs and marching bands and a promposal to remember? I've read articles."

"That's kind of like getting down on one knee or whatever. I don't know why people do that, but it's probably because of the patriarchy. If you put on a big production in public, it's hard for the girl to say no. Patriarchy, I say."

I considered this. Some crazy gesture might be fun, but she had a point. "I wouldn't," I said. "Say no to you."

"Do you want a public spectacle?" she said. "I have recent new experience in the public art known as yarn bombing."

"No, no," I said. "Yarn bombing? What . . . you know what, don't tell me." I leaned toward her. "Grace?"

"Yes?"

"Will you go to prom with me?"

"I would love to. Would you go to prom with me?"

"Yes," I said.

We both grinned stupidly at each other, and then I became engrossed in cleaning up our Sheetz MTO wrappers when the moment made me feel like rainbow unicorn sparkles were about to explode out of the dress pockets.

Afterward, we went back to her car, and she drove me home in silence. The windows inside were lit up, so I knew Dad was home. We sat in the car for a second. I didn't know exactly what to do.

"Thank you. For tonight," I tried. "It was fun."

"We should do it again sometime."

"Definitely," I said. I slowly picked up my bag from the floor.

"Millie, no worries if . . ."

I let go of my bag and took Grace's face in my hands. "Can I kiss you?" I said.

"Yes," she breathed.

My lips met hers and my heart beat joy through every vein until it filled my entire body.

"Wow," I said.

"Agreed." She grinned.

The porch light came on then.

"Guess my dad noticed the car pull up," I said. "I should go inside." I didn't move.

"Guess you should," she said.

We kissed again.

This time the front door opened.

"Night," I said.

"Night."

I got out of the car and walked up to the porch.

"There you are, Millie!" said Dad. "It's so unlike you to be out!"

"Oh. Yeah. Saw a documentary on the Constitution."

"Excellent. I had the best date! Do you want to hear about it? I'll make tea!"

Dad chirped around me as I sat at the table remembering Grace's freckles and the dimple in her left cheek.

"Anyway, Sheila's really great, and I know you'll like her. She has two small children I'm sure you'll love. I met them tonight, and she wants to meet you. I don't know why we've put that off."

"Oh, sure, yeah," I said.

Dad beamed. "Great, honey. We're going out again tomorrow, too! And how was the movie? Did you find out more about truth and freedom and all that?"

"I did, Dad. I really think I did."

MARCH 12: PRETRIAL DISPOSITIVE MOTIONS

"YOU KISSED HER?" SAID CLAIRE.

"Yes," I said.

"Like, *kissed her* kissed her?"

"What does that even mean?"

"Did you kiss her like you meant it?"

"I meant it. So. Yes?" I said. A little part of me regretted telling her. I knew this was the reaction I'd get.

"But I thought you didn't like . . ."

"I like affection. She was good at it."

Now I could hear Claire pout. "I am good at affection."

I rolled my eyes. "You do not want to date me. You never have. One—I will give you *affection* but no sex. Do I contradict myself? No. I don't. People want all sorts of different things. Two—you require far too much attention. Three—you are currently in love with a girl from *Our Town*."

"We *are* in love. We are going to last forever. Or at least until June when she moves back to England. Her dad is here for a work thing. I'll be available for you in the summer."

"Will you be doing Steelton Three Rivers Theater Festival again?" I said.

"Yes, of course."

"Then no freaking way. There is more drama offstage than onstage, and it is bad enough being a bystander to it all."

"Strong words there, lady; watch it." Claire laughed. "But you have a prom date! That's so cool!"

"Right?"

As if summoned by the power of a consumer god, my phone beeped.

"Oh, it's my mom. I should take this," I said.

"Okay. The ol' man at home tonight?"

"Nope. Another date with Sheila. He's talking about another 'play date' with them soon. This time he wants me to go."

"Oh God. We'll talk about that tomorrow. Night."

I clicked over to the other line.

"Hi, Mom," I said.

"Hey, baby doll! It's been a while. What's happening?"

"Well . . ." I said. I hadn't told Mom about college. Or Grace. Or much of anything.

"Everything okay?" she said.

"Yeah, actually. I . . . I heard from a few schools," I said.

"And?" I could hear Mom fighting to sound casual.

"I got in."

"That's amazing, honey! Why didn't you call immediately? This is fantastic. Matt! Guess what? Mills got into college!"

I heard someone whoop in the background.

"Thanks, Mom."

"Where did you get in?"

I sucked in my breath. I should tell her. But I'd just be getting her hopes up. I mean. I didn't know where I'd go. And even if I moved to Ohio tomorrow, what was our relationship?

"Nothing is sure yet," I said.

"I understand. You probably have a month or two to decide. Where did you get in?"

"And cost is a factor, obviously."

"I know. But your dad can pay for it. I wish we could help more, but your dad makes plenty. Where did you get in?"

Dad always said I got my persistence from somewhere, and it wasn't him.

"Well, I admit my top choice right now is—" I took another breath. And another one. She obviously didn't know Dad very well if she thought he'd shell out cash for any old thing I wanted. "Ohio State."

"Wait. What? Are you kidding? You applied? When? Why didn't you tell me? I mean, I mentioned it. I thought . . . You got in? Matt! Matt! She got into OSU!"

"Are you kidding?" I heard in the background. "If we throw the baby in the car now, we could be there in four hours. I will paint the house scarlet and gray."

"Matt went there, you know," said Mom.

"I did not," I said. "That is not why I applied."

"Oh, honey, I know, I know. He's actually dancing. He played football there all four years."

"I still know people. We can go to all the games," he yelled.

"Do you hear him?"

"Yes. Mom! I might not go, you know."

"There's no telling him that. He told me it's okay if you went somewhere else because maybe the baby would continue the legacy. But, honestly, he's been praying you'd go anyway."

"Why?" I said. I barely knew the guy.

"Oh, he knows I'd like to have you close."

She would? Since when? Why? It's weird that the stepdad seemed to care more about me then the father I lived with.

"Wow," I said.

"This is just such exciting news."

She was happy, even if I knew telling Dad might make him never speak to me again.

"Okay. I have more," I said.

"What could possibly be bigger than Ohio State, home of a top-ten Mock Trial team?"

"I also wanted to tell you I have a date for prom."

The woman actually squealed.

"I'm going to hang up if this continues," I said.

"I'm sorry. I have to catch my breath. You swore off dances in middle school. Said they were a waste of time. I figured prom would fall into this category. Do you want me to send dresses? I could send a flat-rate box, and you could just send back the ones you don't want. Or maybe I could drive out there some weekend."

"Mom. It's fine."

"Do you have a dress already?" she said.

"No. I . . ." What? I did not have a dress. I could go shopping with Claire, I guessed. She'd be the same as Mom. "Okay. Well. Maybe you could mail them. You have eerily good taste in clothing for me."

"Yessssss," she breathed. It was like I was talking to Claire. "Fantastic, baby. You will send pictures. We will stream it so I can have input."

"Sure, Mom."

"Who is your date?" she said.

"Pardon?" My heart started beating in my chest. It was one thing for Mom to squeal over dresses. It was another to tell her about Grace.

"Your date has a name, I assume?"

"Hey, did I tell you about how I got into Ohio State?"

"Is it someone I knew?" said Mom.

"Sorry, you are breaking up. Connection weird. Bye, Mom!"

"Millie . . ." I could hear the laughter in her voice.

I tapped off the call.

I flopped back on my bed, exhausted. Mom and Claire took a lot of energy out of a person. I knew they were happy for me. But sometimes it felt like that happiness came when I fit into the neat little box of their expectations. Claire wanted me to obsess over girls (or whoever, but girls preferred) so that I could be where she is. Mom wanted me to giggle over fancy dresses and then move to Ohio so I could literally be where she is. Would they love me if I moved to California and adopted four loyal huskies?

Actually, that didn't sound like a bad plan. But if I wanted to clerk for a Supreme Court justice, I probably wouldn't be home enough to take care of the dogs.

I heard the door click open downstairs. Maybe I should tell Dad about the whole college and prom thing. I did live with the man.

"She's probably asleep," I heard him say. "She is really busy in school."

Wait, did Dad actually bring his date *home* this time?

"I know she must be lovely," said a woman's voice.

I crept quietly to my door and pushed it closed. I eased myself back into bed and clicked off the light. I wouldn't even risk brushing my teeth or going to the bathroom. Sheila was in my house. Where were her little kids? Was she staying over?

The idea was too gross to think about.

I turned over and plugged in my phone. I started my bedtime calming meditation on the lowest volume possible. I breathed in peace; I breathed out thoughts of my dad and mom and Claire and Ohio and prom dresses. Ohio and prom dresses fought back, dancing around behind my eyes.

"Focus, Emilia," I told myself. Maybe I shouldn't let myself get distracted by anything. Or anyone. Prom was around the same time nationals would be. I liked Grace, but wasn't this doomed to failure? It'd be another instance of someone leaving me. Or me leaving her. The thought of hurting Grace made my stomach ache. There were still several trials to go before I could relax.

In more ways than one.

MARCH 13: DEMANDS

DISTRICTS WERE THE REAL DEAL. THE BIG-gest of deals. The deal closest to bartering for life and death and one's soul.

Or it felt like it, anyway.

Cambria County rarely went to states, and as far as I knew had never won. Pittsburgh or Philly or the fancy suburbs always did that. Six teams competed today, and two of them could make states. They had to stagger the trials, because two teams were going twice because of snow dates or something. So they had to determine which of those teams got to come in the afternoon for districts. This left plenty of time for near panic before the event.

I prowled around the downstairs, stopping briefly to nibble at a croissant, scowl at the dishes in the sink, inhale peace and exhale terror in the living room, and resent Dad in front of his office door. The circuit almost had grounded my inner being until Dad emerged, a big smile on his face.

"Sheila is coming over later, and she's bringing the kids! They are excited to play on the snow mountains in the yard. I'm thinking we should do something special for dinner. Maybe pizza? Or would homemade make more sense?"

Was I supposed to know she was coming over? Probably. My ears had perfected the art of filtering out all mention of his love life.

"You are going to cook?" I said.

Dad laughed. "Well, I admit, I might need your help for that part. But I would take you shopping."

"This is today?" I frowned. "I have Mock Trial today, Dad."

"You do? But you are still here. Isn't it usually in the morning? And haven't you already had half a dozen trials already?"

"It's this afternoon. This is our third and is the qualifier for states."

Dad's face fell. "Will you be back for dinner?"

I probably could be back for dinner, if I came home right after the trial.

"I don't know. It depends on how long it goes."

Fortunately, Dad had never actually attended a meet, so he didn't know they were timed.

"That's too bad. Everyone was looking forward to you being here." Dad glanced over to the sink. "When are you leaving?" Clearly the man was thinking how the current lady of the house could help him tidy.

"My ride will be here any minute. I was just going to go outside to wait."

This was a total lie. But CinderMillie did not have time for this.

"Oh," Dad said. "Okay."

"Sorry, Dad."

He didn't say anything.

I wasn't being the team player he needed.

Something caved inside of me. My fear over losing (and the secret fear of getting closer to Grace amid competition and graduation season) gushed out like a dam breaking. Under all that was a red-hot rage. So hot it kept me warm as I trudged down our long woodland drive carrying my backpack and trial box.

Pick me up, I texted Claire, praying that would work. *I'm running away from home.*

She showed up at the bottom of my hill in ten minutes flat.

"You okay there?" she said.

"Dad wants a servant, not a daughter. I feel like I should warn the new woman."

"No. She won't believe you. They never do. It's up to her to do due diligence."

"Okay," I said.

"Glad I could get the car today. But I can't be out too late."

"That's fine."

"Millie, seriously, are you okay? You are kind of growling your words."

"Fine," I said.

Claire knew to leave me well enough alone.

She and I went into the courthouse, where Nikita, Izzy, and Grace greeted us, arms folded, watching other teams shuffle around. I shook my head at them.

"Hey," said Grace.

"There are an awful lot of boys here," said Nikita.

"That happens," I said.

"I like that one," said Nikita, nudging her chin toward a guy who was so ripped you could tell under his suit jacket.

"Is he even in high school?" I said.

"Totally. And his short friend." She elbowed Izzy. "You can have that one."

"Who says I like short guys?" she said.

"You did. At the last meet you liked that guy from Squirrel Hill. The one with the glasses."

"Oh yeah. He was pretty short. It's good to be able to look them in the eyes."

"Actually, I think he's the same guy. Maybe he's wearing contacts," I said.

"No, that other guy had longer hair," said Izzy.

"Maybe he got a haircut," said Nikita.

"I feel like it might not be meant to be if I can't tell whether he's the same guy. And to be honest, it's hard to date straight cis dudes. I look for the queer among us."

"We should get them to put pronouns on our name tags. Would that help cull the numbers? You know what, if we get their names, we can find them online," said Nikita. "There's five other schools at this meet. There must be more queer people here to pick from than just at Steelton, right?"

"I go by 'they' as well as 'she.' I could put that on my name tag. That would put the word out on my end. But that can sometimes backfire around here," said Izzy.

"Have you seen my high kick? You point out any haters to me. I'll take care of it."

"Oh my God, you two. This is not the time," I said. "We are going up against those people, and if you two are trying to get dates . . ."

"Prom is coming up. That guy would look good in pictures," said Nikita, pointing in the most unsubtle manner possible. "Do not underestimate the importance of prom."

"We have to win this trial to advance to states," I said.

"I need to advance to prom," said Nikita.

"I can't with all of you. I. Can. Not." I grabbed Nikita and Izzy and dragged them into our courtroom.

Ms. McClain, Kay, and the rest of the team were waiting for us inside.

"Ready?" said Ms. McClain to us.

"Always," I said.

Kay started talking. "This team is known for its strange psych-out tactics. They don't win by playing by the rules. They make up objections and try to rattle you. Watch out, everyone. Stay on your game."

"How'd you learn this?" asked Ms. McClain.

"I have my sources," said Kay. "But you girls are whip-smart and on your game. You are tough and dynamic. I believe in you."

"And so do I," said Ms. McClain.

Raina closed her eyes and breathed in with her diaphragm.

"You got your vocals ready?" I said.

"I am getting into the moment."

The bailiff came in. They did a group swearing in of all the witnesses; it broke the fourth wall of this whole show, but it took up less time. The defense had won the coin toss, so they got to go first. Nikita's guy gave the opening. He really was nice to look at. Dark wavy hair; light brown skin; dark, dark eyes. The way his arms flexed under his coat. He turned a little to look at us over on the prosecution team (well, probably just Nikita), and the way his collar outlined his neck made my chest feel tight against my blazer.

Grace's opening was elegant, and Izzy burst into tears as Jane Marsh, partner of the deceased Jess King. That freaked out the defense, Izzy was so good.

"Brilliant," I mouthed.

"I watched sad puppy videos on the ride here," she whispered back.

When it was Raina's turn, the bailiff gestured for her to sit in the witness stand.

Veronica questioned her first.

"Please state your name and position for the record," she said.

"Laura Cheney, bomb-squad technician," said Raina.

"Could you please describe for the court what a bomb-squad technician is?"

"Certainly. I was, until a few years ago, an explosive ordinance disposal specialist in the army. I'm trained to recognize . . ."

"Objection, Your Honor!" said a kid on the other team.

The judge looked taken aback. "Pardon me?" he said.

"The witness clearly could not have been in the army."

I stared at him. No one on the defense looked alarmed, so they must have known what the strategy was going to be. The witness statement clearly said Raina's character was in the army and that's where she first learned about bombs. Millie wasn't kidding about this team's odd strategy.

"Counsel," the judge said to Veronica, "is this the information your witness has in her sworn statement?"

"Yes, Your Honor. It's in the first paragraph of her biographical data. I was asking because . . ."

"Oh, I know why you are asking," the judge said. "Overruled." He looked at Raina. "Continue."

"I actually started with the army in college. I joined ROTC during my undergraduate years at MIT. I got a degree in electrical engineering. I always loved puzzles, putting things together and taking them apart. And my family are all kinds of thrill seekers. I sought this out because I was bored in the lab. I could use my knowledge *and* serve my country."

"Objection, Your Honor!" said the other team.

"Overruled," said the judge. "If you are going to try to refute the sworn statements of the case, do it on your own time."

Veronica tugged at her sleeve. I tried to send her calm vibes. Hecklers gave me life.

"So, you know about bombs, then?"

"Yes. After I retired from active duty—two tours in Afghanistan and one in Syria was enough—I entered the private sector. I now consult with the government agencies and help with domestic issues should the need arise."

"Domestic issues?" said Veronica.

"I assess internet chatter about new destructive tech. Help form emergency-response plans. Analyze bombs used. That kind of thing."

"Objec—" said the same kid.

"Overruled!" the judge shouted. I didn't know what that team's game was, but it wasn't working with our judge.

I heard Ms. McClain whisper to Kay behind me. She sounded pretty ticked off. But there wasn't much advisers could do at this point.

Veronica's face grew more determined. Surely, she faced worse than this on the rock wall or even on the *Puns of Steel* magazine staff. "Are you aware of the circumstances surrounding the death of Jessica Marsh?"

She dug in. The other team pushed and pushed the bounds of what I think was even allowed, but the judge wasn't having it. Eventually, the other team seemed to give up. They asked Raina a few forgettable questions and sat down. The judge left the chamber to deliberate.

"What the hell was *that*?" I said.

"Kay was right. Bishop Flannigan High always does this. They are known for it. They try to pick apart the witnesses for being high school kids instead of the people in the parts. They go off book. Sometimes it works with judges who aren't paying attention or who haven't read the case. It seems like that team did their research and the other team wasn't prepared. It's cheating. Not even *good* cheating. But we got a good judge."

The fact that our shot at states hung in the balance with this team was wrong. Somewhere, in a courtroom across the building, the Steelton guys were competing for a shot at states as well.

"Waiting is the worst," said Nikita.

Seconds ticked into minutes. I got up and stretched.

"You were great," whispered Grace. Her hand brushed mine.

I sat back down so I didn't pass out.

Finally, after an eternity, the judge came back.

I leaned forward on the edge of my seat. Everyone, even Nikita, couldn't take their eyes off the judge.

He leveled his gaze at us.

"As I imagine you all know . . . or *most* of you, anyway"—he threw some side-eye to the other team—"the burden of proof lies with the prosecution. There were compelling moments on each side, but given the way today's case unfolded, I am going to rule in favor of . . ."

I held my breath.

"The plaintiffs."

A little whoop went out on our side of the room.

Holy. Crap.

We won!

"Staaaaaaaates," said Veronica.

Kay and Ms. McClain high-fived. They left the room to pick up materials for states from the registration table.

"What if we won because the judge hated the other team's tactics," I said, "not because of the strength of our case? I even thought Chris was guilty when we were running the defense, but I didn't see us having proved it beyond a reasonable doubt. That's the tricky part."

"Why does it matter?" said Raina.

Ms. McClain returned to the courtroom. "We're prosecution," she said.

"See? We've learned so much. We have this in the bag!" said Raina.

"Okay," I said. *Be in the moments that bring you joy*, I thought.

Nikita walked up to us. "Got his number," she said to Izzy.

"But their tactics!" I said. "You want to go out with a guy with questionable ethics and terrible strategy?"

Nikita shrugged. "Might make for an interesting first date," she said.

We heard whooping coming at us from across the parking lot, so I didn't get a chance to talk Nikita out of it.

"We're going to states!" yelled Mr. Darr to Ms. McClain.

"So are we," she said.

"What?" he said.

"What?" she said.

"We won our trial, and we are going to states."

"Yes, so did we," said Ms. McClain.

Mr. Darr blinked. "Oh," he said. "That's. Uh. Great." He clearly hadn't expected to hear that.

"Don't look too excited, Barry."

"It's overnight," he said.

"Yes," she said. "I read that."

"We will have to get a hotel."

"Yes."

"The budget is only for . . ."

"We'll figure it out," said Ms. McClain. She waved her had dismissively at him. "This is about the students. Be happy for them."

I made an extra note to never get on Ms. McClain's bad side.

She turned to us. "Dinner on me, girls. Where to?"

I could feel my phone vibrating in my bag. I searched for it while the others debated options. I noticed thirty-five missed texts.

Are you coming home, honey? When did you say your trial ended?

I could use some help cleaning this place up!

Guess we'll get pizza. Ran out of time to get to the store.

Call me when you are out of your competition! Little kids are such a handful.

I sighed. Honestly, did he even listen when I spoke? Maybe I should try to get back. He obviously needed me.

"There's a Cracker Barrel a half a mile from here," said Grace.

"Cracker Barrel, *yes*," said Raina. "Sister needs some apple butter."

"Do you girls need to get home by a certain time?" said Ms. McClain.

"Nope," everyone said.

The phone buzzed again. *Sheila and I hope you can run after the rascals! It will give you a chance to make up for not helping out more today*, Dad texted.

My hand brushed against Grace's as she put her phone away. Warmth traveled up my wrist from where she had touched it.

"Nope," I said, shutting off my phone. "Me either."

RAINA PETREE,	:	IN THE COURT OF
	:	REVENGE OF CAMBRIA
Plaintiff,	:	COUNTY
	:	
v.	:	
	:	
THE WORLD,	:	Case No. LIFSOVR20205
	:	
	:	
Defendant	:	

MARCH 15: COMPLAINT FOR ACCESS TO PUBLIC RECORDS

MONDAYS ARE APPARENTLY A GOOD DAY for town hall meetings. Most of Steelton streamed into the auditorium of Steelton High, since it was the biggest public gathering space other than the Moretti Performing Arts Center, which probably had a college production going. I met Grace in front of the huge metal doors.

"You've switched to a garbage bag to hold the yarning?"

"I was told to bring any abandoned projects or spare yarn," she said. "I tried to get Millie to come to this, but she had to do something with her dad and his new girlfriend."

"Bummer. Oh hey, over here!" I waved Carla and Alex over to us as they walked toward the auditorium.

"Excellent. Glad to see you girls." Carla eyed Grace's bag. "Do you also quilt?"

Grace laughed. "I have in my life. I brought some of my fabric. I went through a duvet phase but got bored. I'm much more a yarner than a sewer. Figured I could donate my good intentions to the cause."

Carla nodded. "It's going to start soon. Follow me."

Carla, Alex, Grace, and I shuffled to the very front of the huge room, next to pretty much the entire LYS crew. Beatrice and Gretta had brought their entire families. I had underestimated how many grandchildren and great-grandchildren each of them must have had. At least a dozen more people I recognized from the store sat behind them with yarn and needles. They all waved to us as we sat down.

Onstage, someone had set up a podium next to two long tables with four chairs, each chair having its own little individual microphone. Behind it, scaffolding peeked out from behind the nearly closed blue velvet curtain. I realized that it was probably for the set of fucking *Our Town*. I couldn't dwell too much on it because someone came to the podium. The ambient buzz died down around me. Carla turned and nodded to our group. Everyone began pulling out their yarn.

"Welcome to the Steelton town hall meeting. I'm Peter Jones, Steelton city manager. You might recognize me from my recent terrible performance in the administration's basketball game against the Weston municipal employees."

Laughter rippled through the crowd.

"At today's panel, we'll hear from some of our elected officials. Each has a few updates from their respective offices, and then there will be time for questions at the end."

The audience politely applauded.

"In order from left to right, we have: Joseph Adams, our financial director; Malik Novak, the chief of police; Fateh Agarwal, Steelton planning director; and Herman Wise, our new district magistrate."

The sound of metal needle against metal and wood needle against wood gently scraped around me. No one in our section clapped, though Carla was able to keep her eyes trained on the stage as stitches flew around her Addi Turbo circulars. I wondered how long I'd have to practice until I'd be able to do that.

They went through the line, with all the updates from around town. Malik Novak told everyone about officers trained in Narcan dosages and the new app to report needles in public spots. Fateh Agarwal talked about zoning changes in the Warnerstown and Roxam neighborhoods, and how the city planned to make up the budget deficits from the infrastructure improvements. Joseph Adams chimed in there, saying that they didn't anticipate having to cut many services but that they were exploring options to phase out a few early-childhood programs and a domestic-abuse hotline.

"Isn't 'phasing out' services the same as 'cutting'?" said Grace.

"Yes," said Carla. At least, I think that's what she said. It sounded less like a word and more like some sort of growl.

Finally, Herman T. Wise got to speak. The knitters who knew what they were doing picked up their stitching pace.

Judge Wise talked about equity and justice and how he'd lived in Western Pennsylvania his entire life, so he really understood the community's concerns and issues. "And I hope to bring a fair perspective to all the people I serve," he finished.

I could visibly see Gretta and Beatrice seethe into their wool. Their stitches grew tighter and tighter until I worried their wooden needles might actually snap. I half expected to see smoke coming from the Addi Turbos around me.

When it came time for questions, residents lined up in the center aisle behind a microphone. People asked about sponsored addiction-treatment options, new playgrounds, garbage pickup times, you name it. Carla, without breaking her cabling rhythm, rose and maneuvered herself to the end of the question line. My shoulders tensed in anticipation.

A guy asked a question about parking meters, and then it was Carla's turn to speak. "My question is for Judge Wise," she said.

Judge Wise sat up a little straighter. Carla was the first person to direct a question just to him.

"Two of your recent decisions have made the news, and both of them seemed to demonstrate a bias against women. You seem to favor the aggressors' stories over victims'—"

"Alleged aggressors and alleged victims," he said into his microphone.

"Aggressors' stories over victims', and isn't it true that during your days in legal practice you gave several interviews to the *Tribune Republican* where you stated that you believe accusations of assault or sexual misconduct are often exaggerated or fabricated?" Carla's voice got louder with each word until she was practically shouting into the microphone.

Judge Wise cleared his throat. "I . . ."

"With such a bias, how can you possibly bring a fair perspective to half of the population? Or any of the population?"

Now the rest of the crowd started to murmur. Something needed to happen now. Someone needed to do something. And I realized that I wanted that someone to be me.

Moved as if by the needles around me, I stood up. Then Gretta. Then Beatrice with the help of her daughter. Then the rest. I glanced at Grace, who threw me a WTF look and stood. I filed out of my row, and everyone followed until we stood with our backs against the side door wall of the auditorium in a long line. I resumed my knitting.

Judge Wise turned his head toward us, then across the audience, and back to us. My angle and proximity to the stage put me directly into his line of sight. Judge Wise locked eyes with me for a second before he looked back at Carla.

"Actually, I'm afraid we're about out of time," said Jones. "Judge Wise, you can answer if you want, but in the interest of brevity, we could hold off on this discussion until the next meeting."

Another murmur rolled through those assembled. Judge Wise sat back in his chair and folded his hands on his stomach. He nodded to Jones.

"Okay then, folks, thanks for coming out! We will see you next time!"

Alex moved up the aisle, so people could leave through the side exit. The rest of us spread out so that we weren't blocking any doors.

Carla came over to us. A few people smiled at us or nodded to Carla on their way out. Eventually, she led us to the parking lot as well. "Nice move, standing up," she said. She squeezed my shoulder.

"What did that accomplish?" said Beatrice.

"It put his past out there," said Carla. "It added a little context to his time on the bench, so maybe more people will start to pay attention. It put him on notice that people—*voters*—care."

"That's not enough," said Gretta.

"No. I agree," said Carla. "Let's just give it a few minutes, shall we?"

We stood in a conspicuous circle outside. Five minutes went by. Then ten. Everyone kept knitting, but no panelists ever came out.

"Do you think they parked on the other side?" said Grace.

"Probably. They might have left from the other doors. Cowards," said Gretta.

"Well, that confrontation will have to wait. But we have other plans." Carla glanced over her shoulder, her mouth set in a determined grimace. "Okay, folks. Get out your fabric and find someone with a car for a ride. We have to travel to this mission. It's go time."

MARCH 17:
MEMORANDUM AND ORDER

"WHEN IS THIS, AGAIN?" SAID MOM.

"State Mock Trial? In about a month. A little more than three weeks. From today. It's a weekend. I'd go there overnight."

"Oh. That's great, honey. That's great that you won."

Dad had gotten an offer of a full dollar more per mile extra or something for another run, so he hadn't come back for his planned time off. Mom had been a little out of it the whole weekend, since he was supposed to have been around but wasn't. Then she had a double Monday and Tuesday. Her brain hadn't recovered yet.

"It's a lot of fun. It's great just sitting in the courtroom. Maybe I should be prelaw," I said.

"Mm-hmm," said Mom. She started scrubbing dishes in the sink.

"I mean it. It could be my thing. I know I'm a witness, and I'm basically acting. But the opening statements. The questioning. The reasoning of the courts before you. It's fascinating, Mom."

"Great, honey."

She didn't turn around.

I went over to the sink and gave her hug from behind. She missed Dad more than I did when he left. He'd been gone so much of my life that it actually felt weird having him around.

"Daddy said to call him the second you find out about getting into college," she said. I could hear her holding back tears. "He's really proud of you going for it."

"If I get in," I said. I knew how unconvincing I'd been as a turkey.

Mom didn't say anything. She concentrated on the pots. There wasn't a lot more that I thought I could do for her.

"Going to school. Bye, Mom!"

"See you," she said.

I thought the tears would follow as soon as the front door shut behind me. I knew from past experiences of this very thing that she gave herself one full day of grief over the Dad visit disappointment before returning to her stoic keep-calm-and-carry-on routine.

When I arrived at school, I stopped at my locker to switch my books. I rounded the corner to get to homeroom and almost ran smack into Brandon.

"Watch where you're . . . oh," I said.

"Oh. Yeah. Sorry." He shifted his backpack and looked over my head, as if an escape hatch might open from the drop ceiling. When one didn't materialize, he looked at me. "Get the new case materials yet?"

"What?"

"For states. Or nationals."

"Oh. Not yet." I gazed at him.

"Oh. Well. Maybe the Steelton team will go all the way this year," he said. There was something in his voice. A tone that I recognized. He was saying something without saying something. A lot of people couldn't pick it up, but I could.

"Maybe," I said.

"It'd be nice if our hard work all these years would pay off."

I searched his face, but it was no longer mine to read. Something was off, here. But I found I didn't care. Brandon just wasn't the kind of guy who was worth crying over anymore. Or wasting time thinking about what he was trying to tell me.

"Well, see you," I said.

I turned and left him standing there.

In the hallway after homeroom, Millie was in rare form.

"We got the materials," she said as soon as she saw me before homeroom.

"I heard," I said.

"The new case. For states and nationals. It's freedom of speech. You are going to love it."

"Do you have a copy I could see now?" Heaven knows I had no interest in my impending America lit discussion of *Ethan Frome*, the most soul-sucking book ever written.

"No! After lunch. Ms. McClain is making us each a packet."

I sighed. *Ethan Frome* it was. How anyone could take the joy out of *sledding*, I didn't know. I walked by a table of kids selling tickets to the spring play on the way to my locker. I should try to persuade the freshmen to put on *Ethan Frome* next year as their play. I still had some sway over the new people, even if they thought I'd lost my mind. It would serve them right for picking fucking *Our Town*.

"Raina," one of them called. "Are you going to come to the play?"

She looked so eager and happy. I couldn't resist. The school play I wasn't in didn't make me sad. I just wanted them to succeed.

I bought a ticket. Despite what my mom believed, because school productions weren't packing them in, it was open admission. I could go any night. Maybe a group of us could go. It might annoy Claire to see me there. And I bet Millie would want to support her. Win, win!

After lunch, I could hardly wait to get the trial documents in my hands.

"Okay," said Millie. "What we have here is a case involving freedom of expression."

"That has potential," said Izzy.

"A group of nonbinary and female-identifying students put together a discussion group to discuss issues around gender, sexuality, and culture. They called themselves the 'Social Justice League.' Members of the group made posters and art, which they put up on the school free-expression boards. They also had a few social-media accounts to which many members post frequently. The school principal has refused to acknowledge the club because he says it is exclusionary and promotes 'lewd and lascivious behavior.' Postings on the free-expression board are removed. Some satirical art has been circulated, and it is rumored that the group was responsible for the 'rainbow yarn bomb incident' involving the principal's car."

"Yesssssss," said Grace and I together.

"Thus, the principal claims that the club has violated school policies by creating threatening content and a threatening environment. The club members believe that the school is infringing their First Amendment rights. They are suing both the school district *and* the principal in federal court."

"Amazing!" said Grace. "Yarn bombing isn't permanent. If they did his car, he could just cut a row, stitch it up, and have himself a Pride duvet. I don't see what he's so mad about. Though, I do know people get defensive about this sort of thing."

I knew she was probably thinking of the Honorable Herman T. Wise incidents.

Izzy snickered.

"What's the plan, boss?" I said.

Millie looked at the three of us witnesses. "Can you divide the parts up again?"

"I imagine we can," I said.

"I'll talk to the lawyers."

We huddled in our respective groups.

"Okay," said Nikita. "There's Cortney, who is the Social Justice League president. Justina Peters, the social-media monitor, and Blake, a member-at-large. I can be the last one. It sounds the least complicated."

"I will be the social-media manager," said Izzy. "Because I would bet money Raina wants to be the president."

"You know me so well. Okay, for the defense we have Charlotte, the principal. They also have Taylor, captain of the soccer team, and Eden, president of the Real Love Club."

"Real Love?" said Izzy. "What's that horror?"

I shuffled through the stack of papers. "It appears to be a club that supports 'traditional values.'"

"Are these people trying to create a riot in the courtroom?" said

Nikita. "I don't even want to know how they define traditional values."

"I'm not playing her," said Izzy.

"Me either," said Nikita.

"I don't want to, either," I said.

"Someone has to do it," said Nikita.

I looked at the two of them. Izzy was shaking her head as she read the witness statement, and Nikita sat with her arms crossed in front of her.

"I'll do it. But don't hate me. I'm doing it for the team," I said.

Izzy turned to Nikita. "I'll be the principal."

"Yeah, okay. I could be a footballer."

"Witnesses are set!" I said.

There seemed to be more tension on the lawyer side of the room.

"Millie, what side are we in our trial?" said Veronica.

"We are plaintiffs for states," she said. "I assume you've read some of the case now?"

The lawyers didn't seem happy.

"What, the plaintiffs are the Social Justice League ones. Why is this bad?" I said.

"Because it means if we make it to nationals, we might be the defense. They are . . . a little contrary to what I believe in," said Grace.

"We have to make it there first," said Millie. "Why worry now?"

Grace looked at her like she wanted to say something, but then didn't.

"Grace, Imma need a crocheted vest. Can you help me?" I didn't like discord in my happy place.

"I believe I could. Carla would love that. But . . ."

"Hells to the yeah, she will," I said. "But what?"

Grace frowned. "This case. The defense. One side of this, the defense side, is arguing that people don't have the right to exist. At least, that's how I'm reading it. The whole traditional-values thing seems to be hate. And that certain types of people are morally wrong and should be excluded from public life, or whatever. It's not cool. Why would they even *make* a case like this? I'm really uncomfortable with it. It's seems manipulative and wrong."

"Well, we're the plaintiffs at the moment. You can knit us all matching vests! We're chicks with sticks," I said.

"No," said Millie, who looked distinctly like she was trying to avoid making eye contact with Grace.

"You won't keep doing the puns, will you?" said Nikita.

"I have many *purls* of wisdom."

"No," said Millie again.

"Stop," said Nikita.

"What can I say?" I grinned. In the face of possible tension in the group, it seemed wise to try to lighten the mood. "Knit happens."

MARCH 23: JUSTIFICATION FOR NONDISCLOSURE

I LIVED AND BREATHED THE NEW CASE. I'D only had the materials a few days and even Megan was now pretty well versed on First Amendment precedents. It wasn't that hard to inhabit the character, since there was only five pages of it. Also, a drama queen, yarn-bombing high school senior really wasn't that much of a stretch. At this point, I didn't even know if it could even be considered acting.

I rolled into The Dropped Stitch prepared to curse out vest patterns. Considering how a pair of socks caused my eye to twitch in frustration for about a week, I was hoping Grace would do most of it. She could finish an entire reproductive system in the time it took me to hook a foreskin.

"Good *evening*," I said to Grace. I helped myself to cornbread and what looked like chili.

"Compliments of my sister," said Carla, "visiting from out of town."

"Thanks," I said. Or tried to say with my face stuffed with free food.

Grace appeared unusually somber.

I swallowed. "You okay over there?"

"Have you studied the case more?" she said.

"The one for states? Yeah. Millie would psychically sense if I hadn't."

"Does it bother you?"

"Bother me? How?"

Grace shrugged. "I don't know. It seems pretty clear cut. The plaintiffs seem so righteous to me. The Real Love group took over the entire free-expression board. The picture of what they did is included!"

"I saw," I said. The visual had been in my witness materials.

"Look at all it. 'Marriage is between one man and one woman. Gender is determined by God. Blah, blah, blah.' Are you kidding? Could they be any more obviously trite or cliché? Then the Social Justice League took them on for their shit, and then they were called out by school administration? There. Are. Pictures. Here. The Social Justice League posted about toxic behavior in their community and was unduly punished. The defendants are hate-mongering jerks. I know Izzy and maybe Veronica agree with me. I tried to talk to Millie about it, but she either doesn't see it or doesn't care because she wants to win."

I hadn't gotten that out of the witness statements. At worst, everyone seemed a little too attached to a school bulletin board.

Grace kept going. "But Millie says that if we go to nationals, we will have to dig into the case and mount the best defense possible. I mean, we might not make it to nationals so maybe I'm worrying for nothing. And it feels like she's pulling away from me. Things were great there for a minute, but then it's like she panicked."

"This is so important to Millie. But she can see reason. I say, since you like this side of the case so much, you might as well put your energy into pounding the defense into the ground." I didn't know about the second part. Millie and I didn't talk much about dating, beyond me occasionally bursting into Brandon-induced tears.

"Yeah," she said. "I just wished she could see where I'm . . . where *we're* coming from. How we might not be comfortable with it."

"Let us cross this bridge when we must," I said. My dad always said that. "For now, please help me knit a vest for the cause of justice."

Grace laughed in spite of herself. "I'd bet all the chili that you just want me to do it for you."

"I didn't say that," I said.

"You know you can do it, don't you? I'll help if you need."

She might have been right. I was getting better every day.

"Okay, people, listen up," said Carla. "There have been developments, and we are moving to phase four of the resistance."

"What were phases one through three?" I whispered to Grace.

"Probably the vaginas and courthouse steps and the town meeting, don't you think?" she whispered back.

"Okay, good point," I said.

"People think knitting is for young women from the fifties, knitting sweaters for their boyfriends. Or for old biddies, making baby booties. Gretta, am I right?"

"Yes, dear."

"But we know that's not true."

"I finished those penises that you wanted. Were they for someone in particular?" Beatrice said.

"We'll talk about it later. But this is what I'm saying. If you look at a tombstone, and you see the years there, you know what is between them? A line. A simple line. But to me that line is a stitch. It represents that the fiber arts weave life. Blankets for births, socks and scarves and sweaters for birthdays, a prayer shawl after a death. But needles are sharp, and sometimes you need to stick them into politics.

Some of you might be too young to remember, but the AIDS quilt is an example. Crafters have to come together."

"Carla?" I raised my hand like I was in school. "Did something happen?"

Her eyes flashed. "Oh yes, it did," she said. "A certain local magistrate decided to make life a little worse for some people last week *again*. So did some Supreme Court justices. So did a lot of people in power. And we had a chance to make one of them answer for it, and he didn't. Another man had his back and shut that down before we could even get it started. And I've had it up to here."

"I see," said Grace.

"A couple of police officers visited the store yesterday. They seemed to think we might have something to do with recent shipments of anatomy to elected and appointed officials. Or the courthouse street art. Or the giant yarn bomb after the town hall," said Carla.

"Apparently the knit placentas in trees scared people. Or maybe it was the 'consent' blanket. Or any of the various items we left in the gardens and shrubbery and windows at City Hall," Alex said.

"Are you going to jail?" I said.

Alex winked at me. "You're in Mock Trial. You tell me."

"I'll let you know after states," I said.

"Great," said Carla. I'd never seen her so fired up, which was saying something. "Anyway, apparently the police are visiting several local yarn stores, and rumor has it, a certain big-chain-that-shall-not-be-named. They are trying to deter 'vandalism.'"

She kind of spat out that last part.

"Just awful," said Beatrice.

"The craft community from the surrounding counties wants to do something. We are holding a crafting circle on Sunday."

"Here?" said Grace.

"At the Inclined Plane. There's that little park across the street. That will do nicely."

"What are we going to do there?" I said.

"Knit uteruses. Cross-stitch 'Screw the Patriarchy' samplers. Embroider rage. Quilt apoplexy. Whatever. There are some plans to get it onto the actual trolley cars so you can see it when they ride up and down the mountain on the tracks. I expect all of you to be there. It's going to be in the sixties, so it won't freeze Gretta."

"Don't you worry about me, young lady. You forget I was a girl in Canada. We didn't have plumbing until we moved here when I was seventeen. Cold doesn't bother these old bones as much as you might think."

All of us blinked at Gretta. Her tiny, bent frame wouldn't alert you to how badass she actually was.

"Great. Well. There are public restrooms around there. No need to relive your younger years, Gretta."

"Whatever is needed for the cause." She raised her wrinkled fist, the delicate skin as thin as vellum but probably tougher than all the rest of ours put together.

Carla handed us flyers to put up on our way out. "You bring as many people as possible. There is power in numbers. And it doesn't have to be fiber arts. Photographers, painters, comic artists. Whatever. Bring them. At least two people each, please."

"I'll do my best," said Grace.

"Wow," I said. "Shit's getting real, here."

"Seriously," she said.

"You are new to town. Have you ever been to the Incline?"

"Aunt Kay took me when I came to visit. Leave it to Pennsylvanians to build a trolley into a mountain. Are we going to yarn bomb that?"

"I don't know how that's possible. At least in the middle of the day. But I wouldn't put anything past Carla."

Grace laughed. "Hell hath no fury like a LYS owner scorned," she said. "She's at her knit's end."

"Aren't we all," I said. "Aren't we all."

MARCH 26: ORDER DENYING INJUNCTIVE RELIEF

THE MOCK TRIAL TEAM WAS NOT AS EXCITED about the Inclined Plane as I had hoped they would be. The division over the case had lowered morale considerably in a matter of days.

"What are we supposed to be doing there, exactly? I have a manicure at ten that day," said Nikita.

"Crafting for social justice. Like the people in our case!" I said.

"Is this trying to get us into character?" asked Izzy. "I don't actually knit."

"Do you paint?" I said.

"No."

"Take pictures?"

"I act," she said.

"You could start to learn to knit. Or crochet. Keeps your hands busy. Calms the mind. It's good as a preshow ritual. Or if there's something else you should be doing, like homework, you still feel like you are accomplishing something if you yarn instead. I call it 'procrastiknitting,'" I said.

Izzy shook her head at me.

"I got my chic new walking boot," said Veronica. "I could come."

"I count you as my person!" I said. Megan agreed to come because I told her we could get Em's Subs afterward. "This gives me two. I'm doing my part for freedom."

"I don't know what that means, but I'm happy to help," said Veronica. "Gives me an excuse to get out of another Sunday playing video games with my little brother."

"Millie, you have to come," I said.

She glanced at Grace.

"Uh. I'm not much of a crafter," she said.

"But Grace will be there!"

Grace opened her mouth to speak but closed it again. She looked down at the ground.

"Isn't this against the magistrate? What if he ends up being one of the judges we see at states? There aren't that many judges who do this," Millie said. She looked over a Grace, as if she hoped for reassurance. Grace said nothing.

"What are the odds of that? It's in Harrisburg. Come on, Millie," I said.

"I'll see."

"You would make two for Grace. We have quotas to fill."

She didn't say anything. Grace turned and walked over to talk to Ms. McClain without looking at either one of us.

"Grace isn't too happy with me," said Millie.

The bell rang and I didn't have the chance to investigate further.

Later that evening, I took the city bus to support Steelton High theater. It felt like a million years had passed since I'd been on the auditorium stage, even if it'd only been a few months. I went inside to the mostly empty theater and found Millie dead center.

"Hey there," I said. "How's it going?"

"Fine," she said stiffly.

"It doesn't seem fine. Something going on with you and Grace?"

Millie wilted a little. "She's so bothered by this case. And I told her it's fiction, but she said it's based on reality. She doesn't want to play the defense. She said all I cared about was Mock Trial. I didn't want to hurt her feelings. But I want to win."

"That sucks," I said. "But we have to get to nationals for this even to be a problem."

"Yeah," she said.

More people filled in the seats around us, including Megan. Millie didn't seem like she wanted to keep talking about it.

The lights went down, and Mr. Cooper came over the loudspeaker, warning us all to turn off our cell phones and threatening our lives over the use of flash photography. The curtain rose on the sparse set. The Stage Manager took the stage. Some freshman kid I didn't recognize. I wondered why Claire didn't go for this part. She was probably too annoyed.

The Stage Manager started talking.

"I don't get it. Is this a play within a play?" whispered Megan.

"It's a metaphor," I muttered. "Fucking Thornton Wilder."

They didn't have an intermission. Maybe they wisely thought we all might flee the single-most produced play in all high schools everywhere.

At the end, Claire rose from the dead as Emily Webb, the woman who died too soon. I watched Claire act the day of Emily's twelfth birthday. Watching Claire's face turn from utter joy to the somber realization that people don't appreciate the simple joys of life made my chest hurt. My throat burned.

"Take me back—up the hill—to my grave," said Claire. "But first: Wait! One more look. Goodbye, goodbye world. Goodbye, Grover's Corners . . . Mama and Papa. Goodbye to clocks ticking . . . and Mama's sunflowers. And food and coffee. And new ironed dresses and hot baths . . . and sleeping and waking up. Oh, earth, you are too wonderful for anybody to realize you. Do any human beings ever realize life while they live it—every, every minute?" Claire placed her face in her hands.

"No. The saints and poets, maybe they do some," said the Stage Manager.

Ugly tears over Claire's performance of fucking *Our Town* rolled down my face, right there in front of everyone. I quickly fished a tissue out of my pocket. There was sniffling all around.

After the curtain call, Megan took another tissue from me.

"I'm going to hug my mom and clean my room," she said.

"I should apologize to Grace," said Millie, wiping her eyes.

Maybe I shouldn't have quit. I could have made people openly *weep* through that overdone play, damn it all. That was what I wanted, to have people feel what I wanted them to feel. To not just hear my words, but to *live* them *with* me.

We left the auditorium and hung around just outside. As theater kids milled around to meet their parents and rides, Claire emerged positively glowing.

"You were brilliant," said Millie. "I cried."

"Same," said Megan. I don't know that she'd ever spoken to or even met Claire.

"Thank you," said Claire.

Millie held out flowers to her. "A placeholder for your Academy Award," she said.

"Love you," said Claire.

"You were great," I said. It was true. I couldn't even deny it.

"Raina." Claire looked taken aback. "Were you *crying, too?*"

"Of course not," I lied. "Allergies."

"Sure," she said. But I could tell she knew she'd *moved* me.

Afterward, Megan and I went to Eat'n Park. It was a postshow ritual, even if I wasn't in the show.

"I'm also going to be nicer to my sister," she said. "I barely talk to her since she went away to school."

"Oh my God," I said.

"I am. And I'm really going to give swimming my all at college. I've been half-assing on the municipal team. But at school, I'm going for it. You have to appreciate the moments in life. Because you can't go back once they are over."

I kicked her under the table. But after I got home, I went up to Mom's room and curled into bed next to her.

She rolled over. "You okay?" she said.

"Yes, Mommy." I kissed her and snuggled close.

"You sure?" Mom could go from a dead sleep to lifesaver in three seconds.

"Yes," I said.

"Okay." In another three seconds, I felt her deep breaths against my chin.

"Fucking *Our Town*," I whispered. But then I shivered in delight as I breathed in the scent of the clean sheets and my mom's hair, which I probably hadn't done since . . . I was twelve years old.

MARCH 28: CONFIDENTIAL MEDIATED SETTLEMENT AGREEMENT

THERE IS A CHURCH CLOSE TO THE INCLINED Plane. I watched as men and women and little boys and girls in dresses and suits left the building carrying long palm fronds. A little boy jabbed one into his sister's face.

"Cut it out! This is a symbol of peace!" she yelled.

The mom grabbed the little boy and moved him to the other side of her, out of palm-violence range. Church bells echoed on houses and hills, the clear blue sky climbing up forever around gathering crafters.

"Morning." Alex yawned. "What'd you bring to work on?"

"A baby blanket? I think? Squares for Carla. Possibly to go on"—I paused and looked at the Inclined Plane car rising into the air—"that?"

"Shhhh," said Alex. She glanced around. "That's on the down low."

"You asked," I said.

Alex put her finger to her lips.

"I am here," said Megan, coming up behind me. "I am the best of all best friends."

"You are," I said. "I'm sorry I didn't text you. I don't have my phone. I hope it's at home."

Veronica hobbled over, followed by Grace. "Hey, knitter dorks," she said. "My gran was so excited to hear about this, even if she didn't understand what I was talking about."

"Same," said Megan.

"Oh, hey, you came," said Grace, clearly surprised.

I turned and saw Millie joining the group.

"Yeah. Well. Emily Webb," she said.

Grace threw her a blank look.

"The rest of you are here. I wanted to be a team player," she said.

"It wasn't enough that I asked you to come?" said Grace.

"I . . . It's just that . . ." said Millie.

Just then, an aggressively loud siren pierced the air, and my skeleton nearly jumped out of my skin.

"Hello, crafters!" said Carla into an incredibly effective bullhorn. "We're here to quilt new beginnings! To macramé justice! We are here today to stitch a new world!"

A cheer rose up from the crowd. Gretta and Beatrice and all the other Dropped Stitch ladies had brought friends and family. The two of them alone were forming a whole generation of male knitters.

"Should we get a bench?" said Megan.

"We should probably save those for the elderly."

"Good idea. Let's sit on the grass. Glad it's warm."

We spread out our jackets on the wide-open space behind the benches. Soon everyone was yarning or painting or drawing or just talking. A reporter and photographer from the *Tribune Republican* were there and everything. They asked if we minded getting our picture taken.

Then someone cleared his throat behind us. I turned, and there stood two police officers, city manager Peter Jones, and none other than Judge Herman T. Wise.

All day I noticed that Grace and Millie sat near to each other but didn't really interact. It felt like a wall had fallen from the sky between them. Once in a while, one would move to touch the other or speak, but then that wall grew an inch and they just couldn't. Now that her worst fears had been realized in the arrival of a potential Mock Trial judge, Millie looked like she wished she had never met any of us.

Judge Wise went right up to Carla and Alex. "You weren't in the courtroom. Newspapers only say so much. You don't have any idea about the eccentricities of any of my cases. Then *or* now."

"You represented the perpetrators," said Alex. "Never once do I recall a time you fought for any victims."

"*Alleged* victims. I represented the accused," he said. "And they deserved a fair trial."

"You got them off!"

"Because they were innocent. Innocent until proven guilty is how it's done in this country."

"Why are you here? To defend yourself? You didn't think you could do that onstage in front of all those other people?" said Carla.

"I'm here because if you are going to hold me up for trial in the court of public opinion, I wanted a say."

Judge Wise surveyed the crowd. A bunch of us just stood staring at him. Part of me still liked the guy. He'd never been mean to *me*. And he'd come out here to what was sure to be an unfriendly audience to defend himself. He looked at me and Megan and Millie. I could see in his face a flash of recognition, like he thought he might know us from somewhere but couldn't place from where.

Millie's face turned her deep shade of mortified crimson.

"Pardon me," Judge Wise said to the reporter, "I'd like to speak to you as well."

Judge Wise and Peter Jones guided the reporter away from the crafters.

"Oh, I see," said Carla to us. "He's here to control the press on this." She watched him talking, waving his arms around for emphasis. She moved toward them, but one of the police officers subtly shifted in her direction. Carla stopped.

"Not worth it," she muttered.

Eventually, Judge Wise and his companions finished talking to the reporter. Everyone had committed to ignoring them out of loyalty to Carla, so they unceremoniously retreated to wherever they had come from.

Millie didn't speak to any of us after Judge Wise had shown up. She gathered her things, got up, and left without a word as soon as the judge was a safe distance down the block.

Grace didn't even try to say goodbye.

Around four o'clock, angry gray clouds gathered overhead. I stretched out my legs, which had fallen asleep for the sixth time that day.

"Em's Subs is calling us," said Megan. "We can split a super deluxe torpedo. No hot stuff, though."

"That is the best plan ever," I said.

A bunch of us "rows before bros" regulars took our various creations over to Carla before heading out.

"Wonderful, wonderful," she said. Delight radiated off of her. "This will all be put to good use. Law enforcement be damned!"

"How?" said Grace.

"Don't you worry about it," said Beatrice. "Here's a Mock Trial term for you: plausible deniability."

A woman who looked like Beatrice, only with dark hair and less wrinkled skin sighed. "Mom, please don't make me post bail. Both kids need braces."

"I can post my own bail, thank you very much," she said.

"Mom, I swear . . ."

I laughed. I turned toward Grace, who looked like her puppy had just died. "Grace? Yinz all want to be a part of this torpedo action?"

We'd probably have to get a few. Megan trained year-round like an Olympian. A twenty-two-inch sub probably fed only her.

"Oh, no. I have to go home. Family stuff," said Grace.

"You sure? I said.

"Yeah," she said.

I raised my eyebrows as Grace walked away. If Claire's performance hadn't been enough to heal that rift, I worried nothing could.

Megan gave me a ride home, which was good because I'd eaten so much Em's I thought I might explode. Mom was at work, so I put her favorite roast beef grinder in the fridge for later.

Damn brilliant Claire for making me a better daughter.

I found my phone in my room. It'd been hard being separated it for a whole day, even if nearly everyone I'd have texted was with me.

I picked it up and the screen lit up at the movement.

"Fifty missed texts?" I said.

Some were from Megan, but the rest were from Claire. I swiped to see them.

Admissions decisions! Oh my God!

They dropped!

I didn't know because I was busy with the play.

Two of these schools sent it out days ago, OMG.

Bet you forgot. Check your admissions portal.

Actually, whoa, a bunch dropped!

I got innnnnnnnnnnn, she said. OMG, my mom is going to freak if I tell her I want to move to New York. I didn't want to go, but that's when I thought I didn't have a chance.

Sorry, that last one was for Millie. I'm not actually trying to be a dick.

My stomach flipped a little at that last one.

Where are you? Wait, there was a knitting thing. That's probably why Millie isn't answering. Damn it.

I put down my phone. Shit. This was it? I was a few clicks away from one of the most important moments of my life? Should I call Mom? Megan? The whole Mock Trial team? Brandon and I always used to joke that we'd do this together, even if one of us had to wait. He was always going to go to Duquesne political science, but I didn't know if that was still true.

I sat on my bed and opened my laptop. This was it. I could call people after.

I logged in to my CMU portal. My heart lodged itself into my throat when I saw the message in the inbox.

Dear applicant, it started.

There was a particularly large, talented pool of applicants this year. The admissions committee had hard decisions to make.

And I was . . . wait-listed.

Wait-listed? What?

Claire got in.

And I . . . didn't. Not yet. Not right off the bat.

Since we'd applied to pretty much all the same schools, I went to all the portals.

Wait-listed.

Wait-listed.

Wait-listed.

I had been put on the wait list for every school I applied to.

Every single one.

I stared at my computer in disbelief. What did this mean? Had there been some kind of clerical error? Was my computer acting up? It didn't have the spinny wheel of death. It seemed kind of statistically unlikely that I'd be wait-listed at *all* of them. What was the word my dad used to describe this situation? It was a church word.

Purgatory. This was *purgatory*. I wasn't rejected, but I was . . . what?

Still waiting.

I picked up my phone to text Megan. But I saw Claire's text.

. . . *innnnnnnnnnnn*, it said.

I grabbed my bag. Are you kidding? Wait-listed? I was a turkey. I was the best turkey the world had ever *seen*. Please. Even if I wasn't at my most prepared. Or motivated.

My knitting grew tight. Small. Pissed. I thought I added a stitch at the end of the row, so I ripped it out. In that row, I was Raina, Brandon's girlfriend. It had to go. I tried again. The next row still cinched in a way that didn't match the rest of it. I ripped it out again.

That was Raina the CMU actress. It took about nine tries until I calmed down and got back to the neat pattern that matched my previous work. *There* I was. I was in the rows that flowed with the others. What was I making? It could be anything. A scarf. An afghan. A blanket for an elephant.

I didn't know, but there were so many possibilities untangling with every stitch.

APRIL 4: MOTION FOR SUMMARY JUDGMENT

"I AM A DISTRICT MOCK TRIAL CHAMPION, and I was rejected from *everywhere*," I said to my mom. "What should I do now? I am open to suggestion."

"To be fair, the schools didn't know you were such a winner in Mock Trial, did they? You advanced after you filled out applications. Also, you were wait-listed. There's a difference. I read about it. You can send them a letter appealing it if you don't hear and you are still interested. Do that. If you are still interested. Or take a gap year. Get a job. Do theater around here. Maybe take yourself a lover," she said.

"I can't just . . ." I stopped and stared at her. "I'm sorry. Did I just hear you say '*take yourself a lover*'?"

"You were a lot more relaxed when you were with Brandon. As relaxed as you get, anyway. I'm guessing it was the sex, because the conversation always seemed pretty forced."

"Mom, you're telling me to have sex? Isn't that against the mom code or something?"

"Okay, well, have safe sex, then."

"*Mom*," I said.

"You are eighteen. Maybe get yourself a nice vibrator. Safest sex of all. If you clean it properly."

"OH MY GOD, WHAT IS THIS CONVERSATION?" I put my head in my hands and tried unsuccessfully to purge the fact that my mother mentioned a vibrator in my presence.

"All I'm saying is that you have options. You thought you'd shrivel up after Brandon, and look at you. You found a new passion. Several passions, actually. Working for a year could give you some money for school. Go to community college first, then transfer. Never underestimate the importance of artists *or* lawyers not having too much student-loan debt."

"I thought I had life figured out. And then I didn't. This is so *unfair*."

Mom kissed me on the head. "Life is hard, Raina. I don't know who ever led you to believe it is fair. Especially in a competitive field like theater. Suck it up, baby. Good things can come with the bad only if you keep going. I believe in you."

I went upstairs and started knitting again. Mom had so much perspective on life. She'd wanted to be a cellist. She was good. Incredible. But Grandma died when she was little and then Grandpa died and then she got pregnant with me. She played for me when I was little, but she doesn't much anymore.

How goes? Megan's text buzzed my phone.

My mother told me to buy a vibrator, I texted back.

That's amazing, she wrote.

It's horrifying, I texted.

Your mother is my queen, she wrote back.

Claire got into all the schools, I said.

Megan just called then.

"Do you want to egg her car or something?"

"No. She's great. She deserves it," I said. I shook my head at myself. I actually meant it.

"If you stayed around town, you could do the community theater productions without worrying about homework and the school plays. And you know you'd have your choice of lead roles. Who is going to challenge you?"

"No one," I said. "Especially if Claire is gone. I'm by far Steelton's best."

"There's my girl. And what about states? Use the pain."

"Yeah."

"There you go. I have given you a life plan. You are welcome. You have a . . . uh . . . trophy to win? Medal? Gavel? What do they give you at national Mock Trial?"

"I don't know. Millie is giving us a few days off to regroup. I think she needed some Millie time. She is possibly trying to figure out a way to disassociate with people connected to the Judge Herman T. Wise resistance. Also, because I think some of our teammates hate our parts for nationals. But I can ask on Monday."

"Good. Because I want to know. Nana and I will knit a cozy for whatever you win."

"You are knitting with your grandmother?"

"We knit together remotely now over the computer. To spend more time together."

"That's beautiful," I said.

"Fucking *Our Town*, you know what I'm saying?" said Megan.

"Do I *ever*."

EMILIA GOODWIN,   :   FAMILY COURT
                         :   OF DAUPHIN COUNTY

Plaintiff,   :

                            :

v.   :

                            :

MR. DARR,   :   Case No. USHLDNOBTR2

                            :

                            :

Defendant   :

APRIL 11:
FIRST CAUSE OF ACTION

"THIS IS COZY," SAID VERONICA. SHE AND I lay side by side in our double bed, after celebrating our win yesterday into today. Raina and Izzy shared the other.

"Isn't it just?" I said.

Because of budget constraints, we were sleeping four to a room at the Quality Inn Riverfront for states. Nikita and Grace were in the room next door with two girls from another school. I hoped they weren't cute.

Maybe I should have pushed the room assignments.

Though, Grace was as clear as I was on her utter lack of interest in sex.

And in being in the same room as me.

Or possibly the same state or nation.

So help me, they better not cuddle.

"*Focus*," I said to myself.

"What?" said Veronica.

"Nothing," I said.

In the morning, it took two hours before each of us got a turn in the bathroom. I could only imagine what was happening with our neighbors, since Nikita made it known she needed at least an hour for herself. My eyes burned and my back ached. Veronica was a very respectful bed cohabitator, but I slept poorly because I didn't want to turn and accidentally drool on her. The rest of the team looked like the experience had been similar.

"Bye, Michele and Andrea!" Izzy called.

Two girls waved and walked down the hall.

"They are two East Philly Prep witnesses. They were pretty cool. Though, I'm pretty sure they hate their team for voting them into our room."

"Probably," I said. We walked down to the grand ballroom, where the day's trials would be posted, and met Kay and Ms. McClain. There were four bouts in the morning and then the final in the afternoon.

"It's us versus Weston High," I said.

"Let's do it," said Ms. McClain and Kay simultaneously.

The two of them may have been spending too much time together.

The morning trial went fine. I stumbled through cross examination, and the other team kept objecting and having those objections sustained, but we got through it.

The same thing happened as the day before.

The judge left.

We waited.

Raina kept telling us all to breathe.

"All rise," said the bailiff. We stood, and the judge came back.

Then he didn't give his ruling but told us all to register to vote and to always make sure to show up for jury duty. He complimented our passion and preparation.

"That was kind of anticlimactic, right there," I moaned. I lay back on the ground. I sat up. I wondered if waiting for verdicts like this was meant to replicate the speed of the real court system. I bet the Steelton boys' team was just waiting for its victory. I hoped the boys failed in spectacular fashion.

We sat around the grand ballroom as Kay helped Ms. McClain pass out our box lunches. The finalists came down to points awarded, and we didn't even know if we'd won our case.

"Why do they make us sit here?" I glared across the room at Brandon and the boys. One guy hung off a post while others threw cookie wrappers at him. Their ease annoyed me.

"It's for the drama. Or maybe they just need to calculate scores. No matter. You already have so much to be proud of. We've made it this far," said Kay. She delicately picked up her veggie wrap, eyed it, and placed it back in the box. "So few teams can say that."

"I agree," said Ms. McClain. "Keep in mind that four months ago, there was no all-girl Steelton team. But now here you are."

The doors of the ballroom opened. The local organizers streamed in, carrying a piece of rolled up butcher-block paper.

"This is it," I said, barely able to get the words out.

It would be okay if we didn't make it. Like Ms. McClain said, we'd come so far already. I'd gotten so much already.

The organizers reached the front of the room, and one picked up a microphone.

"Hello, Mock Trial state qualifiers!" The room whooped. Most teams stay for two nights, unless they are local. The room was still filled with Mock Trial kids who wanted to be a part of the audience at the last trial, even if they weren't participating.

"It's been a great two days of competition, and we are here to tell you the results are a fascinating twist ending for all of us."

Chattering erupted across the room.

"What does that mean?" said Izzy.

"Were we all disqualified?" said Veronica.

"Maybe there's a tie?" said Grace.

"Since its inception in 1984, the United States High School Mock Trial Association . . ."

"They are actually trying to give me a stroke," whispered Ms. McClain.

The woman up front talked for a solid five minutes. Finally, she said, "This year's competitors in the finals are . . ."

Someone started pattering on their knees until others joined in.

This was it.

"Steelton High versus Steelton High!"

The pattering stopped.

Kay's mouth dropped open.

The room sat completely hushed, everyone stunned by this development.

"It's a first, we admit. The rule changes this year don't prevent such a thing from happening, and this is how the scores aligned. Teams, observers—we will see you in Courtroom A in"—she looked at her watch—"exactly an hour."

"Oh my God," said Grace.

"Didn't see that coming," said Nikita.

The boys' team came over to us. We'd be piling into the same van to go over there. Mr. Darr smiled at Ms. McClain and Kay.

"We meet again," he said.

They ignored him.

"Kay, let me help you with those trial boxes," said Ms. McClain.

"Excited, Millie?" Jeff said to me. "We finally made it to finals."

We hadn't done anything. I was getting there with my team. Not him.

Focus, I thought. *I am the dawn of a new day of self-actualization.*

"You look kind of tired," he said. "Long night?"

His stupid smirk looked oddly well-rested.

"Two people to a bed was a little crowded. What, you didn't mind?"

Jeff looked at me. "What?"

"Didn't you guys have four to a room?" I said.

"Nope. Only two per room." He laughed. "Guess you just got whatever budget was left over."

"I'm sorry, did you say what I think you said?" said Nikita. "You only had to share your bathroom with one other person?" Nikita advanced on him. Jeff took a step back.

"Uh . . ." he said.

"I slept in a cot so the Philly Prep girl could have the bed," said Grace. "I probably have weird indentations in my spine from the bar in that thing. And you got your own room?"

"California Kings!" said Brandon.

"You are *kidding* me," I said.

"All right, all right. What's done is done," said Ms. McClain, holding up her hands. "Everybody get into the van. And don't kill each other. No one from Steelton will win if you all commit homicide before we even get over to the courthouse." But she glanced at Mr. Darr. "Is that why you wanted to check in separately? So, I wouldn't know?"

Mr. Darr at least had the decency to look sheepish.

For not the first time in my life, I felt like punching someone. Brandon, maybe. But I wouldn't, because that was illegal.

All of us buckled into the van in silence. Nikita kept trying to calm her frizzing hair. If stares could burn people, every dude on the Steelton High "varsity" team would have been incinerated where they sat.

THE RIDE BACK OVER TO THE COURTHOUSE for the final was *odd* to say the least.

Grace wouldn't even look at me. She moved away when I tried to maneuver myself into the seat next to her. I think Raina saw what I was trying to do and even climbed over a seat to free up the space next to Grace. But then I ended up giving the spot to Veronica because she had trouble getting in and out of the van with her foot, and Kay and Ms. McClain were talking strategy in the front.

We arrived at the courthouse as the other teams streamed in around us. Most competitors liked to watch the final, to learn about the competition for next year or to pick up winning techniques.

Inside, the four original courtrooms were designed to mimic a season. We'd compete surrounded by the inspiration of spring. The wood gleamed blond and cherry, the carpet and heavy curtains a deep green. Large windows splashed sunlight onto the floor in the square formed by the judge's bench and witness box one on side, the defense's and prosecution's opposite them, and the jury box opposite the window wall.

The whole place had a quiet dignity about it, so it felt disrespectful to speak above a whisper. The teams and their observers talked quietly as they went in. Ms. McClain gathered us into a huddle in the lobby outside.

My heart thrilled a little, to be back in this place. This was what I wanted. This is what the guys *almost* took from me. They could still take victory.

"Team," I said, "I am so proud of all of you. The three trials to get us here. Now, even though you might not have liked this particular case"—I looked over at Grace, who stared at the ground—"you committed to it. Whatever happens now. No one can take that."

"Like we said, you've come a long way. And even if you don't win . . ." started Kay.

Every one of us turned our heads toward her at the same time. It was as if gravity gave up its weight on the team. Each of us stood taller. Ready.

"I am going to crush them myself," said Nikita. "For my hair."

"I am going to take them down because of my back," said Grace.

"I am going to defeat them because they stare at me," said Izzy.

"I am going to win this because they laughed at my boot," said Veronica.

"I am going to squash them because Brandon," said Raina.

Everyone looked at me.

"I am going to win because they thought they could just get rid of me," I said. "And they were wrong."

Ms. McClain looked at Kay. "Remind me never to mess with angry girls," she said.

The six of us marched in there like pure squad goals, in step with one another. I felt like my breath and heartbeat synchronized with them. Jeff tried to do his psych-out smirk to me, and I just blankly stared past him.

Not today, Jeff.

Emilia Goodwin representing the plaintiff, Your Honor. And I will clearly show you the tools on the defense have no idea what they are in for.

"Fair is foul, and foul is fair," Jeff said to his team. "They better watch out."

Raina and Izzy gasped.

"What?" I said.

"They've done it now," said Izzy.

"They don't even know," said Raina.

"Huh?"

"He just quoted"—Izzy looked around—"a certain cursed play I shall not name. It's terrible luck. *Terrible*." She looked at Jeff.

He shrugged.

"Don't worry, Millie," said Izzy. "This is now in the bag."

For some reason, I believed her.

Veronica did the opening and the room went silent. No one could take their eyes off of her.

Jeff did the opening. He was fine.

Chad the sophomore questioned Izzy and Nikita. By the end, Chad looked like he was about to burst out into tears.

Then Raina took the stage.

And Brandon stood.

They looked at each other for what felt like a year but was only about ten seconds.

"So, Ms. Tunis," he said. "Could you please tell us the name of your, uh, club?"

"I am the president of the Social Justice League. So-called because we witnessed a lot of bullying, a lot of unjust things happening in our school. We wanted everyone to feel heard and valued and seen. Anyone can join. Even faculty or staff. All we want is for our school to be inclusive and create the most comfortable learning environment possible." She leaned forward. "And I dedicated my *life* to that."

Raina really knew how to get into character. The last few times we'd done the trial, Raina had just said "the Social Justice League."

"Oh. Okay," said Brandon. I could see Jeff trying to get his attention. Jeff furiously scribbled onto a notepad, presumably to give Brandon some direction.

"Can you tell me who in your club knits?"

"Not just the girls," Raina said.

"What?" said Brandon.

"Knitting isn't just for girls. The boys in the club do it, too. Maybe everyone knits, actually. It's an important art often considered women's work. But the Social Justice League believes in stitching equality."

That was also new.

"Objection, Your Honor," said Jeff from the table.

The judge cocked her head toward Jeff. "Young man, you are objecting to your own teammate?"

Jeff realized what he had done and put his head down. "Oh. No, Your Honor. I'm sorry."

Things did not improve from there for the guys.

Raina left the bench with a bigger smile than the time she'd beaten out Claire for Rosalind in *As You Like It.*

Veronica and Grace nailed their questioning. They moved so swiftly and deftly that the defense didn't even raise any objections. The boys seemed stumped.

Varsity, my butt.

By the time it was my turn to question my witness, the entire boys' team looked dejected. The guy who took the stand in front of me was one of the freshman boys who beat me in "auditions." I picked up my clipboard, and I heard him make a faint, terrified squeak.

Triumph coursed through my body by the time I stood to give the closing statement. I wouldn't say winning didn't matter—it did. But I'd gotten up in front of the team that just tossed me aside like I didn't matter. And, at its heart, that's kind of what this case was about, too.

"Your Honor," I began. "You've heard the argument that the Social Justice League was responsible for creating an unsafe environment at their school. Their social-media posts, targeted art activism, and general presence felt 'threatening to some.'"

I looked over at Brandon, Jeff, and the kids who replaced me.

None of them were smirking now.

"But I think through the testimony of our witnesses, you can see that the SJL was actually the group seeking to *protect* safety, civility, and students who were othered. It was their core purpose to bring kids together who felt like they had no one else. To bring community through art. They were bullied by some of the very people you heard testify on the defense's side." I tried to restate the testimonies from my notes I'd taken during the trial. "In conclusion, Your Honor, as the counsel representing the plaintiffs, it is our responsibility to prove our claims with a 'preponderance of evidence.' The burden of proof is on us. Given the testimony of all the witnesses, we contend that our arguments are far more likely true than not. Thank you."

I took my seat next to Grace, having left it all up there at the podium.

"Great job today," I whispered. "You are brilliant every time."

"I believe in what I'm saying," she said, "for this side of the case."

I waited. She offered nothing else.

"I can tell," I tried. Maybe this was for the best. She was going to college; I was going to college. It wouldn't work. It couldn't. People didn't stay together.

I at least wanted her to look at me.

She didn't.

An hour later, all the teams had assembled for the awards ceremony back at the hotel.

Once again, the organizers entered the room with some drama, quieting everyone assembled. The timekeepers got little stopwatches. And the seniors got pins. I immediately attached mine to my backpack.

"And now for the moment you've all been waiting for!" said the president of the Pennsylvania Bar Association. "The winner is . . . the Steelton High Mock Trial team for the plaintiffs!"

It took a moment for that to register.

Holy crickets.

That was us. We had won! *States*. Bossy, over-opinionated, too-talkative-for-my-previous-team's-comfort Emilia Goodwin had led the girls to victory.

The room cheered as we got our plaque and medals.

"We won!" I said to Grace.

She could congratulate me. She knew how important this was to me. I thought it meant a lot to her.

"I can't be on the defense."

That was all she said.

Even though Grace still hated me, it seemed like I was in a dream. But at the same time, I felt like I was waking up to who I was for the first time in my life. This win was changing me.

Or maybe it had started before that, when I'd decided to form my own team. I felt braver. More myself.

If only I could be myself and have Grace.

But this would have to do for now.

RAINA PETREE,	:	IN THE COURT OF
	:	REVENGE OF CAMBRIA
Plaintiff,	:	COUNTY
	:	
v.	:	
	:	
HIGHER EDUCATION,	:	Case No. YMENONO18
	:	
	:	
Defendant	:	

APRIL 15: MOTION TO QUASH SUBPOENAS FOR DEPOSITION

I LOVED THE WAY THE LIBRARY SMELLED. Worn cloth covers, embossed titles rubbed smooth with the thousands of shelvings and reshelvings. I'd volunteered for the library the summer before ninth grade. There was such a feeling of satisfaction in helping someone find the perfect book, on just the subject they needed.

Maybe I could be a librarian. A really theatrical librarian. Or a theatrical *law* librarian. Who even knew? Not this wait-listed girl, that was for sure. Who invented the system where you had to figure out what you wanted to do with the rest of your life before you could vote or buy a vibrator? It was the worst system ever. Bet the patriarchy had something to do with it. It always did.

"Raina, are you here with us?" said Millie.

My head snapped up. "Yes. Sorry. Just thinking about . . . uh . . . never mind."

"No problem. Okay, everyone, as I was saying, you were fantastic this past weekend at states. Absolutely superb. I loved every second of your performance. In one sense, it's fortunate the way it worked out for nationals because our draws mean we will present the plaintiff cause for all rounds except the final. The unfortunate thing is that we'd end with the less sympathetic side. The witnesses as we've seen them played were awful."

"Less sympathetic?" said Izzy. "You mean bigoted?"

"Wait a second. We are leaving for this when?" said Nikita.

"You think the witnesses were just *played* awfully? Did you read those statements? That's because they *are* awful," said Grace.

"May sixth through May ninth?" said Nikita. "That is the weekend we are supposed to be in Pittsburgh?"

"Okay, okay," said Millie. "One thing at a time. Yes, Nikita, it's on Mother's Day weekend. But as I mentioned a while ago, we are going Thursday morning and coming back Sunday night."

"No," said Nikita.

"Yes," said Millie.

"I'm sorry. But I think the more important point here is that some of the team members have concerns with the parts we are expected to play. Frankly, I am also one of them," said Veronica.

"Listen, I understand . . ."

"I can't go to the national competition," said Nikita.

"WE CAN WORK THIS OUT!" shouted Millie.

"Everything okay, girls?" said Ms. McClain, appearing from around a bookshelf.

"Prom is Friday, May seventh. I am going to prom," said Nikita. "I can't go to nationals."

"Our prom?" said Millie.

"Yes."

"The one they are selling tickets for right now?"

"Yes," said Nikita. "I already bought mine, they are nonrefundable, and my dress is being shipped from California. I'm going with my boyfriend. Who I met at Mock Trial. I kind of owe that to you. So, I'm sorrier than I would have been. Which is not at all sorry."

"You have to go to finals," said Millie. "We don't have any alternates."

Nikita shrugged. "I'm not missing prom."

Ms. McClain slowly backed away, back into the stacks. Some things were just above her pay grade, I supposed.

"But this is a once-in-a-life-time opportunity!" said Millie.

"So is prom."

"You are a junior! Go next year!"

"Who knows if I'll have a boyfriend this cute next year. He's going to look amazing in our pictures. No way." She glanced around at the Mock Trial circle. "I really am sorry." And she walked off.

"Prom is stupid! This is life!" said Millie. If anguish had a color, it would match Millie's face right now.

"I was looking forward to it. Got a suit," said Grace. "Guess that option's out." Grace leaned back in her chair and crossed her arms in front of her.

"Some people like prom. Like me," said Veronica.

"And this case sucks," said Izzy.

"But Mock Trial . . . we worked for this. All the hours spent studying and practicing and meeting. We've wanted this for years."

No one said anything. We knew she was talking about herself. But we'd joined on knowing that. I also knew what she was thinking. We'd had a hard enough time finding exactly enough people for the team as it was. How could we replace Nikita? And if we lost both of the other lawyers?

"Listen," I finally said. "I have a confession."

Everyone looked at me. "I have been rejec—wait-listed at all my colleges. All of them. Maybe I'll get in, maybe I won't. Maybe I'll study theater, maybe I won't. But my mom said something that stuck with me, which is really saying something because I usually try to ignore her. But she said, 'Good things can come with the bad only if you keep going.' And something about life not being fair. And possibly something else about having casual sex to chill out."

"Raina, what is the point here?" Millie sounded so tired.

"The point is that maybe the defense in this case sucks. Playing the defense means we go in there and argue that discrimination against people should be allowed in school. We are arguing that it's okay to post stuff against people who get made fun of or bullied for stuff they can't change about themselves. Maybe it's actually offensive. But life is offensive and unfair. The law is offensive and unfair. But it doesn't have to be. There are lawyers and judges who fight for what they think is right. And people who fight them when the lawyers and judges get it wrong. And then there are the people who give up. All I'm saying is that we should give this a second look. There is more to this than meets the eye. I'm not ready to just throw all this away."

Everyone looked anywhere but at one another.

"I guess . . ." said Veronica. "I guess I might as well stay. I didn't find a dress yet. And really, the boyfriend will be relieved he doesn't have to go again. Maybe I can find a way to subvert this hot mess."

"Yes. Subversion. Perfect," I said. It was a start.

After a few moments, Izzy said, "I could take a second look at it."

The bell rang. I looked at Grace. She grabbed her bag and got up and left.

I squeezed Millie's arm on my way out. "This isn't over yet," I said. "The jury is still out."

"Thanks, Raina," she said. She turned and walked toward Ms. McClain's desk.

This was bad. Very bad. We were down a witness, possibly a lawyer, whose aunt also happened to be our adviser. My only comfort was that things couldn't possibly get any worse than essential parts of the team almost quitting.

APRIL 22: STANDING ORDER

FOR MY MORNING RITUAL DURING THE weeks I had rehearsal or a show (which were most of them), I would get up, do vocal exercises in the shower, eat breakfast, and then run lines in my head or out loud, depending on how many other people were around. If Mom were home, I'd talk to her, but I would often recite soliloquies or sonnets. She didn't seem to mind or was possibly too tired to bother arguing. These days, I thought over my Mock Trial character development. I didn't have lines, just a statement, so there was more freedom there. But now one of my characters was also kind of a jerk.

On the bus to school, I racked my brain to come up with ways to make Eden Ward, president of the Real Love Club, seem more human. Eden was not a fan of gay marriage. Or gay anything, really. She believed, as did her group, in the preservation of "traditional family values," which meant a couple had one dude, one girl, and then a lot of babies in the bounds of matrimony. The men went to work; the women stayed home. She seemed to blame the suffrage movement for many of society's ills. She seemed almost like a parody of a real person, so much so that I wondered if Mock Trial case designers were having a bad day when they wrote Miss Eden Ward. Though I could think of a few people here in good ol' Steelton that could have hung with Eden on the daily.

I wandered into the library before the first bell to return some books. Millie was there at the desk.

"Hey," I said.

She jumped. "Oh. Hi."

"You okay?"

"Mr. Darr just went into Ms. McClain's office with Jeff and Brandon."

"Oh?" That did not sound good.

"Something's up. I can tell. I came here to try and brainstorm a solution to the Nikita problem. I've been avoiding it since we canceled practice the last two days because . . . you know."

She didn't want to say "the team was on the verge of splitting up." I nodded.

"I wish I could hear what is going on in there. We need a heating grate," she said.

"What?"

"Or maybe we could put a glass to the door. Does that work?"

"I don't know about heating grates or glasses, but I can tell you the walls are pretty thin. Maybe Ms. McClain has super librarian ears, but the woman can hear if you and your boyfriend have a make-out session in the study room next to her office."

"Gross."

"I'm beginning to agree with you on that point. Come with me." I grabbed Millie by the arm and pulled her to the quiet study room next to Ms. McClain's office. Just as I thought, you could hear what was going on in there just as easily as she could always tell what was happening in here. Especially if you pressed your ear against the drywall.

"And it's only fair," said Mr. Darr's voice.

"I'm sorry. I don't think I understand what you're saying. You boys worked hard," she paused, "but it was the Steelton girls who qualified for nationals. Not you."

"And that is just the thing. According to national rules, there is no girls' team or boys' team. That was a special state exception brought on by a technical loophole in our district. Almost anywhere else, that wouldn't have worked. But nationals recognizes the school as a whole. As such, we can send any students we want. They do not have to have been on the winning team."

Ms. McClain's office fell silent. Or maybe they had started speaking so quietly I couldn't hear. I strained my face against the gritty plaster.

"No," came Ms. McClain's voice.

"Connie," said Mr. Darr. "I'm the Mock Trial adviser of record. Some of the girls can go. I understand you might need some more team members as it is."

"Being the Mock Trial adviser of record means you filled out a piece of paper years ago. That's it."

"Be that as it may, the principal agreed with me that we should send the best team possible to represent the school."

"And my girls have proven that *they* are that team. If you were supposed to go to nationals, then you would have placed first."

I made a mental note to send Ms. McClain flowers on National School Librarian's Day. Or, if there wasn't such a holiday, to start learning how to invent it and make it nationally recognized. I turned to Millie to ask if she knew about Librarian's Day, but I realized she wasn't next to me anymore.

"Millie?" I said. I did a full three sixty. She'd left.

I tried to casually emerge from the study room as if I'd been in there for a nonspying-related purpose. The library looked empty from my vantage point.

"Millie," I tried to whisper-shout again.

Ms. McClain's door opened. Mr. Darr walked out, followed by Brandon and Jeff. Brandon wore his guilty face, but his posture appeared irritatingly triumphant. Stride long, head up, back straight.

"Raina, can I . . ."

"I WAS RETURNING BOOKS," my internal volume sensor kicked to bits by a sudden, intense rage. "THEY WERE OVERDUE FROM A CLASS PROJECT AND I AM SORRY."

"Oh, it's okay, a few days . . ."

I advanced on Brandon. Jeff was a nonissue and it was probably illegal to yell at a teacher.

"Listen, dickwad."

"Ms. Petree, perhaps . . ." Mr. Darr said.

"Sorry." I smiled sweetly at him. I drew in breath to my core, stomach out. You need to engage those muscles not to strain your vocal cords. But real power comes from holding back. Feeling the emotion but letting it out in a long, cool strain could be just as effective. A power pose, like feet hips length apart, balled fists at your waist, completed the picture. "It might seem like Jeff, or your adviser, or your team, but I know you came up with this idea. You are the smartest of all of them."

Jeff sniffed at that. I didn't bother to look at him.

"You checked the rules. You knew all along that this could happen. You tried to taunt me with it, that one time a few weeks ago. I get it now. But know this."

I stepped close enough to kiss his neck.

Or headbutt him.

Instead, I just smiled. "You didn't win states. And you won't win now. You can never win against me again, Brandon."

Grades and graduation be damned, I turned to Mr. Darr. This one was for Millie. "And I don't know who you think *you* are." I surveyed him up and down like I did when I tried to psych out my audition competition. "But I'm pretty sure arguing that men should take what women earned isn't going to play well in the newspaper. I've been in it enough, representing this school in every theater festival ever. I know they'd be *intrigued* by this story."

"You should be careful how you talk to a teacher, Ms. Petree," said Mr. Darr.

I was a wait-listed woman. That may technically mean I still had a lot to lose here, but I didn't care.

"Then maybe you should consider how you treat students."

Mr. Darr glared at me, then Ms. McClain, and turned and stormed out. Brandon backed away from me, and he and Jeff ran after Mr. Darr.

"That," said Ms. McClain slowly, "was an interesting strategy, Raina. How did you know what happened in there?"

"I was eavesdropping," I said.

Ms. McClain sighed and rubbed her temples, like Mom did so often.

"Did he reconsider? Did I miss something?"

"No. He's pretty convinced there should be auditions again for the national team."

"Can he do that?"

"He seems to think he can. But from me to you, that whole *adviser* thing doesn't mean much. We don't get paid extra. He has been administering the team budget since I didn't push it. Even so, he doesn't control it. And the principal owes me about eight years of favors, so I'm not worried." She looked me in the eyes. "He seemed to think there was some dissention in the ranks. That we might not have a full team. Is that true?"

"If we had a full team, you're sure we would be the ones to go to nationals?"

"Oh yes," said Ms. McClain.

"Then we have a full team."

"Promise?"

"Okay, at the moment we technically don't. But we will. I promise." I held up my pinkie, and she linked hers with mine.

"I consider this a binding verbal contract, young lady," she said. "You make sure we have a full team, and I will get us to nationals."

"If there's one thing I live and die by, Ms. McClain," I said, releasing my hand from hers, "it's that the show must go on."

APRIL 26: NOTICE OF INTENTION TO OFFER EVIDENCE

THE SHOW WAS MAKING A FANTASTIC ARGU- ment that it would not, in fact, go on.

I had tried pretty much everyone I could bear to ask to join Mock Trial, and they had all been a no. Millie was ignoring calls, and she wasn't responding to texts. I searched the school for her until I reached the girls' bathroom.

Once inside, I recognized the sniffles immediately.

"Hey, Millie," I said.

No response.

"Ms. McClain can fight Darr. My money is on her any day."

"But we need a team."

"We will have one."

"We are down a witness." She blew her nose. "Grace won't even look at me. Izzy and Veronica are on the fence."

"We will find a witness. We have—" I thought about it. "Two weeks. I got this."

The stall door opened.

"That's nice of you to say, but I just don't think we can do it."

"No," I said. Maybe it was the smell of ammonia-based cleaning products; maybe it was that I wasn't ready to let go of my newly found interest in pretrial motions. "This is where it began, Millie." I gestured around us. "Remember? You and me? This is where it started. This is *not* where it ends. I swear. You brought us together the first time. You helped me. Now it's my turn."

A tear ran down her cheek.

"Really? You won't give up yet? Just give me two days. Two days and we will have a team. Er. Maybe till Friday. But we will have a solid team by Friday."

"Okay," she said, wiping her chin. "I will believe you."

Millie didn't sound convinced, but it was a start.

She blew her nose again and washed her hands. She looked back at me. "You'd make a decent lawyer," she said. "You are very convincing."

This did not prove true later in the day in my attempt to make good on my bathroom promise.

"Nikita, *please*," I begged. I full-on knelt on the cafeteria floor, hands clasped as if in prayer to the god of proms and ill-timed extracurricular events. "You went to the prom last year. I saw you there with that senior guy with the beard."

"Ah, Mallik," she said fondly. "He went to Stanford, you know."

"Good for him. Nikita, this is more important than pictures. Think of it—glory. Renown. College applications. Surely that is more compelling than overcooked chicken and a few *balloons*."

Nikita chuckled. "Listen. I hear what you are saying. And I'm going to tell you a secret, that you better not let get out. Because it will make me look sensitive or weak or something, and you can't have that on the dance team. The dancers are vipers, I tell you." She moved toward me. "My grandmother is really sick. She's had lung cancer twice and beat it, but this time it's bad. She lives at home with us and loves this kind of thing. She was proud of the trial stuff, thinks I can be lawyer like my dad. But she's been going on about not seeing me and my sisters in our weddings. Caught her crying in the garden about hemming clothes for great-grandchildren. She's finishing my dress from my aunty in LA, and she seems happier than she has in ages. And did you see *Our Town*? Made me realize I should be home more. Not to mention that maybe I could be on the Mock Trial team next year."

That hadn't occurred to me. A team existing after we graduated.

And what could possibly trump a sick grandmother?

"Okay. I understand." I slumped. "I don't suppose you have any dramatic friends who would like an all-expense paid trip to Pittsburgh over prom weekend?"

"Sorry," she said.

"For the record, family love is not weakness!" I said as she turned and walked away from me. *Damn Emily Webb*, I thought.

But then it struck me.

The truth had been staring at me this whole time. The dark, gloomy, unfortunate truth.

"Do any human beings ever realize life while they live it? Every, every minute," I muttered, left study hall, and marched with grim determination to the drama room.

"Well, hello! This is a nice surprise," said Mr. Cooper.

I smiled at him because the man seemed to mean it.

"To what do we owe the pleasure?"

"I need to talk to Claire." I looked down at her bored face. The off-season in Drama Club is painfully slow. All they did was study plays for next year. She was pretending to read the *Merry Wives of Windsor*.

"I desire you in friendship, and I will one way or other make you amends," I said.

She glanced down at the script she was holding and tossed it on the table.

"Say no more," she said and followed me to the library.

APRIL 29: NOTICE OF TRIAL READINESS

GETTING EVERYONE ASSEMBLED HAD NOT been easy.

Izzy said she'd do it if Veronica came. Veronica said she'd come if Grace came. Grace had been the last holdout, but I bribed her with incredibly expensive yarn donated by Megan's grandmother for the cause.

Claire came without question.

"Okay, everyone," I said uneasily. The vibe in the room was not one of conquering defense strategies. "Nationals is in a week. Or a week-ish, anyway. As you may have heard, the dudes could take our spots if we can't come together. Claire here"—I waved to her—"has generously volunteered to be our sixth team member."

Izzy grinned. "Awesome!"

Claire flashed her annoyingly straight smile. Girl had never even had braces. God, her effortlessness still annoyed me. But this was for the cause of justice.

"We have a full team. The issue we have to resolve, then"—I looked at Grace and Izzy—"is that some people are uncomfortable with the defense."

"They don't like gay people," said Grace.

"I don't know who they *do* like," said Veronica.

"Yes. True," I said.

Millie just sat there.

"I can't be a defense lawyer on this. I just cannot," said Grace. "My heart isn't in it."

"I can be a lawyer," said Veronica. "But it will be wild."

"Okay, okay. I thought about that and I have a suggestion." I felt a little light-headed. What I was about to suggest was so far out of what I thought I'd be doing this year that I surely was dreaming. "Grace, could you play a witness?" I said.

"Play a . . . what?"

"You don't have to be a lawyer. You could take Taylor Quinn, the soccer player. She doesn't hate anyone except distractions from the big game. And you *have* mentioned how you always wanted to try acting. This is a good venue for that. Trust me."

"Yeah . . . I mean, I read her statement. I just . . ."

"It was Nikita's role. Claire will take mine."

Grace considered this. We sat for what felt like three years in silence. "Yes. I would be okay with that," she said finally.

"Really?" I said.

"Really?" Millie said, her head popping up.

"Yes," said Grace more firmly. "I could do that. But who would be the third lawyer, then?"

I drew in my breath. Feet hip's length apart. Fists on waist.

"Me," I said.

EMILIA GOODWIN,	:	NATIONAL HIGH SCHOOL
	:	MOCK TRIAL ASSOCIATION
Plaintiff,	:	OF THE USA
	:	
v.	:	
	:	
THE ANYTOWN USA	:	Case No. 1LSTCHANC0
SCHOOL DISTRICT,	:	
	:	
Defendant	:	

APRIL 30: EXTRAORDINARY WRIT POSITIONS

I STARED AT THE NEEDLES IN MY HANDS.

I looked back at the video on my computer.

I looked at the needles again.

"Why don't you go back to affirming with that app of yours," said Claire. "Or your motivational quotes book." She rolled over from her stomach onto her back on my bed. She flipped through a shiny brochure for Carnegie Mellon University. "Or channel the energy you use to rant about the current makeup of the Supreme Court."

"It isn't enough," I said.

Plus, Grace liked to knit. Maybe this would help things with her. Maybe we couldn't be a thing, whatever we were. But I hated how every day our relationship seemed to devolve a little more. Raina had saved nationals by persuading Claire to finally join and by switching her role to lawyer. We had six girls again, so the least I could do was to try to make sure all the others were speaking to their team captain.

"Slipknots are hard," I said.

"Give me that." Claire sat up and took my needles. She expertly cast on a few stitches.

"How'd you do that?" I said.

"Summer camp counseling. Drama only took up half the day. Other half—crafts. God knows I didn't want to be a lifeguard, and I don't like the feeling of glue on my hands."

"I never even knew," I mumbled. I had to learn to cast on myself one day. But it was way easier once something was already on the needle. Even moving to the next row felt less daunting than beginning a new thing I wasn't even good at.

Knitting could be a metaphor for Grace.

I breathed the thought out of my head. Best to combine my calming strategies.

"You bummed about prom?" she said.

"No," I answered a little too quickly.

"How's the woman?" she asked.

I shrugged. "She is so upset about this case. I see her reasons. I *agree* with her reasons. The case is crap. Every day, I think about what I would do if I went to our fictional case school in real life." I looked up from my knitting. "But it's not real. It's Mock Trial, right? I've wanted to win this for so long, so I need to do what I need to do?"

Claire looked at me. She and I both knew I was trying to convince myself of that rather than her.

"I see you, Emilia Ann Goodwin," said Claire.

"My middle name? Really?" I said, though it did make me smile. "What do you see?"

"I know you love Mock Trial. It's your life. And real trials will be your life. But I also know you don't do it because you want to win. Not really. You do it because you believe in it. You believe in the law and the court and fairness and justice and all that stuff that I usually call a pile of flawed shit."

"Are you encouraging me, here?" I said.

"I'm just saying I know you'll do what you think is right. For the last few years, you haven't had any personal connection to the case. This is different. And I know you'll figure out what you need to do."

"Wow, Claire. That's deep," I said.

"I'm an actress, darling. I'm always profound."

I threw my yarn at her. It didn't get very far because my yarn was wound so tightly.

Appropriate.

Just then, we heard the front door open.

"Honey! We're home."

"We're?" asked Claire.

The boisterous, high-pitched squeals of Sheila's four- and six-year-olds rose up the stairs.

I sighed.

"Wow. Kids coming over at seven o'clock at night," said Claire.

"They don't go to bed until about ten. Even then, they talk for an hour."

"You've stayed over at their place?"

"Nope. They've stayed here. Twice this week already. They are in the bedroom next door. The older one takes the bed, and the little one has an air mattress."

"You haven't told me that," said Claire.

"I'm in denial. Dad isn't happy with me for not being thrilled he has a girlfriend. I fear next year I will be expected to be the nanny in addition to whatever household chores my father thinks warrants tuition."

"Millie," said Claire. "I love you and will miss you, but are you sure you can't get out of here?"

"I was thinking about it. If we won nationals, there'd be scholar-ship money that would help me out. A *lot*. It'd be tough without it. I am not going to live with Mom because I still feel kind of weird about her leaving. And I don't want to be a free babysitter for my brother, cute as he is. But maybe if I took out loans or went part-time or worked, I could do it. After a year, I could get in-state tuition."

"That sounds . . . hard."

"Yeah."

"I guess we just have to win nationals, then. Piece of cake!" Claire sounded so confident.

I laughed.

"Mills! Can you watch the kids until Sheila gets dinner ready?"

The laughter died in my throat.

"At least he found a new servant in Sheila," said Claire.

This time, I threw a pillow at her but not very hard. What she said was mean.

But true.

Claire got her stuff and fled before the kids could even speak to her. I made sure to lock my bedroom door before I came downstairs. I'd never locked it in my life, but the first time the kids stayed over, one dropped my laptop off my bed. It was fine, but my life was in there. I'd worked at a stuffy office for three summers to buy it.

"There you are," said Dad. "Hiding in your room again."

"Bye, Mr. Goodwin!" said Claire pointedly. "Thanks for the help on the school project, Millie."

"Oh. Uh. No problem." I smiled gratefully at her.

"Oh! Goodbye, Claire. I didn't realize you were working."

"Hi! Who are you? Can I touch your hair? Look at your clothes! Can I see what's in your bag?" said Victor, Sheila's little boy.

"Gotta go!" Claire said, and practically hurled herself through the window to get out of there as fast as possible.

"Millipede!" said Nina, Victor's sister.

"Please just call me Millie," I said.

"Millipede, millipede, millipede!" both of them sang.

I vowed right then to never have children.

"Millie, what would you like to do? Play with the kids or help Sheila with dinner?"

Neither. What I wanted to do was study First Amendment case law and try to find a way out of this defense or make it acceptable or maybe try to get Grace to speak to me again. I'd already done a load of laundry and mopped when I got home from school.

Victor spilled his milk on the floor.

"I'll go in the kitchen."

"Okay. Clean this up, too, would you?"

I gathered paper towels, wondering if it'd kill the man to do this. If he and Sheila ended up getting married, would he do more to help her?

In the kitchen, Sheila hummed around, stirring things and poking something in the oven.

"Emilia, how wonderful!" Sheila said things like that. "How wonderful," or "Splendid!" Maybe she was attracted to Dad because his idea of family structure matched how she talked—straight out of an old black-and-white sitcom you'd watch late at night.

I didn't bother telling her to call me Millie. She was the nickname averse type.

"Anything I can do?" I asked.

"Set the table, please," she said in a voice I was sure came from dealing with Victor and Nina every day.

I did as I was told, a house specialty of mine.

"Did your dad ask you about next weekend?"

"No. I've given him the details I have. We are leaving early Wednesday."

"What?" said Sheila.

"What weekend are we talking here? May eighth?"

Sheila cocked her head. "Yes."

"Yes."

"So, you are good with it?" she said.

"Yes? We've hit some bumps in the road with this last case, but we still have a team, and that's the important part."

"Oh good. I didn't know if you'd be ready for such a big commitment. Wait. Did you say case?"

"Yes. Mock Trial. Isn't that what we are talking about?"

"Oh, no. Greg! Could you come in here?"

Something crashed in the other room, followed by giggles.

"Yes?" Dad walked in.

"Millie is confused about next weekend." Sheila gave Dad a death stare that she managed to throw 50 percent my way. Something was my fault here, and I wasn't sure what it was.

"Sorry, sorry. I meant to tell her, but work stuff . . ." He trailed off. The trail-off was kind of Dad's signature move. In speaking and in life.

"I'm going to the Mock Trial national's competition next weekend. Remember how we won state? I can do *this* week. Or the weekend *after*." I didn't know what they wanted me to do, but from the way the conversation was going, I would bet good money they wanted me to watch the kids. My brain tried to knock itself against my skull in protest, but never let it be said that Emilia Goodwin wasn't a team player. "But not *next* weekend. As this is the thing I've been working toward all year and have mentioned on at least half a dozen occasions these past few months."

"Oh. Well, the thing is, friends of Sheila's have a lake house that is free next weekend, so we were hoping you could watch the kids while we have a few days away," said Dad. "A Mother's Day gift!"

"I haven't had a vacation since they were born," said Sheila. "It'd mean a lot."

"Can you do this week?" I needed water. My tongue practically stuck to the room of my mouth, it had gone so dry. But Emilia Goodwin was still a team play—

"No," said Sheila.

"Any other weekend, other than nationals?" I said.

"It's usually booked up. It costs about two-hundred dollars a night. This would be a real treat. *It's Mother's Day*," said Sheila.

"Then I'm sorry to hear that. I'm going to my national Mock Trial competition." I wasn't sure why this woman thought Mother's Day would mean anything in this argument. My mother left and lived in Ohio.

Sheila glared at Dad. Dad glared at me. I would have glared, except Victor ran into the room and knocked me into a chair and then ran out again.

A beeper sounded. Sheila sighed like Claire and Raina do when they want you to know how *hard* their lives are. She turned to get the food out.

Oh, Sheila. This will be your reality if you move here. You're getting a third kid.

"Dinner's ready," she said.

For the first time in my life, I was grateful there were two small bodies trying to ram themselves into my chest and shins or both.

"So, what's this case, Emilia?" asked Sheila. "That will be keeping you away?"

"It's the national competition. For Mock Trial. We are going to try to defend this club. They don't believe in great stuff, but free speech, you know?"

Sheila really could cook. Her pesto salmon rivaled anything I'd ever tasted. But it swam on my plate in front of me.

"What do they believe, exactly?" she said.

"Oh. You know. It's like they picked things directly from the news. Stereotypical stuff. Marriage is only between a man and woman. Gender is binary."

Nina kicked my chair.

"That seems pretty cut and dry to me," said Sheila. "Must be pretty easy to defend."

"No, actually," I said. I thought of Grace. What she said about it challenging people's rights to even exist. "It's basically trying to defend hate speech."

"How is saying marriage is for men and women hate speech?" she said.

"It's the way they said it that was so awful. And it excludes a lot of people. Like all the men who don't want to marry women. Or women who don't want to marry men. Or people who aren't men or women."

"Well, you're trying to defend this club, right? Thank God. They aren't promoting hate speech. They are promoting the truth. I know you were raised with the right values. I'm sure your dad would have something to say if you were going against them," she said. "Right, Greg?"

Dad said nothing.

"*Excuse* me?" I said.

Sheila shrugged. "It's almost over, so there's not much to be done now. But I'm glad I'll get a say in your life from now on. You need a woman to talk to." She winked at my dad, and he smiled.

My mouth dropped open at that.

"Okay, time for dessert!" Sheila said, even though all of us had barely touched her wonderful salmon. The kids looked at each other, knowing this was a way to get out of eating real food.

"Yay!" they said.

"I'm full, thanks," I said. I turned and didn't bother to wait for anyone's reply or permission. I had had it up to my bangs with Dad forgetting or just not valuing me or his general awfulness, which was really coming into full display.

Maybe he loved me, but love has to have some action behind it to count.

Sometimes when people spoke near the heating grate, I could hear their conversations from my room without even trying to snoop. That's how I knew Mom and Dad were cruising toward divorce long before they told me. I heard Dad and Sheila talking after the loud children had been put to bed.

"She's a little old for a rebellious phase," said Dad. "She's always been so . . . what was the word her teachers used . . . dutiful."

"I don't think she likes me. Maybe she doesn't want to share you."

Well. Those were words of someone who didn't know me at all.

Dad laughed. "Could be. We'll have to have a big talk before college. She hasn't mentioned it, but our plan was always commuting. We'll make sure to get her license this summer and that her schedule gives you a break from the kids and house stuff sometimes."

And, those were even more so.

What was truly laughable were the assumptions Dad was making. That I'd go to school nearby. That I'd live at home. That I'd want to be some sort of servant. The thing is, I would have watched the kids *any other weekend than nationals.* I still did most of the cooking and cleaning for Dad and me. I remembered my grandparents' and his secretary's birthdays. I managed all the holidays and reminded him to go to the dentist. To Sheila, I must just look spoiled because maybe she thought Dad did that. But the ironed shirt he was wearing? The clean-ish house her children destroyed?

That was all me.

Maybe I should warn her. Let her know that she was getting a nice-enough guy (or maybe not?) but a pretty crappy partner. But then would she listen? I decided it was on Sheila to do due diligence, like Claire said. If she asked, I'd tell her the truth.

I knew she'd never ask.

I ate a granola bar and some chocolate kisses. I was still hungry, so I made myself some ramen in my little microwave attached to the fridge Mom had gotten me my last birthday. It was the single most satisfying meal I'd ever made.

". . . wedding in the summer," said Dad.

Sheila laughed. "Sounds good to me."

"And I'll talk with Millie. She'll have to get used to the new setup sometime. Might as well be now," said Dad. "School is important, but family comes first. She'll see that your views make sense."

Oh.

Dad.

No.

Just . . . no.

Two things happened in that moment.

The first was that I knew I'd be moving to Ohio the day after I graduated, one way or another.

The second, harder thing, was that I realized what I had to do about the national's case.

MAY 4: SENTENCING MEMORANDUM

I HOVERED AROUND THE OUTSIDE OF THE Dropped Stitch. My needles stuck awkwardly into my yarn. There was another bus heading right back toward my house that I could get on in fifteen minutes. The night air clung wet and warm to my bare arms. I really should have worn a sweater. This was a bad idea. Grace should have this to herself. Grace and Raina. I turned to leave.

"Hi!" said a nearly ecstatic voice. "OMG, did our civil disobedience-ish craftathon inspire you?" said Raina. "What do you have there? A scarf? A blanket? A vulva?"

"I don't know yet. I just started knitting rows," I said.

"Then it could be *anything*," said Raina. She seemed calmer, more at peace these days.

"True," I said.

Grace, who had been messing with a car door that didn't seem to want to shut, came up beside her.

"Hi," I said, quieter than I meant to.

"Hey," said Grace.

"I have to check out some new wools that Carla emailed about," said Raina. She ran to the door and went inside.

"She okay?" I said.

Grace shrugged.

"Are we okay?" I said.

"I don't like this case. Defending hate speech. Standing up there like I believe I'm not supposed to have rights like other people. That I shouldn't *exist*. That *you* shouldn't exist, Millie."

"I know."

"I don't want to do it."

"I know that, too."

"I thought about quitting, still. Even as a witness."

I sighed. "And I told you that would screw us all over. We have a full team again, and Ms. McClain fought for us to go to nationals without any of the guys who tried to screw me in the first place."

"Yes, you did."

"It was hard enough to find a team. We're finally hitting our stride. Claire is probably literally the only person who can do this. We will have stiff competition at nationals. I know this case has some hard stuff to it. But I didn't pick it," I said.

"I know," said Grace. She kicked a tiny pile of stubborn snow that had refused to melt. "I should just suck it up."

"I don't think that's the only solution. I tried that for a long time. Don't suck it up. Get angry," I said. "Get so angry you can't keep it inside and put it all out there in your opening. In your testimony now. I mean, don't harm someone. That'd get us disqualified. But I just don't think hating something means you take yourself out of the game."

"Are you just saying that because you need me to win?"

"No. I told you all this already! Darn it. Does no one pay attention when I speak?" My head buzzed.

"I'm sorry, I'm sorry. I know you didn't pick the case. It just felt like you didn't care how I felt."

"Grace," I said, fighting hard not to sound like my dad. "Of course I care how you feel. I care how Izzy and Veronica feels, too. But I also care about Mock Trial. Not more than any of you, but I've cared about it longer. Because it's been a part of me longer. It's a long story I have never told you, but winning nationals could make my life better in so many ways. You need to appreciate that."

Grace gave me a long look. "I do appreciate that."

"With our draws we won't have to be defense unless we make the final round. Then you can do what you want with this witness. Like I've been saying in every practice since we qualified—put everything you want to say out there. It just eats you from the inside if you don't. Trust me. I'm practically an expert on that."

"Okay," she said.

"Okay?"

"Yes."

"Really?" I said.

"I think so. I hear what you are saying," she said. "And I'm there for you. Not the case, maybe. But for you."

"Good," I said.

I can be open to the possibility of love, I thought.

"Because . . . you are more important to me than winning. So much more. You always were. I'm sorry if it ever seemed like that wasn't the case. I was freaked out because I've never felt like this about anyone. You're so . . . I just . . ." I trailed off, unable to fully explain.

"Really?" Grace walked over to me. "I'm more important than winning?"

"Oh yes. Really."

She took my face in her hands. "Really, really?"

"Yes. You really, really are. I also really, really was looking forward to going to prom with you, too," I said. "I'm sorry nationals was the . . ."

Her lips met mine and my unnecessary apology faded into the softness of her kiss. We melted into the brightness of the spring moon above us. We only broke apart when someone else tried to get around us to get in the door to the shop.

"Are you coming here for *me*?" She grinned and glanced up at the yarn store.

"Mostly," I admitted. "But I like having something to do with my hands while I watch trial videos. It's like affirmations for your fingers."

Grace considered that. "I have no idea what you are talking about. But I'll take your word for it."

I smiled. "Also good."

"Let's go in. If we stay out here too long, Raina is going to finish the cake," said Grace.

"Lead the way."

MAY 8: FORCE AND EFFECT

MS. MCCLAIN WAS IN RARE FORM. WE ALL sat in a circle of chairs after our semifinal round at nationals, listening to her. I tried to pay attention, but it was hard to move my mind away from the fact that we were one step from the finals or one step from going home.

"Trying to send the boys' team instead of our girls. I don't think *so*. So I said to the principal, so help me, if you try and pull rank on me, I will never run a fundraiser or athlete study hall again. And you know the football team relies on those to pass," she said.

"You said that to your boss?" said Kay.

"Oh yes. Threatening a football team's well-being will work every time. I've been saving that one for just the right moment, and it practically presented itself on a platter."

"You should run for office. I would manage your campaign," said Kay.

"Nah. Though, I'll tell you what platform I'd run on. Book-buying budget."

The two of them laughed.

I paced back and forth, trying to breathe in peace and breathe out panic. When I tried to open my phone to use my meditation app, I saw a bunch of passive aggressive texts from Dad about chores when I got home. That only made my breaths come out faster.

"Don't hyperventilate, Millie. You pass out, we'll have to forfeit," said Veronica.

"It all comes down to points," I said. "We did okay in these initial plaintiff rounds, but what if we actually . . ."

"Been there," said Izzy.

"Done that," said Grace. She put her arm around me. "We got this."

"Okay, but in the first nationals round, I almost totally choked when I questioned Claire," I said.

"I couldn't tell," said Claire. "Besides, I am a professional. And so are you."

"You are such a great witness," said Izzy.

"Thanks! Listen, you have to have range. And sometimes a character outside your comfort zone is just what you need. You can't be Emily Webb all the time." Claire nearly retched at the thought. "When we make it to finals, I don't care if I have to be the worst. I don't have to *like* my character. I don't have to want to hang out with her. I just have to try and embody her. Briefly."

"Better you than me," said Izzy. "I respect your commitment to the craft."

"Okay, but what about the second round, then?" I said. "My closing—"

"Millie. Stop. You did a great job," said Veronica. "We all did."

"Here, here," said Grace, raising her diet soda to me.

I let myself lean into her. They were right. After all the drama with facing the boys at states, and then almost losing the shot of coming here *again* because of the boys, I was having trouble letting myself believe them.

Nationals had the same kind of pomp and circumstance as states. Only two of the four teams that had made it to semifinals would advance. Part of me didn't want us to make it, didn't want to do it, because I knew what I had planned. I knew what the right thing to do would be. I didn't want to do it. It'd be easier just to lose now and get our honorary plaques and go home.

The nationals officials entered the room to music over the loud-speaker. They had the same build up to the ceremonial unveiling of the two final, championship teams here as they did at states.

I watched the administrators take the stage to announce them.

I didn't clap.

I couldn't even move.

"It's okay if we don't . . ." I said.

Grace squeezed me.

"The two teams advancing to the final round of this year's National High School Mock Trial Tournament are . . ."

I held my breath.

"Waverly High from Reno, Nevada, and . . ."

I exhaled. Well, it was good while it lasted.

"Steelton High, from Steelton, Pennsylvania!"

Oh.

Holy.

Crickets.

I stood up but then immediately had to sit down again. The moment weighed heavily of joy and terror.

"Sh—crap," said Raina.

"You aren't joking," said Veronica.

"I knew we'd do it," said Claire.

"I . . . I just . . ." said Izzy.

Grace knelt down in front of me. She looked great in a gray suit. "You ready for this?" she said.

I looked at her. "One more to go."

We only had an hour before the afternoon's final.

"In the worst-case scenario, you'll get second place. In the country. Not too shabby, girls," said Kay.

Ms. McClain walked over from the faculty and staff room.

"I have some news, ladies."

We looked up at her.

My plan faded from my mind. What had seemed like a shiny silver idea instantly tarnished. Obviously, I should have the team do everything I could to win. I couldn't blow it with my crazy ideas.

"It seems our old friend the Honorable Judge Herman T. Wise will be hearing this year's final case."

Those words sunk in.

I knew him. He knew me. Well, not me per se. But Raina and Grace. Lordy. It was a perfect storm. The stupid defense of this terrible case. And now the judge who got more and more awful with every article Grace showed me.

"You're kidding," I said.

"You *must* be," said Raina.

"Afraid not."

"Is he the guy from the knitting thing? Well. *Things?*" said Claire.

"Oh yeah," said Grace. "That's him."

"Don't count yourselves out! He is meant to be fair and impartial!" said Kay, but she didn't sound convinced. He hadn't shown evidence of that before.

I sat there, in that moment. Trials can go a lot of ways. You never really can tell how something is going to turn out. Sometimes history decides great events. Sometimes small acts of free will that don't matter much in the scheme of things are everything to one person.

We could win this. I knew we could. I had the best witnesses, I was sure. My lawyers would rally. We could win and we'd be recognized at Mock Trial colleges and I could move out and be free.

But Grace looked like she was going to throw up at the thought of going in for the win defending hate speech. Defending the right of people to use their fake moral voice to keep other human beings down. Izzy's face had turned a greenish shade that didn't look like it was humanly possible. This was personal for her. For me, really. For all of us.

And my dad thought it was the right side to be on.

But there wasn't really any reason to listen to him anymore. There wasn't a compelling argument anywhere to make me listen to anyone but myself.

"All right, everyone," I said. "We need to talk."

"I will be the best soccer captain I can be," said Grace. "I can embrace my part for the greater good."

"An actress is an actress," said Izzy. "I will play my part."

"Obviously, we are going to win this," said Claire. "Millie, we got you."

All three of them still looked uneasy, even Claire. She had the worst part in this whole thing; her character was written as such a jerk.

"I'm ready," said Veronica.

"Same," said Raina. "I've been practicing my speech in front of the mirror for days. I can lie to the Dropped Stitchers."

"Ms. McClain, Kay, excuse us, please." I looked around at the team. "Huddle up, team."

Ms. McClain and Kay obliged.

Everyone circled around and looked at me.

"You lot have been amazing. From the beginning, you've given everything you had. And listening to all the arguments and winning by defending these people can't feel great. It feels . . . too much like someone else's beliefs and arguments. Which is what Mock Trial is, but I'd always been able to believe in it until now. So . . . why don't we rebel a little?"

Silence greeted me.

"What?" said Izzy.

"We are still the defense in name. But what if we got out there and just put out what we thought? Play it like it really is. That this isn't a safety and respect issue. That it's a free-speech versus hate-speech issue. That our side is wrong, and we know it."

"You want us to throw the case?" said Grace. "For real?"

"No, not throw it. Just be a little truer to ourselves."

"Wouldn't true to ourselves be winning?" said Claire.

I straightened up to all the height my full five-foot-one inches would give me. "I thought so. For a really long time, I thought so. But now I've realized that sometimes the winning side and the right side aren't always the same thing. Especially when it comes to the law."

Or living in my own home.

"I know I've been the one holding out on this jury. But I've been swayed. And I say we side with the case that we think is the *just* one."

I looked at Grace. She grinned. She put her hand in.

"I'm so angry," she said.

"Livid," said Izzy.

"Motivated," said Veronica.

"I'm not sure what you are saying," said Claire. "But I trust you, Millie."

"I'll explain," said Raina. "Emilia Goodwin, with the dissent. Who'd have thought?"

"Let's go be angry," I said. "Or motivated. But triumphant, either way."

The courtroom felt electric. It's as if everyone around us could feel that something was different this time. That the defense had fire burning through us that everyone couldn't see, couldn't understand, but could feel.

The Honorable Herman T. Wise came in as we stood, witnesses were sworn in, and the air of incredible anticipation hung in the air. Here I was, at nationals. Not how I thought I'd get here, not doing what I thought I'd be doing. But it felt right.

"Welcome, teams. I see we have one from Nevada—Welcome to the Keystone State!—and one from . . . well, well, well." He looked up from his notepad. "If it isn't Steelton High." He glowered down at us for a second. I couldn't tell if he looked pleased or annoyed. Maybe he just wondered how we could get this far and end up together.

At least, I wondered that. It was fitting, though, for what we were about to do.

He looked like he was going to say something directly to Raina or Grace but thought better of it. "Very well. This is an interesting case. Defense, I understand you won the coin toss. When you're ready."

I stood. "Thank you, Your Honor. Fellow humans of the court. We are here today representing Charlotte Gray, principal of Anywhere High School in Anytown, USA. She posits that a club called the Social Justice League has targeted her for harassment and made the learning environment unfriendly and unsafe for people of opinions different than their group. We will prove, beyond the burden of all proof, that this is the truth. The Social Justice League makes the environment unsafe for bigots, racists, and defenders of unfair social policies meant to keep others down. My client is one such person, in a district filled with small-minded people just like her."

I paused, to let the audible gasp from everyone in the audience and the plaintiff side die down.

"We will present to you Ms. Gray, who believes firmly that love is not love. That it must conform to a narrow idea that I can't even call antiquated. Because throughout history, consenting, adult people have paired off in every imaginable configuration. We will then present to you Eden Ward, founder of the Real Love Club, which for that same reason is allowed to exist despite its policies of discrimination and targeted harassment against the Anytown High School LGBT community. And finally, we will hear from Taylor Quinn, a student who doesn't seem to care about her fellow humans, just about whether the actions of a just few will disturb her team's chances at reaching the championships. Through this testimony, we will show the court that we believe hate speech is, in fact, protected by law, whereas arguments to the contrary are not. Because arguments to the contrary challenge the status quo, and we can't have that and maintain law and order. Thank you, Your Honor."

I turned, nodded to the plaintiffs, all of whom stared back in wide-eyed awe.

"What are you doing?" said Kay quietly.

"The right thing," I said.

RAINA PETREE,	:	IN THE COURT OF
	:	ALLEGHENY COUNTY
Plaintiff,	:	
	:	
v.	:	CIVIL ACTION-LAW
	:	
NO SMALL ROLES,	:	Case No. CMUWHO22
	:	
	:	
Defendant	:	

MAY 8: RELEVANT
PERSONS AND ENTITIES

I LOOKED UP AT JUDGE WISE. HE STARED AT us. But what could he do? We weren't violating any rules, exactly. We were presenting our case.

The plaintiff team got up.

"The defense started the case by bringing up points essential to our argument . . ." she began.

We questioned our witnesses and theirs, pointing out each time the Social Justice League was penalized for doing the exact same thing Real Love was. And when they questioned us, it became evident that no one really thought the knit rainbow was threatening.

Except maybe Judge Wise.

Finally, I walked over to the podium for the closing. I looked over at the stunned team from Nevada and flashed my most radiant actress grin.

"You've heard from the plaintiff's team that this is a matter of right versus wrong," I began. God, I felt so alive. I loved this speech. I'm glad I spent two years studying improv. "The freedom of speech is guaranteed by the founders of the United States. And surely, they meant all manner of discrimination, bigotry, and outward cruelty to their fellow persons," I finished. I turned to sit back down but then went to the microphone one more time. "Also, more than ninety to ninety-eight percent of sexual-assault claims are credible. False reporting just isn't generally a thing, and agents of the court should know that. Rape culture is what makes anyone think otherwise and maybe we should work to change that. Thank you."

The plaintiff's team just sort of restated what I said, minus the rape culture bit.

Later that night, at the awards banquet where our nationals' fates were to be decided (well, if Millie hadn't gone all superhero lawyer), the team from the Reno team came over to us.

"That was the most epic thing I've ever seen," opening-statement girl said.

"You should have seen us at state. We were defense. It felt gross," said one of the cross-examiners.

"*I* didn't feel gross. I almost got kicked off the team for seeing the validity in the defense's argument when we presented it," said closing-argument girl. She rolled her eyes. "But I'm glad we probably won."

The other two shook their heads at her and went back to their team table. Even if I didn't agree with closing-argument girl, I understood her motivation.

Claire sat next to me. "How are you feeling?"

"Strangely powerful," I said. "I don't think Ms. McClain is so happy with us."

"Oh yes, she is. She just has to put on that teacher face. I heard her telling Kay how proud she was of all of us. If we are going to go down, might as well go down for a good cause."

"Agreed."

"You know, I actually saw on the news that something like this happened near us. Only it was at a community theater. They had groups who could come in and perform local playwrights' scripts. One was this horrible piece detailing how the world would be better when men completely controlled women's reproductive health. Like that isn't almost reality, you know?"

"Shut up. Are you kidding?" I said.

"No! I'll send you the article when I get home. I saved the link on my school email."

I clenched my fists. I could think of a certain local scriptwriter who would be receiving knit responses to his work. Maybe I could write plays to put on at this place to counterprogram this nonsense.

Just then, the pomp and circumstance arrived for the Mock Trial national competition closing. It wasn't that exciting, knowing that there was absolutely no chance we were going to win.

And we didn't.

We collected our runner-up awards before the Reno team got the biggest, goldest, most glorious trophy I'd ever seen.

Millie looked at it longingly.

"I'm number two!" said Claire, holding her certificate up to the light to see its watermark.

"This will complement the wait-list letters on my wall nicely," I said.

"You printed them out?" said Claire.

"They were a wake-up call, like breaking up with Brandon. I needed to figure out what I wanted."

"Have you?" said Claire.

"Not quite," I said. I looked at the trophy we gave up across the room. It glinted like the aluminum size sevens in my bag. I liked the idea of winning an award, but I liked having a cause to fight for and something to create for myself even more. "But I'm getting there."

EMILIA GOODWIN,	:	IN THE COURT
	:	OF ALLEGHENY COUNTY
Plaintiff,	:	
	:	
v.	:	
	:	
GREGORY GOODWIN,	:	Case No. FUDAD2021
	:	
	:	
Defendant	:	

MAY 8: UNDISPUTED FACTS

THERE WERE COLLEGE REPS IN THE AUDIENCE of national Mock Trial. I'd always heard rumors that a few came, but it seemed unrealistic. Usually that sort of thing only happened to athletes.

They handed out pamphlets to the winners.

"I've already committed to Columbia," said one girl.

"No one is perfect!" said the man, shoving a folder into her hands. He looked at another kid. "What grade are you in?"

"I'm a junior," he said.

"Can I get your info? We have an express link for scholarship opportunities," he said. The man noticed me watching him.

"Bold move in there," he said. And turned back to the kid from the winning team.

I sighed and walked over to Kay and Ms. McClain.

"Thank you for all that you did. You got us here," I said.

"No, thank *you*, Millie," said Kay. "It's been a blast."

"And even though I don't quite understand what you did in there," said Ms. McClain, "I still respect it immensely. This is because of you. You brought us all this far."

"My team did, too," I said.

Another woman came over to us.

"Hi there," she said. "I'm a reporter from the *Pittsburgh Post-Gazette*. I was wondering if I can get a quote from you. I'm told you are the team captain from Steelton High."

"You bet," I said.

"My biggest question for all the competitors: What did you learn from this experience? From the competition here and from Mock Trial in general?"

I thought about it for a second.

"I guess . . ." I thought of everything. From my years researching for the boys; doing work for Dad; for being Millie, the dutiful daughter and student.

What had Mock Trial really taught me?

"It taught me that even though it is often important to be a team player"—I paused—"it is also just as important to figure out the right thing to do, and the right time to do it."

"Great," she said.

I realized how true that was.

Sometimes dissent is the best thing you can do, as an angry girl.

For yourself, and for everyone else.

RAINA PETREE,	:	IN THE COURT OF
	:	CAMBRIA COUNTY
Plaintiff,	:	
	:	
v.	:	CIVIL ACTION-LAW
	:	
THE UNFAIRNESS OF A LIFE	:	Case No. BRNDNWHO21
PURSUING A CREATIVE	:	
OCCUPATION,	:	
	:	
Defendant	:	

SEPTEMBER 1: SETTLEMENT AGREEMENT AND RELEASE

EVERYTHING WAS FINE.

Everything was great, actually. Who would have guessed?

I was killing it as the Stage Manager in the Stackhouse Players production of *Our Town*. (Everyone said so, including the reviewers in *This Town: Steeltown* and the *Tribune Republican*. But everyone loved this damn play no matter what you did. It didn't matter.) The admissions department at Carnegie Mellon didn't seem interested in my performance, but I'd accepted that. I was taking classes in political science and "law and government" at the community college to try it out. Alex had moved to Massachusetts to work at a pot store, so Carla hired me on as her replacement.

The door clinked open. The hottest guy I'd ever seen stood in front of me. I stared at his chest, imagining the abs that must be under that American Eagle shirt.

"Hi," he said. "I'm looking for a new LYS. Just started at Penn State Steelton. I'm starting a club there. Row Bros," he said.

Wow, his pants were tight. And just look at his red hair.

"What are you studying?" I wondered if I could get a picture of him to send to Megan. Her head would explode.

"Accounting," he said. "Do you go school there, too?"

"No. I'm focusing on activism," I said. "Take a pamphlet. We are going to be holding a knit-in at a local theater where they produce misogyny."

"I'm in. Took me a while to recover from toxic masculinity myself. I'm still a work in progress." He cocked his head. "Hey, actually, I recognize you. You were in that play they took us to for orientation. You were, like, one of the leads, weren't you?" he said.

"Oh, *Our Town*?" I asked.

"Yeah. I've always *hated* that play. They made us do it every year in high school when I ran tech. But you were awesome in it." He looked around. "It's great that you work here. Can you show me your worsted weights? And, possibly, if you are interested, your number?"

I eyed him. I didn't really need a boyfriend at the moment. I had the theater and the protests and all the fancy yarn I wanted at 50 percent off. "What do you look for in a girl?"

He thought about it. "Enthusiastic consent," he said.

I grinned. "Good start. I'll think about it. Let me show you the colors we just got in."

He was obviously happy to follow me.

I was happy to think about where to lead next.

EMILIA GOODWIN,	:	COUNTY COURT
	:	OF FRANKLIN COUNTY
Plaintiff,	:	
	:	
v.	:	
	:	
ANY OBSTACLE WHATSOEVER,	:	Case No. FUTRS0BR17
	:	
	:	
Defendant	:	

SEPTEMBER 7: PARTIES BOUND

TODAY WAS THE DAY.

I looked in the mirror for the twentieth time. I smoothed the scarlet and gray folds of my skirt. It was my first day of work at the law firm. I was only a part-time receptionist, but I would sit in meetings and organize notes, and experience was experience.

"Millie? Are you almost done in there? I have to get ready for class."

I opened the door. One of my six housemates paced back and forth in front of me.

"Sorry!" I said.

Living with so many people was a pain, but it was all I could afford. I only made minimum wage at my library job, and the law firm wasn't much more. I spent as much time in Grace's dorm room as possible.

If all went well, I'd live on campus next year.

Nervous! I texted Grace, at the thought of her. *Miss you!*

You got this, rebel fighter. Love you, she texted back.

I saw several missed texts from my dad. I thought he'd disowned me for not living out his life plan, but Sheila told him it was better if Victor got my room so he and Nina didn't have to share.

Hey babes, do you remember where the key to the safe is? We need some documents in there asap! Did you see my new dress shoes while you were packing? Are you coming to visit for fall break? Sheila wants to visit her parents without the kids. Can you spare a weekend over Christmas? We might go skiing and could use an extra pair of eyes.

Dad wasn't paying for college, since I was "being willful."

So I willfully blocked his number after the text about Christmas.

And then I also willfully forgot to mention I'd hidden his shoes in the back of the laundry room broom closet before I left. I wondered how long it'd take Sheila to find them, since I knew Dad probably didn't even know the space existed. I'd brought the key to the safe with me to college.

And then I threw it in the garbage when I unpacked.

My phone buzzed again.

When do you get off tonight? Nine? Can I pick you up? texted Grace.

Only if you take me to the late-night cafeteria for chicken fingers, I texted back.

Deal.

A girlfriend with guest meals was helpful.

A girlfriend in general was pretty great.

I rode the bus to my job, excited to get started. They'd said on nights when the partners went home early, I would be able to study. I brought my Intro to Poli Sci book to keep me company.

I didn't even mind that I would have to wait a year to have enough time to do Mock Trial here. The team would be there sophomore year, and nothing felt better than being free to take care of only myself.

I couldn't wait to see what I could do on my own.

ACKNOWLEDGMENTS

As always, thanks must first go to my family and friends, whose support carries me. Particularly Katherine and Charles, who always make me laugh.

Thank you to the Feiwel and Friends team—especially Anna Roberto, who is amazing and wonderful.

Thank you to Catherine Drayton and Claire Friedman, as well as everyone at Inkwell Management. You answer my copious questions and tolerate my dubious ideas with grace and humor.

Thank you to Josh Groban—who is not an angry girl but could play one onstage. Actually, I hope he does.

Thank you goes to my SNHU and Boston University students. TURN IN YOUR ASSIGNMENTS and also MAKE GOOD CHOICES.

Thank you to the real Nikita Varman, a tremendous human being who wanted to be a villain in a book.

I have a lot of people willing to read my works in progress. I am so grateful that you give your time to help the likes of me. I owe so much to Jennifer Mann, Cate Berry, Salima Alikahn, Lindsey Manwell, Rebecca Chernoff Udell, Shelly Nosbisch, Michele Prestininzi, Marianne Murphy, Alexa Donne, and Kristin Brophy . . . You are all perfect.

Of course, Melissa Baumgart and Kathryn Benson are perfect, and help me work through my ideas with eight hundred texts a day. But they also host the brilliant Truer Words Podcast (www.truerwordspodcast .com). Everyone should listen to it to make your creative life better.

Thanks to Dean Gloster, who has always championed my work every chance he gets.

Thanks to Gail Dickert, for caring so deeply.

Thank you to Kim Lloyd, for being strong and kind, as well as a great coach.

My love and gratitude goes out to the Dead Post-its Society and all of my teachers and friends from VCFA. It was the single best decision I ever made falling in with you lot.

I honor the memory of Gracie King, who was epic.

To Corinne Francis: I'm so happy you liked *Dear Rachel Maddow*. I hope you triumph in all future pursuits, spelling or otherwise.

Thanks to CT from Martha's Vineyard, for the tour and for being generally awesome.

My appreciation goes out to Réa, Alan, Amber, Emily, and Cheryl—the people with whom I spend the most time outside of my actual family. All of BU Res Life, really. Thank you for listening to me talk (constantly) about my books and for always championing me along the way. Thank you also to Pauline, who has had to hear about it all for more than two decades.

Thank you to Ellie Moreton. We failed at the Green Line critique group, but you've always stuck with me.

Finally, thank you to all the angry girls.

If you identify as one, then you are one.

Stay furious.

THANK YOU FOR READING THIS
FEIWEL & FRIENDS BOOK.

THE FRIENDS WHO MADE

SIX ANGRY GIRLS

POSSIBLE ARE:

JEAN FEIWEL, *Publisher*

LIZ SZABLA, *Associate Publisher*

RICH DEAS, *Senior Creative Director*

MALLORY GRIGG, *Art Director*

HOLLY WEST, *Senior Editor*

ANNA ROBERTO, *Senior Editor*

KAT BRZOZOWSKI, *Senior Editor*

ALEXEI ESIKOFF, *Senior Managing Editor*

KIM WAYMER, *Senior Production Manager*

ERIN SIU, *Assistant Editor*

EMILY SETTLE, *Associate Editor*

RACHEL DIEBEL, *Assistant Editor*

FOYINSI ADEGBONMIRE, *Editorial Assistant*

STARR BAER, *Associate Copy Chief*

FOLLOW US ON FACEBOOK OR VISIT US
ONLINE AT FIERCEREADS.COM.

OUR BOOKS ARE FRIENDS FOR LIFE.